The Taco Wagon Murders

By

Robert G. Rogers

Also by Robert G. Rogers

Bishop Bone Murder Mystery Series
A Tale of Two Sisters
Murder in the Pinebelt
A Killing in Oil
Jennifer's Dream
The Pinebelt Chicken War
The La Jolla Shores Murders
Murder at the La Jolla Apogee
No Morning Dew
Brother James and the Second Coming

Non-Series Murder Mysteries
The Christian Detective,
That La Jolla Lawyer,
La Jolla Murder Mysteries
French Quarter Affair,
Life and Times of Nobody Worth a Damn

Suspense/Thrillers
Runt Wade,
The End is Near

Historical Women's Fiction
Jodie Mae,

Youth/Teen Action and Adventure
Lost Indian Gold,
Taylor's Wish,
Swamp Ghost Mystery,
Armageddon Ritual

Children's Picture Story book
Fancy Fairy

Dedication
I dedicate this book to Denise, Yarka and Eva for their hard work in editing and making suggestions for improving the
book. I thank all of them.

Prologue

Bishop Bone and Kathy Sullivan, relaxing with their morning coffees, sat on the back porch of his cabin overlooking Indian Creek. Steam twisted upward from their cups from the hot coffee.

They casually watched the furry beavers on the far side of the creek working without pause in their pond. Most of them were working diligently to repair the damn that kept their pond from draining into the creek. A limb had worked loose and water was beginning to leak through the opening. Others worked just as tirelessly repairing their lodges.

"It's like watching a giant bee hive," Kathy said.

Bishop agreed. "Yeah. They work like robots."

The ringing of Bishop's cell phone got him up to answer it. He had left it inside the cabin.

"I'll be back," he told her.

She nodded and continued to watch the beavers at work in their pond and sipping her coffee. In a few minutes, she had to get dressed to go to work. She managed the small town Lawton public library where Bishop had met her. It was five miles from his cabin.

Lawton had its beginnings as a lumber town where men came to harvest the old grove yellow pines that grew like weeds in the layer of clay soil that stretched in a wide swath across some of the Southern states. The clay layer was called the "pine belt" by people who made a living off the trees that grew in the soil. And, since the pines continued to sprout up and grow fast in the pine belt, the town still depended in part on its timber and lumber interests. Nowadays, poultry and some high tech industries had moved in and were prospering.

Because he read so much, Bishop had, sometime earlier, made a decision to check out his reading material from the library instead of buying it and had met Kathy in the process. They soon discovered mutual interests and had been close friends ever since.

Kathy lived in an old Queen Ann home in the small South Mississippi town. It had been her mother's home when Kathy moved there after her divorce. Her mother had since moved into a nursing home in Arizona. In reality though, Kathy spent as much time as possible with Bishop in his cabin where she'd stayed last night.

Kathy had a pretty face with golden brown eyes and light brown hair which brushed against her shoulders when she walked. Bishop loved to see the glow in her hair when the sun caught it while they were outside. She stayed in great shape playing regular tennis with Bishop and looked younger than the fifty she was.

Bishop, a lawyer in his early sixties, stood a shade over six feet, with almost no flab, a consequence of also staying in good shape. His face was rough and showed the beginnings of age lines. He also had light brown hair that was showing some gray here and there and a thinning spot at the back.

He only shaved when he was seeing Kathy or was handling an assignment from a bank, his "work." Bishop stayed busy representing clients, mostly banks. He did that primarily to have something to do.

Both had earlier suffered through messy divorces. As a result, they elected to stay close friends instead of getting married. During the time he'd practiced down and dirty law in California it seemed to him that often when two people were married, they felt the marriage certificate was an obligation they somehow had to be shed and divorce was the only way to do that. He knew that didn't make logical sense, but it seemed that way from the problems had by some of his clients.

Bishop had a decent income from investments he'd made after settling a complaint he'd had with the corrupt developer and his banker conspirator who'd, in effect, chased him out of California and, at least temporarily anyway, ruined his life. They'd framed him on a real estate deal he was handling. The legal battle dealing with that, one he'd initially lost, ended his career, not to mention his marriage and had forced him to retreat to Lawton to lick his wounds. He'd been there years before on a business deal and remembered it favorably.

While he was considering his next move, he inadvertently got involved in the culture and business of Lawton and Mississippi and found that he fit in perfectly.

Thusly rehabilitated with his equilibrium restored, he returned to California to settle the score with the developer and the banker who'd framed him. Afterwards, he came back to live in Lawton and bought his cabin and twenty two acres on Indian Creek. Unfortunately, by the time he'd proven he was innocent of the claim the developer had made, it was too late to salvage his marriage. His wife had remarried and his children had finished college and were married themselves. Since then he had, after a difficult time, made peace with her and his children.

The phone call took several minutes. He hung up and returned to the porch with a puzzled look on his face. Before telling Kathy about the call, he grabbed his coffee cup and left for a warm up. Kathy declined his request to bring her one since she still sipping on what was left in her cup.

Once back on the porch, he explained to Kathy that the call was from Ellen Wasserman, the Chief of Police in San Diego which bordered the Pacific Ocean near the Mexican border in the southern part of California. They'd worked on a number of cases together, all involving murders that had touched Bishop's life in different ways. During those times they had become friends although the friendship was not always amicable. Ellen was not known for her patience.

However, she'd made a reputation for herself over the years as being a straight shooter and completely honest. It had earned her steady promotions including her appointment as Chief of Police in the border town.

He told Kathy that Ellen wanted him to address a convention of law enforcement detectives in San Diego in a month, all expenses paid. Ellen said there'd probably be at least five hundred senior detectives at the convention, give or take a few. San Diego was a great vacation town with many things to do. Families brought their children there just to relax and everyone loved to hold their conventions there.

"She wants me to speak for thirty minutes and answer questions. Probably another ten or so minutes, then fly back."

"Why?" she asked. "You're not a policeman."

Bishop smiled and said, "Good question. I asked the same question. She thinks I can give the detectives something to think about when they get back to their locales and resume their police work solving problems.

A different point of view keeps them from getting into a rut, Ellen thinks.

"She wants me to tell them how I went about solving the cases we worked together over the years. My approach and my execution, but most of all, she asked me to stress tenacity, something she thinks I have a lot of." He smiled again.

"Tenacity is one way to describe a stubborn streak that won't let you give up until you've figured out who did it," Kathy said and added a laugh.

Bishop shrugged and added, "I think anybody who's going to succeed in any field has to have a stubborn streak. Otherwise, nothing would ever get done. No successful person runs at the first clap of thunder."

She stroked his arm. "Of course. I wasn't making light of it, sweetheart. I'm always amazed at how you go after things. It floors me. You play tennis the same way. Go after every ball. Search for a weak spot and pounce."

She leaned over and kissed him on the cheek. "You're my role model. My hero, Bishop. I can see why she wants you to speak at the convention. What'd you tell her?"

"I told her I'd talk to you and my clients and unless you objected or my clients could foresee that I'd be needed for something coming up, I'd do it."

"No objection from me. I know how the world works. You scratch my back and I'll scratch yours. I'll endure."

"Thanks. I'll check with my bank clients and let her know."

After breakfast, Kathy left for the library, and he did just that, made calls to the banks he worked for and asked if they foresaw a conflict for that period. Mostly he was concerned about court appearances or meetings they had planned for one reason or another. Anything that would require his presence. No one he'd called saw a problem. So, he set out to finish all of the assignments he was working on ahead of the time Ellen had told him to come out.

There was one bank officer he couldn't contact, but he'd always called Bishop when he saw any problem requiring his involvement. And, he usually called earlier instead of waiting until the last minute.

"I'll try him again later," he said. *Likely has no problems.*

After the initial round of phone calls, he sat on his back porch and stared at the Creek and thought about what he was going to say during the speech. When he had a pretty good idea, he went inside and typed up his thoughts. After he was satisfied with that part of his preparation, he rehearsed it to see how it sounded and how much time it took. Using his reaction as a guide, he massaged the speech until he was satisfied with everything, the length and the impact.

And then he emailed it to Ellen for her review. He didn't want to give a speech that conflicted with anything she was going to say or anything with which she might disagree.

She said she liked it. It had given her full credit for her contributions to the cases he'd had.

And, that was how Bishop came to be involved in his next murder case, a very frustrating and very complex one.

*****

The bank manager he hadn't been able to reach earlier, Aaron Garman, called. Bishop had left him a message about his trip to California. Garman rarely had emergencies so Bishop wasn't too concerned, but knew there was a first time for everything.

"Aaron," Bishop answered when he saw the name on the phone window. "What's happening?"

Be damned. Probably has something for me to do the day Ellen wants me to speak in San Diego.

He didn't, but, he did have a problem loan, a big one. "The loan to Dalton Parsons is in default. Has been for several months. We've been propping it up but cotton prices are staying low and the borrower has run out of money. Says he has anyway. You recommended getting more security and we turned you down. I have to admit you were right."

Bishop well remembered. It was a good loan, he had said in his report, assuming the price of cotton stayed high. It hadn't but he didn't go into that with

Garman just then. One thing he'd learned was not to tell a client "I told you so." He knew he might get away with it once, but never twice and he didn't want to test that theory. So, he let the manager's comment slide past.

The borrower had needed a loan to get into a new business. He had the idea, backed by a compelling market report, the best that money could buy, to set up fully staffed warehouse facilities to service equipment used by delta cotton farmers. His dad farmed some good delta cotton land and promised his son all of his business. The loan provided for building a number of the service facilities close to the big Delta cotton farms.

If a piece of farm equipment needed repair or servicing, it could be brought into one of the facilities built and furnished by the loan and be back on-line in no time.

Unfortunately, the price of cotton fell and no one was planting much. As a result, not much equipment was being used and not much needed to be serviced or repaired. And, as was always the case where the unanticipated occurred, the borrower was left holding the bag. It was an empty bag and the bank ended up with a loan in default.

His dad had recommended the business to the son and suggested getting the loan. His dad was also a big shareholder in the bank so the loan committee was generous in setting the loan terms.

Bishop, who had been asked to do a market survey in addition to a loan analysis, had recommended getting the dad's guarantee or more collateral. The bank elected to ignore Bishop's recommendation and now was facing a big dollar loan in default.

"The old man won't let the loan go into default," the committee had said.

Well, he did.

The bank had been letting the loan drift, taking into account the dad's position in the bank and the son's financial statement. But, after four months of drift with little or no activity, the bank was calling Bishop.

Garman replied, "I'd like for you to talk to Dalton. See if you can get through to him. His loan is in serious default. We can't let it drift any longer. The regulators have sent us a notice to do something. We don't want to file a notice of default but unless Dalton Parsons can put something new on the table, we won't have a choice."

"It's time for his dad to step up to the plate," Bishop said. "Wouldn't it be better for you to make the call? Keep it friendly. If I call, he'll know he's in deep shit."

"The President doesn't want Dalton's dad to get upset. He'd been talking like he wants to be on the board. Something like this might push him to do that. The regulators would have a field day with that, the father of a big loan borrower being on the board. Favoritism is frowned on."

"Yeah, I understand." So, Bishop agreed to make the call and didn't beat around the bush. The loan was in default and unless Dalton brought it current, the bank would have no choice but to file a notice of default, an NOD as it was called by people who dealt in real estate and loans. Once the NOD period elapsed, the holder of the mortgage could foreclose.

The call went about as expected.

"Bullshit!" Dalton shouted into the phone. "My dad is a big shareholder! Nobody's gonna foreclose on my property. Cotton will come back. It always had and always will. The world needs cotton and the bank needs to learn patience."

"No doubt it will come back, but it's not doing it at this time, when you need it. Banks can't have patience when the regulators are looking over their shoulders. You have no choice. You have to bring the loan current or put up additional collateral so the bank can rewrite the loan and get the regulators off its back."

"Garman'll be hearing from my lawyers! He can't push me into anything. And, you're an asshole. I remember you snooping around, looking at my property, before the loan was approved. Garman said you'd recommended that I put up more collateral or get my dad to sign on the loan. You didn't get your way then and you won't get it now."

Bishop had the urge to tell him it was the bank making the decisions, not him, but let it pass. He knew Dalton was doing what many borrowers did when in default, blame the messenger, which just then, he was.

After a pause, Dalton said, "The world would have been better off if your mother had the good sense to abort you!"

Before Bishop could answer the man's insult, Dalton had hung up.

Bishop called Garman and gave him the gist of the conversations. Later he'd email him a full report including the abortion quip.

"Damnit to hell," Garman said. "I was hoping you could talk sense into him. He's been telling me the same thing." Bishop heard a loud sigh.

"Okay, I'll talk to the President. It's his call but I don't see that he has a choice. He has to give the regulators a report they'll accept. That means we'll have to be aggressive. And that, Bishop, we'll need you to do your thing."

"Well, call me when you get to that point. I'll get out my workbook on being aggressive." He explained that he'd be in California for a few days later on but could always get back in a hurry if needed.

Garman thanked him.

Bishop figured there'd be a couple of meetings before the bank was ready to make a decision. But, he knew that sooner or later the bank would have to face the borrower and the defaulted loan, head on.

Bishop turned his attention to the trip to San Diego and Ellen's request, a speech to the detectives. He was looking forward to seeing his feisty friend.

Chapter 1

Ellen sent someone to pick up Bishop at the airport and take him to the La Jolla hotel hosting the event. It was late so he didn't see her until the next morning, after breakfast.

La Jolla was an affluent beach town just north of San Diego. Some people complained that only rich people could afford to live there.

It was Friday. The speech to everyone was that evening. The convention would break into groups for their Saturday morning meetings. Then, they'd all go out and have fun, golfing, boating, sightseeing and shows, or a relaxing walk on the beach, the usual litany of things people do when a convention's over.

She met him in the hotel lobby where they exchanged hugs and quips about the last time they were together. She announced how pleased she was that he'd accepted and how glad she was to see him again. He smiled and replied with similar small talk that people exchange when meeting for the first time after a long interval. Once the small talk is out of the way, the relationship is usually driven by the events that had precipitated the meeting. What had to be done and who was going to do it, the important questions.

Ellen was African American in her early fifties, and always kept a no-nonsense look on her face. She was almost as tall as Bishop. She stayed in top physical condition to command the respect of the law enforcement personnel who worked for her as well as to discourage anyone from challenging her.

"You're looking good. Thinner than ever," Bishop told her.

"I've taken up tennis," she said. "I play three times a week and am limiting my sugar intake."

He gave her a look up and down. "Well, it shows."

"My tennis instructor put me on a vegetable, fruit diet. She's been running me ragged. I've lost weight." She laughed. "I'm not a bad player, Bishop."

He gave her comment a shake of his head and a smile. "You have the look of a lean and hungry player, out for a victory at any costs. Good."

"Probably some of your bullshit talk, Bishop, but thanks."

He laughed.

They toured the conference room where he'd speak that evening. He stood behind the microphone on the stage to get a feel for the room. He even said a few words with the mic on and was satisfied. He had notes for the speech but had enough pride not to use them.

A couple of placards in the hotel lobby announced a local event, a tennis tournament sponsored by the La Jolla Rec Center in town. Anybody could sign up. There were no restrictions other than the payment of an entrance fee.

During the morning, Bishop accompanied Ellen on a couple of investigations she had been watching develop. Mostly he just stood and listened to her direct the investigators. At noon, he invited her to one of his favorite places, the Bread and Cie French bakery, for a light lunch and cup of cappuccino. It was located in the Hillcrest district of San Diego.

"Always the best here," he told her.

She agreed.

Afterward, she dropped him back at the hotel to get changed into his "speaking" outfit, the clothes he usually wore on assignments from banking clients - khaki shit, pants and light jacket with tennis shoes. He called them his working clothes. Mostly though, he felt comfortable in them. Wrinkling was almost impossible and if he got something on them, most anything could be washed out.

He chuckled to himself, remembering the times he'd been in La Jolla. How men went to the grocery store wearing pajamas to buy their beer. And, women did the same, wearing the scantiest of clothes, to buy something they needed for a snack.

Great place, Bishop thought. *Comfortable living. Practically everybody shows six zeros on the bottom lines of their financial statements.*

*****

For the speech, he used two murders he and Ellen had investigated. One was the hatchet murder in La Jolla Shores. The hostess of a local event at her home was killed with a hatchet. Bishop had to track down the murderer before he ended up in the morgue next to the hostess.

The other was the murder of a "work out" specialist, a hybrid real estate developer, at the opening of his high end project called the La Jolla Apogee. Some of the people Bishop had questioned, hard, tough real estate developers, threatened him if he didn't back off. Since backing off was something Bishop never did, he had to watch his back in that one as well.

He finished the speech a few minutes over his time limit then answered questions for ten or so minutes before Ellen took the mic and thanked him. He did a little bow to the applause of the attendee's and walked off stage.

Ellen joined him back stage a few minutes later after the hall was cleared of the detectives who went in search of something cold to drink in the many "watering holes" in and around La Jolla, most with surf views.

She invited Bishop to a Mexican restaurant down the street for a margarita, always a treat.

"They liked it," she told him after they'd ordered. "Several came up and told me so. They liked the way you used cases in making your points."

"Thanks. I enjoyed it too," he said. "Kind of fun to go back over an old case. It looks so simple once you know who did it. Makes me wonder why I didn't crack it sooner."

"Yeah. Until then though," she said, "it's like looking at a ball of twine with ravels everywhere. Not knowing which ravel to pull first."

He agreed, "And, you're never sure if you're pulling the right one."

"Yeah and some come with barbed ends."

"So true. Barbs that can bite you in the butt," he added.

Their drinks arrived. They touched glasses, took a sip and offered praise for them.

"Uh," she said, "Bishop, I need a favor."

Damn, he thought. *A favor? I just did her a favor.*

The look on her face suggested that he might not like it. His brain automatically began to conjure excuses to back up his "no: if he needed one.

"What?" he asked.

"I agreed to play in the local tennis tournament. You may have seen the poster in the hotel. I have a match tomorrow afternoon. You might not believe this, but I'm one of the celebrities." She added a chuckle.

"I'd have to say that you are one," he said. "Being the Chief of Police certainly qualifies."

But, what's the favor? Do I have to keep the press off your back? Call the lines? What? He wondered.

"Here's the favor. My partner had to drop out. I'm not sure his excuse made much sense, but he's not playing. I suspect he was afraid we'd lose and I'd blame him, which, I might very well have done. So, I'm now without a partner. You play, as I recall, so I figured I'd ask you to substitute for him. My match is at noon tomorrow."

Hell, not as bad a favor as I'd figured. But Ellen? Playing tournament tennis? Well, her instructor said she was a natural. I've never met one and I sure as hell wasn't. Developing my game was like chiseling concrete.

"I doubt we'll last more than one match," she said.

Probably. Most of the La Jolla people play all the time from what I recall and they're all damn good. Cutthroat tennis, they play.

"My flight back is Sunday afternoon," he said. "Maybe I should cancel it just to make sure. Hell, we might win by default and have to play a second match."

She smiled. "So, you'll do it! Thank you! I knew I could count on you."

Hell, she'd do the same for me. People who are really your friend are people who'll do you a favor when asked even if they'd rather not. I guess that makes me her friend.

She took a long sip of her drink and added, "By the way, I took the liberty of bringing you some tennis togs and a racquet, courtesy of my original partner, in case you did."

"Pretty sure I'd agree, were you?" Bishop said.

"Like you, I come prepared to meet all responses."

"Just don't blame me if we lose," he said.

"Not to worry. I don't think we will. My instructor says I've taken to it like a pro. And, I recall that you're no slouch either."

Bishop laughed. *Haven't we all. Ah, the benefit of paying for something. The extras, as in accolades, come free as each check clears.*

She'd leave the tennis togs and racquet at the front desk and meet him at the court where they were to warm up fifteen minutes before the match.

Fortunately the togs fit and the racquet felt comfortable in his hand.

Bishop couldn't know, but a few blocks away in a luxurious office two men were having a meeting that would impact his life and not for the better.

Chapter 2

Snapper (Charlie) Cornwell walked through the office door of the Taco Wagon Investment Company with a casual, if not arrogant, flair. He'd come to see Walter McNally, who actually ran the company and from the expression on his face, he didn't have anything pleasant in mind for the meeting. It was early afternoon.

There was no secretary in the outside office. The company didn't have one. Most phone calls were calls McNally answered directly and most had to do with what the company was doing and more importantly about investing in Taco Wagons.

In fact, that was the main function of the office, the management of those investments. The rest of the business affairs could have been just as easily handled in less luxurious surroundings outside of the high rent district of La Jolla. And, in fact, most of the day-to-day activities were handled by subcontractors out of their offices. However, it was felt by McNally and Cornwell that investors would be more likely to invest in the company if the company looked successful and an office in La Jolla satisfied their feelings.

"Rich people feel more comfortable dealing with people who look rich, like them," McNally had once said. "Birds of a feather."

Snapper was something of a celebrity in La Jolla; well-known and wealthy. However, people who knew him well gossiped that most of his money came from the estates of his wives and primarily his third wife.

In his mid-fifties, he was also considered handsome, with thick, dark hair which required some color now and then to stay that way. His eyes were dark, matching the color of his hair. His square face carried a slight smile, which showed his perfectly shaped teeth and projected the confidence that most women found attractive and inviting. He was six feet tall and stayed in good shape, to a certain extent, by lifting weights daily and taking a turn on a treadmill.

People seeing him for the first time often wondered if he might be a movie star. Some movie stars had homes in La Jolla.

Snapper smiled when he overheard the suppositions and usually responded with a smile at whoever was doing the speculation, particularly if the speculator was a female. And, if she looked interesting, he'd do more than smile.

Since his third wife's death, politicians and media people had called on him with equal frequency to ask for his advice and his money. He had that air about him and was frequently on talk shows and gave talks to financial groups, when asked. More recently, during those talks, he would slip in a pitch for watchers to invest in Taco Wagons.

In the expensive brochures that described the Taco Wagons Company, Snapper was given full credit as the man who'd developed the innovative plan for the company. And, his handsome face was plastered all over the colored brochure.

In reality, however, he'd done nothing, consistent with what he'd done most of his life. McNally, looking for a name, picked Snapper for the position after he'd done all the thinking about and all the organizing of the company. He told Snapper he would be the front man and for that it was agreed that he would receive a percentage of the investments he brought in, directly or indirectly.

The brochures bore the title of The Taco Wagons Investments. The outside cover contained a stylized representation of a "wagon" that resembled an old Conestoga wagon, though smaller. The "wagons" were what a franchisee would get with their franchise along with all that was needed to make it work ... and more important, to make money.

The colored representation showed food prep counters, drawers for implements and cabinets for food and beverages. Like an old Conestoga, a white canvas cover protected the wagon. In addition, a swing out canvas umbrella protected the customers and owners from the environmental elements. It had four wheels and a trailer hitch to enable it to be easily moved around by a pick-up truck.

In addition to showing the Conestoga look-a-likes and describing how they worked, the brochures also talked about the "Investments," offered by the company, the main reason for the brochures and when everything was boiled down, the main reason for the company, the insiders said. It was said that those investments were where the money was and why McNally had put it all together.

The investments were ten year bonds issued by the Taco Wagons Company with an estimated yield of between eight and ten percent, payable monthly. The bonds were sold to fund the business of the company, the development, operation and lease of Taco Wagons to franchisees.

Franchisees paid $5,000 initially to get started and $5,000 every six months thereafter until the company recovered what it cost to have the wagons built. The brochure suggested that there might be price increases as the business developed.

The brochures described how the company was continuously searching for small, but developing and "friendly" cities with sidewalks wide enough to accommodate the Wagons and where electricity was available or could be made available. Although each Wagon had battery backup, they basically ran on electricity.

In some cases, where a city was interested in the business but didn't have wide enough sidewalks, the brochure described how the company would lease small store fronts for customers to walk in and buy the same Mexican food being offered by a Taco Wagon. The amount to be paid by franchisees for that kind of space would have to be negotiated.

Some detail was given about the type of individual the company believed suitable for a franchise. Retired men or women who had experience in management and who were still vital, with energy and ambition; people who wanted to own their own business and earn in the neighborhood of a thousand dollars a week, or more, depending on location and the number of hours the Wagon was open for business.

Snapper was quoted in press releases and interviews as saying, "I want to do something for people who are retired but still have the energy and drive to do something with their lives. I hate for people with skills and motivation to waste it sitting around doing nothing. Those people can still make money and we can make money helping them. Winners on both sides of the table."

He talked about company projections that showed how a successful Taco Wagon business could become so profitable, it could be sold for a profit after a couple of years or the franchisee could contract for another Taco Wagon at another location; in effect expand their business.

All anyone had to do was pay the leasing fee and they'd be in business, assuming a location was available. Usually, there was a waiting period, the brochure said, while a search was on to find suitable locations.

A franchisee would buy all the "fixings" from the company and began selling street tacos and offer Mexican dishes to people looking for a quick lunch.

The brochure stated that a franchisee might have to relocate to the small city where a permit could be issued for a sidewalk Taco Wagon. Such cities were agreeable to have patrol cars frequently check on the Wagons to keep theft to a minimum.

If training was needed, it was available. The clothes the franchisee had to wear to look the part of a street vendor were supplied by the company.

The company wanted uniformity, the brochure said.

The franchisor controlled the franchisee by charging for the quantity of food delivered to the franchisee. If the franchisee claimed more than acceptable waste from the quantity delivered, the franchisee had to pay for it out of pocket or surrender their franchise.

A number was listed for interested parties to call for information about buying a franchise. It was answered by a recorded message. Walter McNally's name was given as the man to call for information about bonds being sold by the investment company to finance its operations. He took those calls himself.

"Snapper brought it to me. I couldn't resist. It was the most innovative idea I'd seen in years." McNally was quoted as saying when the announcement was made about the company's operations. And, although no Taco Wagons were yet in California because of the narrowness of the sidewalks, it was hoped that soon there would be. They were looking at small California towns to see if their sidewalks could accommodate the wagons.

However, the credit given Snapper in the brochure and all the press releases were a complete fabrication although Snapper did handle most of the television appearances and media interviews. In reality though, McNally had developed the plan for the company but needed a "name" to front it and attract investors. He'd seen Snapper's name in the newspaper and made arrangements to see him and to pitch the plan to him.

The phone number given for Snapper was also answered by a recorded message. The publicity for the company consistently said the same thing. Snapper was the mover and shaker for the enterprise.

After explaining the plan over lunch and extolling the reasons why Snapper would be perfect as a figurehead for the company, Snapper laughed and asked, "Why in hell would I do that. Set myself up for lawsuits up the ass if something goes wrong? You want a fall guy. I'm not it."

McNally answered his question, saying, "Well, I'll give you six percent of every investor you bring in and a thousand dollars for every board meeting you attend. You'd be the Chairman. There'll be five board members." He gave the names of the people who'd been approached, all of whom were retired from public service in and around San Diego.

Snapper didn't laugh at that. He looked at McNally pensively for a second or two then said, "I'll take twelve percent."

They settled for ten percent. McNally would do all the work and Snapper would take credit for creating the company and for making it work. He'd handle all the publicity as well, something he enjoyed, talking and having no responsibility for doing anything.

As soon as the office door closed behind him, Snapper said in a loud voice, "McNally! Where the hell are you?"

McNally came out of his office right away – there was only one office in the suite - hurriedly putting on his coat. "Ah, Snapper," he said, forcing a smile. "Good to see you."

McNally was not as tall as Snapper but was much larger, size wise. He had a jowly face, big hands and a stomach that pushed out over his belt. His face was equally broad and marked by smile lines; the consequence of what McNally did, dealing with investors. He never greeted anyone without a big, toothy smile, which he figured projected honesty. He never turned down a beer or a cocktail and he loved deserts when he dined out, which was often.

His eyes and hair were brown and had begun to show signs of gray and some balding. McNally was in his early sixties.

"I bet. Been napping, I'd guess," Snapper said. "Another liquid lunch?"

McNally laughed. "No, just catching up on some book work." That was a lie, something McNally was adept at. In fact, he was napping.

Snapper responded with a grimace and sat down in one of the outer office chairs. He gestured for McNally to do the same, which he did.

"What can I do for you?" McNally asked.

"Indeed," Snapper replied. "What the hell can you do for me. How about a check for what you owe me. The three investors I sent in two weeks ago. I think you owe me five thousand dollars. I'd like it."

Since Snapper was the public "name" for the company, he had become responsible for much of the money invested in Taco Wagons. Not all the people knew he got his money from his wives and thought somehow that since he was "rich" he knew what he was doing.

"Ah, the check. I've written it ... well, I've been meaning to write it. Expenses have cropped up that ate into ... our available cash. I was waiting a bit so our bank balances wouldn't get too low."

"Horse shit! You've got plenty of money. I want my share like we agreed!"

McNally nodded without argument and went back inside the office to write Snapper a check. He brought it out and handed it to him.

"Great job," he said. "You're bringing 'em in. And, I haven't heard anybody complaining yet."

"They like that eight percent they're getting."

McNally nodded. "Our Taco Wagons are selling them tacos faster than our Wagoneers can make 'em, and they're making big bucks," he said, butchering the English a bit. He'd taken to calling the franchisees the colorful name of Waggoneers instead of franchisees.

"Don't let my check drag next time or you may be looking for a new front man," Snapper said. He was bluffing. Having to come to the office and bitch for his selling fee wasn't a big deal but he wanted to let McNally know who was boss.

With that and the check, Snapper stalked out without further comment. McNally watched him leave, also without comment. But when the door closed behind Snapper, he said, "Arrogant bastard. If it wasn't for the money, I'd kick the lazy son of a bitch out."

He smiled. *Ah, the money. Don't forget that ole buddy. I'd put up with the devil if he were bringing me money.*

And, on the way to his car, Snapper was all smiles. "I put that fat asshole in his place."

He'd have a late snack after he'd deposited the check.

Then, maybe he'd go out and hit a few tennis balls with somebody. The tournament was coming up. *Valley will do most of the playing,* he thought. Vincent Valley was his doubles partner for the tournament. However, practically everyone Vincent knew called him "Vince."

Like always, Snapper's mindset was to shift responsibility to somebody else.

Chapter 3

Vince, a man in his late fifties, sat on the edge of a table just below a stage and plucked the strings of his black lacquered guitar as people came into the hall and took seats. Most took the time to look and smile in his direction. He always nodded back.

He was almost six feet tall, had light brown hair and blue eyes. The exercise he did most days at the Rec Center gave his shoulders a nice strong look, like he could hold his own in a confrontation though it had been years since he'd had one. That, with the flat stomach the exercise and his diet fostered, made him look younger than he was.

Vince didn't have one of those square, handsome faces that women turned to look at when he passed or talk about at social meetings. It was what some would call lean and mean, with a good chin covered by a slight beard. A mustache completed his appearance. The smile he most always showed people, except when he was in court, offset his lawyer's "lean and mean" look to a great extent; stoic his fellow lawyers called it.

It was Saturday morning, early summer, the usual time for his "people" talks, as he called them. The hall was small enough not to require a microphone and he never felt taking the stage behind him was part of what he wanted to present anyway.

Regarding the stage, as he told someone, early on, he didn't come to be looked up to, just to be listened to and if they liked it, to come back the next week. So far, his listeners had increased over the weeks.

If the time came when they didn't want to listen, he would go back to what he was going to do before he got there. However, he had to admit, talking to the people like he had been doing and having them, apparently, like what he was saying, kept him from getting out the pills he'd accumulated for the final trip away from everything that he always had on his mind.

The tune he played was *Only the Lonely,* a popular and hit tune by Roy Orbison some years before. For the "meeting" Vince wore casual clothes, a worn short sleeved shirt and pants, without a belt, and comfortable old shoes.

*****

Vince and his wife, Carolyn, were, well had been, lawyers with offices in La Jolla, until almost 5 years before, when his wife was diagnosed with lung cancer, having smoked most of her adult life, the consequences of pressures from an active law practice. The doctors assured them they could cure her with chemotherapy but within a year of the treatment after being told, "We got it all," it was back and she slowly began to die, in pain. The pills they always gave her did little good.

They had two children, a girl and a boy. The girl was a doctor and helped Vince while her mother was dying. Their son was a computer scientist and spent as much time with them as he could.

After the burial, Vince went into a deep depression. Unable to function with any degree of effectiveness, he sold the law practice including the office space to the junior members of the firm. Then he was faced with joining his wife or doing something else but had no idea what the "something else" would be. He'd kept the pills his wife hadn't used so he could join her when the time came. He hoped they'd be enough to do the job if and when the time came. So far it had not.

So, in consideration of the end being near, he also sold their La Jolla home as well and gave the proceeds to the children. He kept his 401k and the income he was receiving from the junior partners but had begun to make arrangements to give it to the children as well. He had decided there was nothing left for him to do with Carolyn gone and the children functioning on their own. So, he got out the pills and put them on the breakfast table to take.

While he was thinking about that and what, if anything, he wanted to do with the rest of his life, he put the pills away and moved into their Airstream trailer which they had been keeping at a camp ground just north of San Diego. There, he spent his days moping under a tree in front of the trailer thinking about the "end" and when that end would be. He just never seemed to be able to make that final decision.

His camper "pad" neighbor, Beatrice, often strolled out to his tree to keep him company. Now and then, she brought out a beer and nuts which she shared with him.

She'd kept herself in pretty good shape, wasn't bad looking and was reasonably sophisticated. If it hadn't been for his circumstances, having lost his wife, Carolyn, he might have looked at her with interest. But, as things stood with his pills, he didn't think he could ever be interested in another woman. And, after thinking about Beatrice, decided he could never be interested in her. She just wasn't his type.

Her camper, which she'd lived in with her husband until he'd died several years earlier, was larger than the weekend camper Vince and his wife had used for short "get-aways."

Beatrice didn't like her camper much but it was all she and her husband felt they could afford.

She'd married her husband after a breakup with the man she truly loved but who, she discovered, hadn't loved her. On the rebound, she somehow took up with a man who had driven a cab after he'd retired from driving a big rig all over the country. Even though she knew she deserved better, she elected to overlook it and accept the life she'd made for herself. As she used to say, "I've made my bed and I have to lie in it."

Her husband drank a six pack every day and always kept a can at the front of his seat and sipped on it when he could. And, although he never drank to excess, he would say, he soon began having slight strokes which increased in size until one took him out.

Beatrice went through a short period of depression but soon recovered and found herself happy that her worthless husband was out of her life. Unfortunately, her living circumstances in a camp ground didn't offer her much of an opportunity to find a replacement, that and her age.

So, she was pleased that Vince had moved into the adjacent pad and tried to kindle an interest in him. She could not and often felt depressed when he failed to respond very much to her overtures.

From the way Beatrice strolled out to visit when he sat down to mope and wonder when he should take the easy way out with Carolyn's left over pills, Vince rightly suspected that she wanted a closer relationship but he rejected that. He preferred to mope in private and his interest was in having no serious relationships.

Nevertheless, he was always nice and thanked her for the beer and nuts. And, he was pleased by the way she always tried to cheer him up even though it was a losing proposition. His only interest, however, was deciding when to leave the place permanently. Practically every day, he thought about it but always found a reason to wait another day to do it.

She was a couple of years older than him, a bit over weight, as many women get when living alone with nothing to do and no one to do it for. However, she was not so much overweight that most men would have found it objectionable should there have been any around, looking. Unfortunately, in the camp, there did not appear to be any and Vince hadn't shown any interest in being one.

Her hair was a light brown with some gray; her face rounded, always with a nice smile and she was several inches shorter than him.

Finally, he made the decision to take enough of the pills he'd accumulated to join his wife, but before he could do that, someone called and asked him to speak to a writer's group in La Jolla. They wanted a lawyer and knew him from a case he'd handled for them years before.

He told the caller he had nothing left to say, but the woman insisted that he could surely speak for thirty minutes on things he and Carolyn had done while they practiced. "I need you," she'd pleaded.

He finally agreed, but instead of talking about legal problems that had confronted them, he decided to talk about things that had bothered him about people and life.

His talk was well received. *Most likely because it wasn't legal and boring as hell,* he thought. He and his wife hadn't had any cases that left the participants laughing.

Oddly enough though, the experience brought him out of his depression and thereafter, he began a program of weekly "people talks" in La Jolla. He'd worry about what to do if and when they ever ended. Barely a day passed that he didn't think about it.

His first talk was in front of ten people. Thereafter it had grown so that some weeks, he spoke to as many as a hundred about whatever had crossed his mind the week before.

He'd gotten some flak from a couple of churches who claimed some parts of his talks were blasphemous and asked him, actually told him, to stop. That made him laugh.

"I'm only talking about what I see and hear," he told those who asked. "If that is a sin, as some folks are saying, the sin is not mine. It's everywhere I look."

He tuned up his old guitar and often used it in his talks.

He didn't play his guitar at every meeting, only those where a song seemed to tie into what he was going to talk about.

"Only the lonely know the way I feel tonight …" he sang while he strummed the chords that went with the song. It reminded him of how he had felt every night since his wife died.

*****

Vince nodded at some of the people who sat in chairs near where he was playing, people who watched and listened to the song. He recognized them as regulars who'd come every week to a meeting. Like Vince, they'd dressed casually. They had come to hear what he had to say, not to make an appearance at an event. About a quarter of those attending were married. Most though were singles, some divorced, some not.

The hall was filing so he stood to be able to see everyone and so they could see him. *People want to know I'm here,* he thought as he strolled down the corridor between the chairs set up for visitors and continued playing.

He was surprised to see Beatrice in attendance. She smiled at him as he passed. He held up to nod and smile back as he played. It was the first time he'd seen her at one of his meetings.

Probably the first time she's come. Must have gotten a ride, he thought. He didn't recall that she had a car but he'd never asked. She did have a car he just hadn't seen it.

He was surprised however. He didn't know she even knew he gave the "people" talks but lately, since there had been more interest, announcements had been in the newspapers.

She watched him pass. *He'll be impressed that I've come,* she thought. *I can make him happy again. I know it.*

Those were her thoughts as she sat there. Unfortunately for her, he didn't know it and didn't want to know it. Being happy wasn't something that was on his mind. Depression hung over him most of the time like a dark cloud.

Two old fans twirled wobbly on the ceiling of the hall, which was a room connected to the recreational facility just off the middle of the town. While La Jolla, which bordered the Pacific in Southern California, was generally cooler than other areas of San Diego Country, it was warm enough for the fans to be welcome even though a slight breeze stirred the outside air. The windowed room could accommodate about a hundred people and chairs had been set up to accommodate them, should that many show up.

Vince's talks usually drew somewhere between sixty and eighty people. He had first spoken in whatever church hall he could solicit when he had begun his talks some months earlier. That stopped when the churches objected to what he was saying. After that, the La Jolla Light, the local newspaper, accommodated him with an announcement about the place and time of his weekly talks.

Cindy walked in with her friend, Amy. They were in their thirties, both in good physical condition and mentally alert. They stood an inch or so over five and a half feet tall. Their faces appeared to be without feelings just then, like no smiles had ever brought a wrinkle to them. But, they were just distracted, thinking about the talk they'd come to hear and the help they would give Vincent.

Their help was voluntary but he was relieved that they were helping. It made things easier for him. They had been helping since they'd met playing tennis at the La Jolla Rec Center where they played regularly.

The first thing they did after they came inside was to place two old felt hats on small tables beside the door. Inside each were cards saying, "donations appreciated."

Donations, if any, from those who came to listen to his message, were dropped into the hats as they left. Vince never asked for anything. He gave his talks because he wanted to share his messages with anybody who wanted to hear them. The idea for the hats and cards came from Cindy.

Cindy had been married once for about a year. When it became clear that her husband only wanted what was free and bitched when she dared to ask for more, she kicked him out and got a divorce. She was glad she'd fought off the impulse to get pregnant. She worked as a paralegal in a law office in La Jolla. She'd thought about getting a law degree but never seemed to have the time or money to do it.

Amy, perhaps less pretty than Cindy, had never been married although, like most young women, wanted to find someone. So far she hadn't. She once said, "When I quit giving out free samples, they quit calling." She worked in a real estate broker's office as a salesperson with aspirations to be a broker as soon as she qualified.

Vince smiled at them with a nod and turned to make his way back to the front of the hall, strumming his guitar and singing, "No more sorrow, but that's just the chance you gotta take. If your lonely heart breaks ..."

Once the guests quit coming into the hall, Vince leaned the guitar against the table and told them, "I was playing *Only the Lonely* because I want to talk about people today and that song is about people. There are lots of lonely people in this world."

They applauded. He gave a nod at their response. He avoided a smile, but did let himself enjoy theirs.

Nice to know that people can still smile. I wish I could.

Chapter 4

Vince began his talk by reciting somebody's theory that when the planet people called earth stopped where it did and began its rotation around the sun, it was covered in ponds of "soup" filled with microbes. He figured that the sun brought the microbes out of the soup and they made decisions to form all living things including, eventually, our hungry ancestors.

"I said hungry because I wanted to tell you this. Some scientist discovered micro-biotic creatures in our guts that send signals to our brains in response to what we eat. Those signals can send us into a depression or anger. I've wondered if that's one reason our ancestors ran around with clubs. Because of what they were eating.

"Somebody, Hippocrates, a Greek doctor I think, once said in the 1800s, we are what we eat. I'm sure that person didn't know about those creatures in our guts, but he was closer to the truth than he might have imagined.

"Okay, enough digression. What I really want to talk about are women, the fairer sex, they are called. Someone, a man I recall, once testified in an old court case I had, 'A womern has a lot put on her.' The man butchered the English but that was his way and no one complained. And, the woman I represented won the case.

"I thought what the man said about women was profound. Just think about it. Right next to man's instinct to survive was his instinct to procreate. We are programed from birth to create survivors. All creatures, all plants, are born with the instinct to make more. I doubt the earliest forms of life understood that but they just did it because the instinct to do it was so strong, it dominated their lives just as, I think, it dominates ours today. In fact, in this day and age, it seems to be the only thing on people's minds, the instinct to procreate.

"Can you just imagine first man and first woman. Both have that instinct, but man, being the dominate of the two, grabs anybody close with the right parts, and begins the process. Thereafter, the women's stomachs began to swell and nine months later, all swollen, they began to experience pain and shortly thereafter, they expelled another living thing that wanted to be fed. Can you just comprehend their shock. Having that bloated body and then a small thing that wanted food. And, the male creature has already left to do what male creatures did in those days. Climb trees and bash other male creatures over the head with his club."

Beatrice smiled broadly, completely agreeing with what he was saying.

"I wonder if they stared at the small thing and said, 'What the hell is that?' Of course the female creature probably remembered what had happened with the male creature, - hell, it might have been fun for her as well – and eventually they must have figured it all out. If they had words in those days, she might have said, 'Be damned.' Instinctively, she would have taken care of it, raised it. It somehow had to be hers, ... somehow, since it came from her.

"Society has finally evolved to the point of recognizing that women can do more than just have children. They can hold political office and make important decisions, just like a man. Maybe one of these days, a child factory will be created to have the children and relieve them of the burdens of child birth. You just tell the factory manager what you had in mind for a child and pick it up at the exit door. Maybe deposit some DNA. As somebody once said, 'Wouldn't that be a note to take to the baby Jesus.' I don't quite understand the quip. I just threw it in. Sounds kind of like it fits though."

After a pause to let that sink in, he said, "Let me digress a bit and talk about evolution. Man no longer sleeps in trees. We wear clothes, cut our hair and bathe. Some of us anyway. You drive down the streets and gaudy signs beckon us to buy something we don't need and will probably throw away when it quits working after we get it home. Sounds like we're making progress, but think about it. We still need bathrooms. Or as I my granddad used to say, 'Can you stop at the next bush?' Excuse my digression. The thought just popped into my head so I shared it with you.

"I want to take questions like I always do but before that, I want to say something about man's instinct to dominate.

"Some men, with no one else they could dominate, turned that instinct on women. Made 'em feel superior to psychologically and physically dominate a woman. Probably couldn't dominate anything else in his life so he picked a woman. Made her feel like she was worthless when compared to a man. In my opinion, such men should be taken into a courtyard and horsewhipped. Instead, if a woman could and dared to, she might consult an attorney who would take the bastard to court. But, that was centuries later."

The women in the hall applauded, Beatrice more loudly than the others. A few shouted encouraging words. Beatrice didn't do that but she was thinking just how sensitive a man Vince was.

Damn. That makes me think I know what I'm talking about, Vince thought. *But, hell, I know better.*

He smiled, nodded and continued, "One more thought on man's domination and I'll be finished. Man could lead and the strongest did and the women had children like they were told to do. That's how nations came into being, I think, to satisfy man's ego. Armies were formed so other people could be dominated to satisfy that man's, the leader's, instinct to dominate. Interestingly enough, the strength of that instinct varies from man to man. That's why some people are leaders and some are followers. But, just to make the point, it has now been discovered that women also have, at least, the equivalent of a dominate instinct. Of course it could be an equivalent instinct that was learned over time or it could just be intelligence or common sense born of experience. At any rate, things have changed and are still changing … for the better."

More applause, mostly from the ladies but men joined in as well. All those who'd come to hear Vincent were reasonably well educated and had common sense.

He talked some about society and the way people lived and how the approach to life had changed over the years and for the better. Even men wholly steeped in the traditional way of life, had to admit that.

"Okay, now that I've got that introduction out of the way, I'll get to what I really came here to say." He grinned.

"I came here to talk about man's attraction to women and visa versa. Knowing people as I'm sure we all do, it isn't hard to imagine that even way back in time, man had preferences. He'd look at some women and want to procreate with them more than he'd want to procreate with one of the others. Well, maybe they didn't start writing poetry or painting pictures or singing songs about women just then, but over time, that's just what did happen. So when marriage was finally created or sanctioned or whatever, when it began, man could indeed look around and find a woman he truly liked enough to marry and build a life."

I wish he'd look at me. I love him so, Beatrice thought.

Vince continued. "I have no doubt that younger men looked around, still do, and see women they "love" enough to procreate with and are willing, maybe they even believe, they can build a life with the woman. Unfortunately, most lack the experience and therefore the judgment to make worthwhile decisions. Probably some women also fall into that category. So, many of those marriages don't last. Only when man has sufficient experience and intelligence can he make a proposal to a woman that can be relied upon. Otherwise, they too end up paying a lawyer to correct their mistakes. Sometimes leaving children behind to grow up without a father they can see every day and learn from."

He looked into the room so see if anybody looked like they might want to object. Apparently not, so he continued, "So, I'm where I wanted to be when you walked in and I was mangling my guitar. Men and woman wanting each other. We all know it just doesn't always happen like we want it to. We see somebody we like and they don't like us back. Or they think they do and the divorce thing I just alluded to happens. What happens then? They become lonely. They don't have what they need to feel whole. They don't have a mate. So, those men and women write poetry, paint pictures, maybe sing songs. I've heard thousands and I bet you have too. Songs about loves, lost loves and unrequited feelings."

I could tell him about love. My love, Beatrice thought as she smiled broadly at him. *I could make him happy.* She was so glad she came.

Vince picked up his guitar and began strumming the strings of *Have You Even Been Lonely*. He walked slowly up the center aisle, playing his guitar and singing, "Have you ever been lonely? …"

When he reached the door, he turned and walked back to the front, singing, "Have you ever loved someone who doesn't love you?" He paused and said, mostly under his breath, *"Damnit."*

My wife loved me and I loved her and I've been lonely ever since she left me. He thought as he strummed.

He stopped at the back and said, "I think we all need to talk about our experiences so if somebody wants to say anything, stand up or not and talk away. We have the time. Somebody once told me if I told somebody about my worries, they'd go away. I tried it and damned if I don't think they were right."

Unfortunately, they just don't stay away, he thought grimly.

A woman stood and talked about a love affair she'd had with a married man who decided he couldn't leave his wife and children after all. But, he'd enjoyed the sex. It had left her bitter but she felt better having heard what Vince was saying about men and women. "You've given me hope to go on living," she said.

Several others also stood and talked about their lost loves and loves that had become corrupt and how they had handled them or how they had internalized them and the resulting effect they had had on their lives and the way life had looked afterwards.

Beatrice half wanted to stand and talk about love but was too shy and too afraid Vince would know who she was talking about.

While they talked, Vince strummed his guitar softly. After more than a dozen had stood to voice their disappointments in life, it was over. No one else wanted to or dared share their secrets.

Vince thanked everyone for coming and for sharing their stories. He said he'd be back the next Saturday at the same time unless he didn't.

"We never know when our last day will be. Sometimes, I think, our bodies sense that we've had enough and decide to do us a favor and pack it in. But, as of now, I'll be back. I have no idea what I'll talk about. I hope something comes to me over the week. Right now, I have to play tennis. Somebody asked me to be their partner and I agreed. Now, I have a responsibility."

The people who'd come applauded as though they'd enjoyed the "talk." Several came up to shake his hand and to tell him how much they enjoyed it. "Please come back next week," was what most were saying in various words. Many of those were ladies who had plans to invite him to dinner as soon as they worked up the courage.

Beatrice told him how much she enjoyed his talk.

"I'll probably see you later," she told him.

He shook his head but wasn't sure that she would see him anytime soon. He had a tennis tournament to play in.

On the way out of the hall, most of those who'd listened to Vince's "talk" dropped a buck or two, sometimes fives, into one of the hats. Now and then, a ten was dropped in but twenties were a rarity.

After counting the money the attendees contributed, Cindy and Amy handed Vince a roll of bills. Cindy said, "Over a hundred. All tax free." She smiled.

"You and Amy take some. The hats wouldn't have been there but for you," he said sincerely and handed it back. He wasn't holding the talks for the money. He was doing what he had just said, talking away his troubles. He still missed his wife, her love. He'd go home after the tennis match and play an old Orbison cd and after that the late Patsy Cline's song, *Have You Ever Been Lonely*.

The two young women looked at each other for a long interval, nodded and took most of the bills, leaving the rest for Vince. He was glad they had taken some. His living needs had become minimal since his wife had died.

They had been going through the same routine every week, same apparent indecision, same hesitancy, same facial expressions before deciding to divide the money. After the first time they went through the routine, Vince almost laughed. However, he knew they probably needed a few extra bucks. The cost of living kept going up.

*****

Most people, including Vince picked up one of the investment brochures Ginny and Amy had left beside the hats. The ladies received a small fee for every investor they brought in.

The brochures were the ones McNally had prepared for *The Taco Wagons Investments*. Vince was impressed by the stylized representation of the old Conestoga wagon, the brochure described as the "Taco Wagon" franchisees could lease.

He also took note of the interest return on the bonds investors were asked to buy in the company to fund its operations.

Not bad. Eight to ten percent. I wish Carolyn and I had bought some. Be damned, he thought, when he saw Snapper's name and the information about how he created the company.

I wouldn't have thought he had that much creativity in him, Vince thought. *Seems like an arrogant son of a bitch to me. I hope he'll play better tennis today than what I've* seen him play. *He plays lazy tennis, watches his partner play.*

Vince had been asked by Snapper to be his doubles partner in the tennis tournament at the La Jolla Rec Center. They had a match scheduled that afternoon. They had played together a couple of times in the past when somebody developed a cramp or something and Vince was asked to finish out the match for him. That's how he came to know Snapper.

Vince acknowledged in his thoughts that Snapper could play, but more often than not, he seemed to dog it and let his partner do all the work. He was about to find out just how right he was.

Vince threw the brochure into a trash can by the door. He wasn't investing in anything anymore and certainly wasn't interested in becoming a street vendor selling Mexican food from a leased Taco Wagon even if it did look charming as hell.

Chapter 5

Bishop showed up at Court 2, with his borrowed racquet in hand and dressed in the outfit Ellen had given him, at a few minutes before one, the time Ellen had said they were to play. He was in pretty good shape, game wise, and had played a couple of days before flying out for the speech. He wouldn't have been worried, but had no idea about the level of competition he'd be facing.

Competition looks pretty good, he thought as he watched the prior match wind up. *They're knocking hell out of the ball.* From the score, he figured the players were fairly evenly matched and looked like they'd be tough to beat. *I hope the team we're going to play isn't that good.*

After the last point, they thanked each other and waved to Bishop. It was his court. Ellen walked up seconds later along with, what Bishop concluded, was an elderly couple. He laughed to himself. *Hell, I'm elderly.* For some reason, but even though he was past sixty, he just never considered himself old. And, the couple that just walked up looked too elderly to be playing competitive.

So, if Ellen is as good as her instructor said, we should be able to handle them.

Ellen wanted the forehand side. Bishop didn't mind. The other side took the opposite end of the court and began hitting the balls back and forth to Ellen and Bishop for a few warm-up minutes. Neither team did much more than get the ball back, not wanting to show their game any more than they had to.

Even so, Bishop felt confident that their opponents would not be able to stay with them, especially if Ellen played as well as she had been talking about when she first brought up the tournament and her need for a partner.

Indeed, when the other side began serving to start the match, it was clear that their opponents hadn't been playing very long. In fact, they didn't seem to mind losing. It was like playing in the tournament was entertainment for them. They laughed at their mistakes and patted their racquets when Ellen and Bishop made good shots.

And, Bishop was pleased to note that Ellen was as good as she'd suggested. They won in straight sets, hardly breaking a sweat.

They reported their score and were told to be back at eight the next morning for their next match. Court 2 again. Bishop was glad. While the other courts had nets between them to catch balls from invading adjacent courts, having to play next to others was a distraction. Court 2 was by itself, with no adjacent courts.

Even though he didn't know them, he stayed to watch Ginny and Amy's match on one of the grouped courts. He thought they played well. They won almost as easily as he and Ellen had against much better players. He congratulated them. They thanked him, both smiling.

He didn't stay to see Vince and Snapper, his partner, neither of whom he'd met, winning on another court. He did see them in a glance and took note that they were playing very well. *Good tennis players in La Jolla. Probably follows with all the good weather. They can play every day.*

*****

Bishop and Ellen showed up the next morning almost at the same time. Their opponents were two young men. They didn't bother to disguise their shots during the worm up, preferring instead, Bishop figured, to try and intimidate them. He and Ellen knew they'd have to play better than they had the day before to win. They didn't have a strategy meeting. It didn't take talking strategy to know they had to play damn good to win.

When they took to the court, Ellen looked at Bishop and nodded toward the other end of the tennis court. Bishop nodded back. He understood. They had to whip them.

Both instinctively adopted a plan to keep the ball in play until the other side became impatient and hit an error. The young men got the first serve and won at love.

Damn, this is gonna be a short match, Bishop thought. He knew there was no need trying to power any shots past them. He was sure they'd knocked balls back faster than he could serve them, for winners. So, he mixed slice serves that nibbled away at the corners with short, almost drop shot serves that confused the hell out of the young men who were accustomed to playing with opponents who felt they had to match their shots, power for power.

Bishop won his game and when the next guy came up to serve, he backed up a stride to give himself more time to get the balls back. Ellen saw and did the same. The guy won his serve but it went to deuce. When Ellen served, she played like Bishop had, hitting soft and slice serves, and also won.

Hard shots to Bishop and Ellen had to be played back as lobs. When their opponents went back for put-aways, Bishop and Ellen got in front of their overhead returns and played for half volleys or short hop returns.

The match stayed even but when it was even at six, Ellen caught a put-away and it dribbled over the net for a winner. Bishop's next serve caught a corner and the guy had to pop it up. Ellen put it away. First set was theirs.

The second set went the same way and Ellen and Bishop were in the next round which, the way things had played out, would be the semifinal matches.

The young men applauded them and wished them well. Bishop could tell they were disappointed however. They had expected to win against their "older" opponents. They left the court with shoulders slumped.

Bishop still hadn't received a call from any of his banker clients so he wasn't worried about that aspect of his life. His only worry was their next match which was against Cindy and Amy whom Bishop had watched after their first match. They had breezed through their sets at love.

Gonna be a challenge, he thought.

Warming up, Bishop could tell they were both very good. Strokes were even and smooth and hard when needed, soft when soft was more effective. They played good, smart tennis, Bishop figured.

Vince and Snapper were playing in the other semifinal match. Like Amy and Cindy, they had not lost a set during the tournament.

Ellen and Bishop lost the first set, 6-4 and felt lucky to have won as many as they had. It seemed like everything they threw at the two girls, they were ready for. And, they were hitting the lines and corners with regularity. Bishop felt frustrated.

He told Ellen, "I'm gonna adopt a drop shot, lob game to see if I can get them off their game. They're like robots, waiting for everything we hit, ready to knock it back like rifle shots. I want them to wonder what we're going to hit next. I want them to think. That ought to slow them down some.

It did and Bishop and Ellen won the second set.

When they started the third set, the two girls stepped in a stride to catch the drop shots earlier. They also tried to overpower Bishop and Ellen. When Bishop and Ellen saw that, they tried to hit the balls back at the girls' feet to slow down their game. They returned the balls, but the returns were defensive and more or less easily handled by Ellen and Bishop.

They were tied at 6-6 in the match game. Bishop was serving. He'd been hitting slices and knuckle ball serves since they'd begun. He decided for the match game to go with his hard flat serves and see if he could catch them by surprise. He did.

With that change in strategy, Bishop and Ellen won the match and would play Vincent and Snapper in the final match the next morning.

Bishop and Ellen breathed a sigh of relief when it was over. It had been a hard match.

Vince and Snapper were still playing when Bishop and Ellen won over Cindy and Amy so they got to watch their last few games.

They were playing very well and Vince and Snapper were winning, but Snapper seemed to be riding Vince after every point they lost. He wasn't hitting the winners Snapper thought he should be hitting. Or, he wasn't serving like he should. And, he didn't cover the lobs like any "decent player" would have.

Bishop wondered about that. He didn't believe riding a partner was a good thing.

At the last cross over, it appeared that Vince took the time to have words with Snapper who frowned and dismissed what Vince had said with a sharp wave. He walked onto the court while Vince was still talking. Even with Snapper's browbeating, they won the game and the match. Vince left the court without speaking to Snapper who didn't seem to care.

"Tennis partners who aren't seeing eye to eye," Bishop quipped to Ellen.

She agreed. "I think the one guy, Snapper, stays so uptight, he doesn't know shit from Shinola."

Bishop laughed. It was an old expression he'd heard many times since he'd been in Mississippi but never in California.

*****

That night, he had a call from Garman. He'd been expecting a call from him. And, he had the news Bishop had also half been expecting since his talk with the borrower about the loan hadn't gone well.

Garman told Bishop he would be needed the next week for a meeting at the bank with Dalton Parsons and bank executives who sat on the bank's loan committee. Parsons would also be bringing his high priced and well known attorney from a big firm in Jackson. So, he expected fireworks.

Garman said the bank didn't want to face the attorney in that kind of meeting without having one of their own present and Bishop was the one they wanted backing them up.

He said he'd tried to get Parsons' father to attend but was turned down. It was well known that the father had sufficient assets to bring the loan current, even make the payments until cotton prices rebounded.

"Anything been done since we last talked?" Bishop asked.

"No. We've exchanged demanding letters. His demanding more time. Ours demanding money."

"Loan's been drifting in default," Bishop said.

"That's right. The meeting will address that and unless some progress is made, a demand letter, probably a notice of default will be filed as well." Garman said.

"I guess Dalton still thinks his father can bully the bank into letting him get away with a defaulted loan," Bishop said.

Garman agreed. "He's forcing us to have a face to face. As I said, he'll bring his attorney. It'll be top level all the way. So, we definitely need you there."

With only one match to go, Bishop told him he would be there.

*****

He told Ellen about the call the next morning when he showed up at the court for their final match with Vince and Snapper.

"I'm glad we're not going on tour," she replied.

"Me too. Right now, I'd like to win in straight sets and catch the next flight to Mississippi."

Ellen looked at Vince and Snapper sitting on their bench and said, "I doubt that'll happen. They had to play pretty good tennis to get here. We'll have to play better than that to take the big trophy home. That Snapper guy looks like he could play in the movies. Handsome son of a gun."

Bishop laughed. "Yeah. He does look like a movie star, doesn't he? Let's see if he can play tennis as good as he looks."

Ellen gave Bishop a brief description of Snapper's personal activities. How he, according to some, had become wealthy by marrying elderly ladies and squiring them around until they either had to pay to get rid of him or they passed away. The children of the women he married played a part in forcing their mothers to get rid of the man they recognized as a leech, a promiscuous leech at that.

She also told Bishop what she'd heard about Snapper, how he had developed some kind of franchise called Taco Wagons that some people said was doing well. The company was selling bonds to support the business. The high yields paid by the bonds had attracted local interest.

"So, he's king shit," Bishop said and thought, *thinks his shit don't stink.* It was an expression he'd heard in Mississippi and thought it fit.

"Thinks he is," she answered with a look in the direction of Vince and Snapper.

It didn't appear to Bishop and Ellen that the two men were speaking to each other. However, when Vince saw Ellen and Bishop unloading their gear on their bench, he walked over, greeted both and extended his hand to Bishop.

Like his partner, he looks weary, Bishop thought. He figured they must have had some close matches. *Maybe we can wear them down a little more.*

"Good luck," Vince told them and walked back to his bench.

"You too," Bishop called. He laughed to himself. *The only luck one tennis player ever wishes another is bad luck. What they leave off when they say 'Good luck' is 'You're gonna need it.'*

He continued the conversation he and Ellen had been having about the trophy before Vince had come over to wish them good luck. "Whichever trophy we get, you can have, Ellen. It's your tournament."

She put up a token argument but it was pretty clear that she wanted any trophy they won, the big one as winners or the small one as runner ups. Bishop was glad to let her have whichever trophy they ended up with. Playing was his favor to an old friend. That was trophy enough for him.

When Bishop and Ellen took the court to warm up, Vincent and Snapper followed them out. After a few minutes of hitting the ball around, Snapper called out. "Looks like you're ready."

Ellen answered. "Yep."

Snapper approached the net, said, "You call it." And flipped a coin. Ellen called heads. It was tails. Snapper's side would serve first.

Vince played like a man possessed, getting to every ball. Bishop and Ellen played very well, but they were no match for Vince's play. He and Snapper won the first set, 6-2.

Vince looked exhausted but seemed enthused enough to play more games with just as much vigor. He drank a bottle of water during the set. From what Bishop could see, Snapper was content to cover mostly the doubles lane on his side and little more, forcing Vince cover the rest of the court.

Vince did what he had to do, however, and did it well, but after each game, he looked even more tired than he had when he first walked up to the court. And, when Vince couldn't get to a ball or returned a shot badly, Snapper let him have it. Vince shook his head with a stare but continued to play like his life depended on getting every shot.

Bishop assumed that was his playing style.

Not only that, midway through the set, Bishop began to take notice of Snapper's calls on their end of the court. Bishop frequently objected to his calls, bad ones, and was told by Snapper, "You call balls at your end, we'll call them at our end. That's how we do it out here. California rules."

The son of a bitch knows I'm visiting. Thinks that gives him the right to be an asshole.

At the turn, he told Ellen softly, "I think the guy who's bitching about everything his partner does, is making some absolutely bad calls. I don't like it."

She agreed. "I'm glad you called him down about it not that it has done any good."

"It hasn't. The man has no scruples," Bishop said.

Vince sat down and drank another bottle of water. The men still hadn't spoken, Bishop noticed.

Ellen thought more about what Bishop had said about Snapper's calls and said before they resumed play. "The guy has tennis eyes. I figured it'd even out over the match but I don't think it will. He's playing a game with us."

Bishop smiled, "Well, it ain't gonna even out. The man's winning the games with his bad calls. He called one of your shots out that was in by half a foot. He tried to get in front of it, but it had bounced twice by the time he did."

"Damn! I think I remember that shot," she said. "Maybe I'll have him arrested."

Bishop laughed, leaned over and whispered, "It'd be a first but I like the idea. Why don't we do this? When in Rome, do as the Romans do."

Ellen looked at him as though she couldn't believe what he was suggesting. She began shaking her head no. "Goes against my grain, Bishop. I'm used to enforcing the rules, not breaking 'em."

"You have to answer this question, Ellen. Which trophy do you want to take home? And, do you want to give the big trophy to a guy who's winning points with bad calls?"

She stared at her feet, shook her head some more then looked at Bishop and said, "I can't do it, but I can't stop you from doing it. If the other side attacks you, I'll help keep them off of you. And, I won't contradict your calls."

Bishop said, "Fair enough."

They took the court. It was Snapper's serve. He had a big grin on his face as he walked briskly to the line to serve.

Looking to wrap up this tournament in a hurry, Bishop thought to himself. *I'll do my best to frustrate all that. I'm going to be the fly in his ointment.*

Snapper hit a hard flat serve into the backhand side of the service court, in the court by a fraction. Snapper turned to go to the other side when Bishop called "Out."

"What!" Snapper yelled.

"What what?" Bishop yelled back. "The serve was long. Second serve."

"The damn thing was in by plenty!" Snapper shouted.

Bishop stood his ground and said, "Second serve."

Snapper did a little walk around, cursing as he did. Finally, he walked up and lobbed in a second serve that was out by several inches.

"Love fifteen," Bishop called out the score.

Snapper stopped, took a deep breath and walked to the other side for his second serve. The first serve was clearly out. The second was in by a couple of inches, right down the middle. Ellen returned it down the middle about as hard as she'd hit a ball all match. The other points went about the same. Anything close, Bishop called out. Snapper tried to do the same, but Bishop always beat him to the punch.

And, Snapper lost his serve. He didn't like it, but there was very little he could do about it. And, that was how the second set went.

Bishop called shots like Snapper had been doing and was still doing. However, Bishop and Ellen were hitting everything down the middle, hitting inside with plenty of clearance. No way even Snapper could call them out and Vince was scrupulously fair with his calls. Also, he never questioned Bishop's calls as if somehow he understood what was going on.

Vince continued to play hard even though it was clear that he was exhausted and almost dead on his feet. Meanwhile, Snapper stayed clearly on his side of the court and cursed at every shot Vince either couldn't get to or had to hit back as an easy shot. And, Ellen was killing everything he put up.

A natural, Bishop thought. *Never takes her eyes of the ball. Lots of us do and shank the put-aways.*

Bishop and Ellen won the second set 6-2 and evened the match.

At the break, Snapper was heard browbeating Vince for not playing harder. They heard Vince's reply. "Listen, asshole, you stand over there like you're daydreaming and let me play the damn match. Get off your ass and join me. Tired as I am, we can still win this thing."

"Excuses. Always somebody else's fault," Snapper shot back. "Is that your excuse?"

"Get your ass in gear," Vince told him and took the court.

But it was clear he had nothing left. And Snapper didn't look much better. Bishop figured he had been hugging the doubles' alley because he was too tired to do anything else.

Bishop and Ellen took charge, breaking Vince in the first game and Snapper in his. When they went up 4-0, Snapper shouted at Vince who'd just thrown himself at a shot, flicking it back for Ellen to put away.

"You look like a fool," he shouted, waving his racquet at the man trying to stand. "Where'd you learn to play this game? I must have been out of my mind to ask you to be my partner!"

Vince staggered over, grabbed Snapper by the front of his shirt. "You're a poor excuse for a human being. Another evolutionary failure." He threw Snapper sideways but instead of following up as Bishop assumed he might, he turned, grabbed his gear from their bench and began to leave the court. "You're so damn good, you can play the rest of the set by yourself. That'd be a change. You haven't played any of it so far," he looked back and shouted when he was at the gate.

Snapper looked at Bishop and Ellen with a pleading look on his face, like there was something they could do, or would do.

Bishop looked at Ellen and said, loudly enough for Snapper to hear. "That's what you call winning by default. Let's go log in our score, Ellen, and get a beer."

Ellen told him as they left, "If looks could kill, that Snapper guy would have died several times during that last set and for sure just then."

Bishop agreed with a shake of his head.

They got their gear and did just that, leaving Snapper standing on the court looking bewildered.

Chapter 6

Vince was nowhere in sight when Ellen and Bishop got to the clubhouse to report on the match, but the manager said he'd come by and reported what had happened. Everybody who'd ever played with Snapper had the same complaint, the manager said. It seemed that Snapper blamed everybody for everything and never accepted responsibility for anything.

The club was about to ban him from playing. They were going to give him a warning first.

Ellen picked up the big trophy with a smile and she bought the beer at a place overlooking the beach.

"Thanks for playing," she told Bishop. "I was getting ready to default my matches."

He told her he was glad to do it and was "damn glad" they won even if they did it by default.

"A victory is a victory no matter how you come by it," she said.

"I agree. My flight to Mississippi is in the morning," Bishop told her. "Glad to have played with you. Your instructor was right. You're a natural."

"You know what they say about us 'blacks'? We got sports in our blood." She grinned and took a sip of beer.

Bishop chuckled. "Never heard that one but I'd say you picked up tennis like you were born to play. Hell, it took me over a year to get to your level."

"When I was growing up, I worked on my grandpa's farm, slinging hay with a pitchfork. Makes for a good back hand. The rest, the forehand and serve just fell in. Maybe I have an instinct for the overheads. I just keep my eyes on the ball. Who knows? Right now, though, I've got bigger problems than my tennis game."

"What?" Bishop asked.

"Hell, two of my guys left to work for the FBI in DC. Another guy is taking over as police chief in San Francisco. I'm glad for them but they've left me damned short-handed. And, we're having a big drug problem. Seems like every corner has a dealer these days. I've heard that somebody's selling corners if you can believe it. Maybe true. I'm seeing an explosion of grass, coke, meth and heroin. The stuff goes anywhere from $15 a gram for grass to $100 a gram for coke. Crystal is $80 a gram."

"People paying to feel good and wreck their health in the process. Makes me think people can't accept responsibilities. They get up tight and have to have something to take them out of it. Use drugs and their responsibilities disappear. They live in a dream world but they have to wake up when the drug wears off.

"I wonder what happened to doing a good job and feeling good from that. Make money with a good days work and it won't kill you, like drugs will. Let me ask you this. Where in hell do all the people get the money for dope? It's not cheap." Bishop asked. "And not all of them are working."

"The ones not working have to beg, borrow and steal, we figure. Problem is, being short-handed like I am right now, I can't stop a hell of a lot of it. Not only that, the dealers are killing each other for the best spots. Like I said, I think they're selling the spots."

"Damn. Sounds like you're up to your back side in it. And, for now, shorthanded. So, you're the chief cook and bottle washer."

"Yep, trying to do it all, Bishop. I'm recruiting but it takes time to go through the resumes, interview candidates and even when you hire somebody, you have to watch the new hires to make sure they don't screw up. Dealers can shoot each other, but let us kill one of them and the shit hits the fan. Police brutality."

"I know what you're saying. I feel sorry for you. Glad it's not me," Bishop said.

"Lucky bastard. You get to speak to strange people you don't know at conventions, get thanked for it, play tennis, drink beer and fly home to a little woman."

"I have to agree," he smiled. "And, you missed a few other things that I won't get into."

"Beaver watching," she said with a grin.

He smiled back without a comment.

They had a second round, Bishop buying that time.

When their glasses were empty, he told her goodbye. He had to pack and get ready for an early morning flight. The hotel had a limo that could take him to the airport.

"Well," she said, giving him a goodbye hug, "See you next time."

"Call me when you need me. Or if you want to play in another tournament."

*****

The *second* thing Bishop did when he got back to Mississippi was to take Kathy out to dinner to celebrate being home. After dinner, they sat in comfortable rocking chairs on his back porch with his creek lights on, watching the greenish-brown waters slowly flowing past. And, they had a relaxing evening together. The next day, Kathy went to work and Bishop did as well, the bank problem loan.

He had a couple of days to get ready for the meeting between the bank and Dalton Parsons and wanted to use it. He figured it'd be a tense and probably brutal meeting with demands and counter demands from both sides. And, from past experience, he figured to be at the focal points of all demands. He knew he had to be prepared and would be.

Parsons dad, also named Dalton, was a big land holder in the Delta, still great dirt for cotton. But, according to Garman, he wasn't growing much cotton just then. Nevertheless, he was accustomed to having his way, and keeping his money, and probably figured the bank would cave in sooner or later. Bishop assumed that was why he wasn't going to attend the meeting. He didn't want to be confronted by a bank demand.

Most likely thinks the bank will make Parsons a deal because of his position in the bank, both as a shareholder and a depositor, Bishop thought.

Bishop had been watching the loan on the bank's reports since it had funded and, anticipating a default, had done some investigating already and had a recommendation ready should he be asked for one by the committee.

He imagined the committee was also getting ready. They were accustomed to dealing with high rollers but they also had the bank regulators to answer. They were in the unenviable position of being "damned if you do and damned if you don't. And, they didn't have any options. The regulators made the rules at that point."

His position was somewhat better but not much. He figured sooner or later, he'd be asked to solve the problem and become the bad guy on both sides. Hell, as far as the Parsons are concerned, I already am.

Chapter 7

The meeting was held in an impressive bank conference room with plush chairs situated around an oval wooden table that probably cost a fortune, Bishop assumed. The borrower and his attorney sat in comfortable chairs on one side and the bank's representatives sat on the other with Bishop.

Somebody had brought in fresh coffee in a silver container with fine china cups. Everyone had a cup and all were friendly before they sat down. At least they gave that impression.

Bishop knew it was all a fake. Behind those smiles they were all as uptight as they could be.

All fighting the urge to go to the bathroom, Bishop thought with a silent chuckle. He'd been there.

When they were all seated, Garman, the bank officer in charge of the loan, officially greeted everybody and gave a brief summary of the loan's status and the issues they would consider during the meeting. The loan was seriously in arrears, he told them, and the borrower was requesting an extension without offering any consideration and without bringing the loan current.

To bring the loan current would require a payment of three hundred thousand dollars. And the bank was requesting that the loan be paid in full since it was in default. The bank had accelerated the due date in accord with the loan terms.

"In effect," Garman said, "Mr. Parsons is asking the bank to re-write the loan for more money including an interest reserve to carry the loan for a year. The bank finds that request unacceptable."

In support of that proposal, Parsons offered another marketing study that said cotton would be coming back in the next year as big as ever. The study recommended that the bank show some patience and give the market time to solve the problem to everyone's benefit.

Parson's attorney, Washington Broadmore, said, "I'm not a cotton expert, but the report was prepared by a reputable company which is an expert in cotton. With a prognosis like that, I don't see how the bank can insist on having the loan prematurely paid off."

Parsons said, "You know I'm good for it," he told everyone at the table. "You aren't going to lose a nickel on my loan and you know it. Cotton is coming back. You just heard it!"

"What we know and what we think are not relevant to this meeting. We have regulators to deal with," Garman told him. "To rewrite the loan, as you're suggesting, would require, according to our regulators, Federal regulators by the way, that you first bring it current. Then, you have to reduce the loan amount by making a substantial principal reduction. Ask Mr. Parsons -"

"I can't do that. Well, I'm not going to. Dad doesn't want to get involved. It's my loan. I'm handling it! You're letting that half assed attorney-" He stopped for a moment and pointed a finger at Bishop with a sneer. "That asshole, tell you what to do. And, you're bootstrapping your demand with what you say the regulators are asking. You can tell them the loan is current if you just rewrite it and establish a new maturity date. Show the old one as paid in full. Dad told me you can do it that way. And, in case you haven't looked, he's a shareholder in the bank."

Everyone in the room knew that and they also knew that his dad had encouraged his son to open the facilities in the first place. But now, it was "his loan."

His dad's equipment would always be sent to the facilities for servicing. That'd guaranty the son steady business. But, that was before the downturn in cotton. The equipment, his father's and that of others, wasn't in use at the moment and didn't need servicing. And, all the service personnel had been laid off. Parsons no longer had a business.

For an hour, the sides exchanged proposals and criticisms as they rejected the other side's proposals. Finally, somebody asked Bishop what he thought.

"Ah," Bishop said. *I've been wondering when the finger would point at me.* "I think cotton will come back. It always has, just as the marketing report says, but the question is when. Notice how the report skirts around that bit of information. I can only guess why. They didn't know. Nobody does. However, in a business like this, a borrower has to, well damn well should, anticipate the ups and downs in the cotton market and be ready for them. In the first place, more has to be charged by the borrower for the services being offered and a reserve established to carry the loan when there is a downturn. I think I said something to that effect in my initial report. The borrower didn't do that and the loan didn't require it and now the ox is in the ditch, so to speak."

When the loan was made, the cotton market looked strong enough to last long enough to get the loan paid down to acceptable levels. The outfit that made the marketing report the borrower had just submitted, had made a similar report when the loan request was submitted and had stated that no reserve was needed. The borrower's prices for the services rendered were set at market rates for the area. The market study suggested that higher prices could force users to go elsewhere. Bishop had noted that the study hadn't shown the prices being charged by other, smaller servicers.

"Okay," Parsons said. "So, we all screwed up. That man," He pointed again at Bishop. "was right. I'll accept my share of the blame. I just want to stay in business. I'm asking the bank to accept its share of the blame. Let's do business not waste time talking about something we can't control. The report says the market is coming back! We'll all get well!"

Garman said, "But, we're not well, Mr. Parsons. The report may very well be right, but no one can say when the demand for cotton will be great enough to get you back in business. And, your loan is in default and is now all due and payable."

Parsons made a move as if to stand up but Bishop began to talk so he sat back down and listened.

"How about this," Bishop said. "You have 500 acres on the reservoir. Prime land. Two nationally known developers, home builders, have already expressed interest in the land and that interest has been rejected by you."

He was citing information he'd discovered during his investigation of the loan when it was made.

"Some of the land, with water views, is worth six or seven thousand dollars an acre. Water and electricity, telephone and internet are in the paved road in front of it. Some of the property is valuable for commercial use. You could sell that land to a developer and use some of the proceeds to do what the bank needs to keep the regulators off its back."

Parsons did come out of his chair then. "Wait a damn minute. That property was never in the financials I presented with my loan request! It's not part of this meeting. You're just causing trouble, like you've been doing since I asked for the loan! You're an asshole, Bone. A flaming asshole! You'll get yours one of these days. The bank made a mistake getting you involved."

"That issue, what I am or am not, is not the one this committee is facing at the moment. I daresay they will never have to. So, let me get back to what IS on the table, the 500 acres you failed to disclose to the bank in your financials. I think that land is now part of your financials, don't you, now that the bank knows about it. I also think it should have been disclosed initially. I think the loan request you signed stated that you'd disclosed all of your assets. Well, it's an asset and you're in need of an asset to take care or your problem. Seems a simple solution to me."

Parsons' face turned red. He stared at Bishop like he was ready to attack. He put his hands on the table and had begun to push himself up, but his attorney interrupted that.

His attorney stood, leaned over and whispered something in his client's ear. The borrower frowned with an angry shake of his head, but nodded and eased down into his chair.

His lawyer took over with a thin smile to counter the frowns on the bankers' faces.

Knows his client committed fraud against the bank by not disclosing the extra property. Also knows the bank, if it responded as it should, would file for judicial foreclosure, put a judicial lien on the property and sell it to satisfy any judgment they received on the suit.

The lawyer said he agreed with Bishop in general. "Without getting into the issues he's raising."

Yeah. Failure to disclose his client's fraud. Let's not get into that. Let's beat around that bush.

The lawyer then apologized for the borrower's "inadvertent non-disclosure" of the 500 acre asset. "My client thought he only needed to disclose sufficient assets to support his loan request. Had the bank needed more, it would have said and the reservoir property would have been disclosed."

He went on to say that the borrower would either sell the reservoir property for development or arrange financing through other sources to take care of the bank loan.

"I'm requesting thirty days to let him do that before you pursue your notice of default."

His father, Bishop thought, *will have to step in. He can't do anything in 30 days. Too much money involved. Negotiations plus escrow time will take more than 30 days even if he found a buyer tomorrow.*

The lawyer promised the bank a proposal they could accept in a week. And, that's how the meeting ended. After the meeting, Parsons told Garman he'd sell the land to his father for enough to bring the loan current and to keep it current for another year.

A decent solution, Bishop thought. *Should have proposed it before now.*

Garman agreed that no re-write would be necessary in that case and would recommend a short delay to allow the borrower to work out that sale. As far as reporting, once the loan was brought current and paying as agreed, their records would be "adjusted" to show that the loan had never been in default. That was the informal agreement made after the meeting had been adjourned. That would keep Dalton's credit unblemished.

Bishop listened to that agreement being negotiated by the lawyer and Parsons. He didn't say anything. *Bank business,* he thought. *Nothing to do with me.*

He wasn't invited to participate in the meeting so he left. He wasn't getting paid for the meeting anyway. *Besides,* my *weeds need hoeing.*

*****

A couple of days after the meeting, Dalton called Bishop and shouted angrily, "I hold you responsible for this whole damn debacle, embarrassing the hell out of me and my family. Making me pay for a lawyer who was ready to sell me out with the first sound of thunder. Forcing me to sell my property, probably at a loss. I won't shed a tear when somebody puts a hole through your head."

No loss if you sell to your father, Bishop thought but said, "Maybe that's why the loan failed. You can't accept responsibility can you? Lived too long at your father's feeding trough. I think you need to talk to somebody, professional. You know what I mean? However, I'll report your threat to Chief Jenkins just in case somebody takes a shot at me."

The man hung up without saying more.

*****

A couple of days later, Ellen Washington called him with a story and a request. Her call wasn't expected and her request wasn't either.

Her story didn't surprise him but her request was one he wasn't ready to consider. It wasn't a favor like playing in a tennis tournament. When he got right down to it, losing a tennis tournament was something he could get over. Her request, if it went wrong, wouldn't be something he could get over.

Like putting my neck in a noose, he thought.

Ellen, in effect, was offering Bishop a short term job as her assistant, a high risk job. A situation the Mayor had suggested. He knew Bishop by reputation and also knew he'd just spoken to a police association and played with Ellen in a tournament they'd won.

She explained to Bishop why she needed him. He cursed to himself as he listened. He didn't need a job like that. Jobs like the one she was proposing sometimes had a dead end, with the emphasis on "dead."

The story was interesting though.

*****

The evening before her call, Snapper Cornwall was driving home from a meeting with investors McNally told her. Snapper lived in an expensive townhouse half a block from the La Jolla Rec Center. Across the street from his townhouse sat a homeless man on the curb, eating an apple. Anyone watching would have assumed the apple was a gift from one of the older women who lived in La Jolla. They often gave handouts to homeless men and women and felt better about themselves for having done it.

However, the sight wasn't what anyone would have assumed from a passing look. The man had bought the apple at Vons and was waiting for

Snapper to come home. He knew Snapper would eventually show up and park his Maserati Turismo on the street in front of his home. The man had been there before to check out Snapper's habits.

Snapper got a kick out of flaunting his money. People stopped to stare when he drove past in his expensive car. Having them stare at him always brought a smile to his face and reassured him that he was better than the ones staring.

The development had underground parking but high flyers like Snapper parked on the street to get inside his townhouse sooner and to get going sooner when they left home. The high flyers seemed always to be "driven" to get to their next "important" meeting sooner where people waited to see and hear them. They believed their time was too valuable to waste going to a garage to get their cars.

Anyway, by the time Snapper had parked and had opened the car door, the "homeless" man had hurried crossed the street and stood beside him. He shoved the barrel of a thirty eight caliber automatic hand gun against Snapper's head.

Snapper knew what was happening. A panicky flash coursed through his mind causing him to blurt out, "Wait, I'll p-" He was going to say he'd pay more than the shooter was getting but he didn't get to finish.

The man said, "No, you have to die, you money grubbing bastard." He pulled the trigger that ended Snapper's life. His last thought process was … disbelieving dismay. He wasn't ready to die.

He was dead before he hit the sidewalk.

After he'd shoved the gun behind his belt, the shooter reached into Snapper's back pocket to take his wallet. Next, he snatched the gold watch from his wrist before hurrying away. Someone found the empty wallet down the street and turned it in to the police. The only fingerprints on it were Snapper's. The watch worth several thousand dollars was never found.

A man from one of the other townhomes had heard what he thought was a shot and looked out a window in time to see the "homeless" man hurrying down the street. He didn't see anything unusual about it but later did report what he'd seen after Snapper was found dead. He described the man as appearing young and in pretty good shape from the way he moved.

A celebrity was dead and no one in Ellen's police department was available to investigate. Her experienced detectives had gone on to better things. The public was raising hell about the killing, the Mayor told Chief Wasserman. He told her she had to have a high level assigned to the case.

Unfortunately she had none left and that was why she was calling Bishop. She need help big time. In effect, the Mayor was her boss and he'd told her to get her problem fixed.

"I want the man's killer brought in," he'd said before hanging up. "Your job is to do it. I don't care how you do, just do it."

The only man with enough experience and intelligence to help her was Bishop. If he was working the case, she knew he would keep the public from raising hell until she could hire someone with enough clout to head up the investigation.

The media reported the killing as if Snapper was the most beloved and dynamic person in La Jolla, not a guy who'd gotten his money from women willing to pay to get rid of him and lately the money he was getting from people investing in the Taco Wagon Investment Company.

*****

"Ellen," Bishop said, trying to sound helpful, "You're asking a lot of me. I have clients here with problems and a good friend I enjoy seeing every morning over coffee. I don't need to be in California chasing around after a killer who might not like to be chased, if you know what I mean. Lord knows, from what I know of the Snapper guy, he must have had many enemies. He struck me as a first class asshole at the tennis match. I think his partner, Vince something, would agree.

"Besides, you have to at least consider that he was killed by the homeless man, like your witness reported. That'll be a hard case to solve. Lots of homeless men running around. Hell, the man may be in San Francisco by now."

She answered, "I don't disagree with what you said, but I'm thinking the wallet and watch were taken to make us think just that, Bishop. In my opinion, the man had too many enemies to lay it on a homeless man who just happened to have a gun and who just happened to be waiting across the street from where the guy lived."

Bishop had to admit she was probably right. "Without the gun, I'd say the homeless man did it for what he could find. The gun, you're right, makes it look damn suspicious. If a homeless man had a gun, probably stolen, he'd have sold it for drugs."

"And, you're the best person to find out which of the people he's pissed off in his time did it, Bishop. The Mayor said as much when he agreed with my proposal. He's been catching flack about all the drug killings and doesn't want another one on his shit list rearing its ugly head." She told him what she was offering and the expense account. It came to over fifteen thousand dollars a month.

"Damn," he said. "That's high cotton."

"I know you're worth it, Bishop. The Mayor does too."

"I don't know it but I like the numbers. I could save enough from that to carry me through my lean times around here. Let me think about the obligations I have on my plate and get back to you. How long do you think it'll take you to get replacements for your senior detectives?"

"A couple of months. Then, I'll need a month for them to get up to speed."

"So, I'd be tied up at least two months, maybe three. Could I fly back here and take care of emergencies, if anything comes up? I have a case cooking in a bank's oven and it's likely to heat up."

"If you aren't in the middle of bringing in the killer."

"Okay. I'll think about it and let you know tomorrow."

Where in the hell would I start an investigation like that? Hell, the man must have had more enemies than he had friends, if he had any friends. I only knew him a few minutes and he made my shit list. His tennis partner has to be at the top of the list of suspects. I wonder about his investment company, Taco Wagons. Does he have any pissed off investors? Or Franchisees? I'd need to check that. I wonder how many he has.

Lots of loose ends. Lots of ravels to pull. Frustrations at every corner. But, I do like the money Ellen's put on the table.

He called his bank clients to see what, if anything, they had cooking that would require his immediate assistance. Unfortunately for him, things were slow. Ordinarily that would be bad news, but not with Ellen's $15,000 job offer on the table. So, there was no excuse to turn her down.

The banks had a few things on their lists to keep a watch on but nothing that was urgent like Dalton's problem with his high priced lawyer running interference for him.

Might be a good idea to be out of town when the bank has to turn Dalton down if his dad won't buy his land. I'll get the blame big time if the bank forecloses and sells the property for a profit.

Next he called Kathy and told her about Ellen's call. He took her to dinner to explain. Easier to hand out bad news over a good dinner. After listening, she said she didn't much like it, but she understood.

"Will you be able to fly home now and then? I need to see you," she said.

"I need to see you too. And will. You can bet I'll have some free weekends. If not, I'll make some. I'll be back. Without you, I have no life."

"You've said," she replied, adding. "I feel the same way about you."

So, she agreed. She would have anyway but having his assurance of coming home periodically made it palatable.

The next morning, he called Ellen and told her he'd be out there the next evening late. She'd have somebody at the airport pick him up and he'd have one of the city cars to use. He could also stay in one of the apartments the city used for such situations.

He packed a bag with two changings. He figured he'd wear one set and wash the other after he'd worn it. He did take a suit just in case but hoped he wouldn't need it.

If I have to play tennis, I'll use the stuff Ellen had for me the other day. Hopefully, the killer will come forward and confess and somebody will pardon him for ridding the world of an undesirable element. Hell, somebody might erect a monument in his honor. Hmm, or hers? A woman might have shot him. Or the child of a woman he jilted or cheated out of money.

He and Kathy enjoyed a last evening together. Neither said, but both wondered as they always did when Bishop went off to "war," would he return this time?

Chapter 8

Bishop was met at the airport by a uniformed policeman in the car he'd use while he was working on Snapper's murder. He dropped the policeman off at one of their stations near the apartment he'd been assigned and drove there to leave his bags.

He grabbed a midnight bite, bacon and eggs, at the nearby Denny's and went to bed. The next morning he did the same thing, had breakfast at Denny's, while deciding on his schedule for the day.

The guy he wanted to see first was Vince Valley. Even though he doubted an argument born of a tennis conflict was sufficient motivation for a murder, he had to admit that it was possible. The fuse of every person burned at a different rate, he knew, and Valley had had a physical encounter with the dead man, Snapper, after putting up with the man's bullshit for over an hour.

From what I know about the man, Snapper Cornwall, he might have goaded Vince afterward and got him so riled up he became mad enough to kill the arrogant son of a bitch.

"Some sensitive people running around this world." He said to himself over his last cup of coffee. "I would have knocked the shit out of the guy on the tennis court if he'd bitched at me like he did at Vince, but Vince might have decided that wasn't enough satisfaction and shot him instead."

Anyway, Vince Valley was first on his list to see and the most logical in terms of a police investigation. A file with his address was in the apartment per his request to Ellen when he told her he'd take the job.

His plan was to give her a report after each day's "investigation." He had called her earlier with his plan for the day and just to say good morning. She was busy so he left a message before leaving to interview Valley. Fortunately, or maybe it was by plan, there was a computer in the apartment. He'd use that to make his reports and to do any research the investigation called for.

*****

After some trial and error, Bishop found the drive to the charming old campground along an old river bed. The camping spaces were shaded by a grove of old trees. He couldn't tell what kind.

He parked in a slot near Vince's space and got out. He could see Vince sitting at a bench under the shade of an ancient tree in front of an old Airstream trailer. The man was more or less staring aimlessly down at a cup in front of him like he was depressed. An old pickup truck for trailering the camper was parked not far from the bench where he sat.

A woman from the camper next to Valley's and wearing gloves, was bent over a rose bush outside, checking for bugs and pruning. Bishop's arrival attracted her attention and she turned to see what was going on. He saw her and nodded.

When it was clear that he had come to see Vincent, she stared, smiled and half waved in that direction. If Vincent took any note of it, he didn't show it.

From what Bishop saw, she looked to be a few years older than Vincent and, like many men and women who'd retired, had put on a few extra pounds but not so many that she'd be considered overweight.

She walked a mile every day and that kept her in pretty good shape and healthy. Except for the few extra pounds, she looked good, always dressed nicely and greeted everybody, especially Vince, with a smile.

She went inside but stayed close to her door to watch what was happening. Vince rarely had visitors. In fact, the man who had come to see him then, was his first he'd had except for the two young ladies who had been there. Their names were Amy and Cindy but she didn't know their names or why they came to see him. She'd later discover that they helped him with the talks he gave at the La Jolla Rec Center.

Bishop walked to where the man sat, said hello, introduced himself and showed him the police card Ellen had given him. As he did, a dog began to bark inside his trailer. Vince called for him to be quiet. The dog complied.

"My dog, Rascal. My daughter gave him to me after my wife died. Probably figured it'd give me something to live for. Maybe she was right. He's a mongrel but a good watch dog. I like him."

"You daughter could be right about that. Some people say as much," Bishop said.

Vince let the small dog out of the trailer. The first thing he did was sniff Bishop's leg. Bishop gave him a pat on the head.

"He'll love you now," Vince said. "He and my neighbor, Beatrice, have a thing going." He nodded at the camper next to his, where the lady watched them from inside.

He continued, "She gives him left over chicken bits now and then and he wags his tail every time he sees her. She visits sometimes." He gave a wave toward the neighbor's camper with a smile at Rascal.

Although Bishop couldn't see it, the wave sent the woman away from her door and into the shadows of her camper. She was afraid he was waving at her.

With a softer voice, he said, "I think she might like me, no husband to get in the way, but I'm not in the market. I doubt I ever will be. My late wife stays in my thoughts."

He gave Bishop a two line explanation about his wife's death. Bishop told him he was sorry for his loss.

Although Vince remembered Bishop from the tennis match, his face still showed surprise as in, *what the hell are you doing here? Oh, he figured it out. Snapper's murder. He thinks I may have done it. That's funny.*

Bishop explained how he came to be investigating Snapper Cornwall's murder.

First, he digressed to tell Vince that he was a retired California attorney with a consulting business in Mississippi. However, he'd retained connections in California and visited often usually at "Chief Wasserman's" request.

"Sometimes she wants me to speak to policemen about something," he said and added that was why he was here and why he ended up as her partner for the tennis tournament.

He also went on to explain how he came to be investigating Snapper's murder. The Mayor had felt the case needed someone with high level experience and suggested that Bishop be hired.

"Chief Wasserman and I have handled several major murder cases together in the past."

"Yes," Vince said. "Now that you mention it, I think I've read about you. You worked on the murder of that La Jolla real estate developer."

Bishop nodded. "Killed at the opening of his last project, the La Jolla Apogee residential development."

Vince said, "I remember. By the way, I meant to tell you, but I left early, you played well the other day. Like Snapper, you have, what I call, tennis eyes. Anything at your end is out even if it's an inch in. I think you were calling 'em that way after you saw how Snapper was calling 'em. He was worse."

"I usually try to be as fair as I can, but when I saw what he was doing, I decided to reciprocate."

"Any eye for an eye, eh?" Vince said.

"That's right. If the other side is playing dirty, you play dirty back."

"It worked. You won, even if by default."

Bishop nodded without going into the details.

"I also noticed how you hit the ball as far from me as possible," Vince said. "Made me run. You must have known Snapper was tired and dogging it. He wasn't chasing anything. I was tired too. But I hate to lose so I had to chase down every ball. Eventually though, I got so tired I just couldn't get to everything. Maybe that's why I lost my temper with Snapper."

Bishop agreed. "That's tennis. Play to the weakness."

"Right. Well, you did that and won."

"Yeah. Well, that's the reason for my visit. I have to ask you some questions about Snapper's murder. Because of your … attack on the guy when we were playing tennis, you're a suspect. Top of the list."

Vince grimaced. "Yeah. Snapper'd pushed me as far as I could stand, as tired as I was. I'd stood it as long as I could, you know. I wanted to win and was willing to put up with some bullshit, but the way he acted in that last set and with us losing the way we were was more than I could take so I let him know. I'm only sorry I didn't hit him."

"Most people would have done the same, I imagine. It was obvious he was too tired to play effectively and you were having to play the match by yourself. It was also obvious to us that you were on your last legs as well."

"Yeah. Cut throat tennis. I know. So, ask your questions. I didn't kill him." He made a gesture with his right hand.

Bishop asked what he did other than play tennis.

He told him about his Saturday talks at the La Jolla Rec Center about what was on his mind. "I call them people talks. Mostly I ramble and tell them what I've been thinking about during the week. They seem to like it. My guess is, most of them agree with what I'm saying."

He said the talks helped keep him more interested in life than death. He explained in more detail how his wife had died and how he had had a hard time accepting it. "Still having it," he added, bowing his head as he did.

Bishop sympathized since he'd gone through something similar when his wife left him and took the children with her. He didn't feel like life was worth living until he'd found reasons to change his mind in Lawton, Mississippi.

"I'm sitting here thinking about my next talk," Vince said. "I've talked about corruption in government, two Saturdays for that one and one about how our cultures have descended into greed as a way of life, for the most part. Before the tennis match, I talked about the relationship between man and woman."

"Sounds like some good ones," Bishop said.

"Thank you. When I run out of something to talk about or when the people quit coming, I'll go back to where I was before I started doing it." *Counting my pills.*

"I understand. Tell me how you do it? Write your talks."

"I decide what I want to say and then I organize my thoughts so I can make a thirty minute presentation. Right now, as I said, the talks and the benefits they seem to give the people who show up are the only thing that keeps me here. I miss my wife. I guess I've half way said that already."

"I can understand about your talks. I'm glad it's you doing it and not me," Bishop said. Having to write a speech every week would be enough to send him into orbit.

"Maybe. My alternative was to join my wife. Still is. I'm not sure about the hereafter religious people go on about. It seems to me if the spirits live on in the other world, they'd find a way to contact the loved ones they left behind. I've never heard of a single contact between people left behind and those that had passed away, so I'm suspicious that there may not be another world. But life without my wife isn't much anyway so I don't much give a shit. Excuse my language."

Life is nothing, he thought. *Everything is nothing as far as I'm concerned. Not a damn thing has value to me. I eat, get ready for my talk, sleep a little and think about my Carolyn. And, when I can't get out of it, I play a little tennis.*

"I've heard other people going on about the same thing," Bishop said. "I just don't know."

He nodded and added, "Frankly, I'm inclined to believe that when you die, everything dies with you. But, I wouldn't mind that. Once you stop thinking, you stop worrying or being worried. If you were doing anything important, somebody else will do it." He shrugged.

"Giving these talks keeps me going for now. Sooner or later though, I'll run out of something to say and take the easy way out." He nodded to the trailer.

"Best to hang in there," Bishop said. "You'll find somebody else one of these days and be glad you did." *I did. Kathy saved my ass.*

"I hope you're right. I drive down the street and listen to the radio and all I see and hear is gaudiness. And the people behind the gaudiness aren't worth a damn thing. Bull shitting people to buy whatever shit they're selling. All any of 'em want is some of what I have and they don't want to give anything of value to get it. It's all a waste of time as far as I'm concerned. Worthless. Everything. It's all just a game about scamming somebody out of what they've worked for. What's the point of living with that?" Vince asked.

"I agree with your point of view, but you have to look ahead. Somebody once said it's always darkest before the dawn. Maybe you're in your dark cycle. The dawn is just ahead."

"I doubt it. I've kept all of my wife's pain pills. I've taken care of most of my affairs. I'm doing these so called people talks just now. Who knows how long they'll last. One day somebody will probably smell something funny and look inside my rig. I'll be laying in my bed, at peace. Somebody will take care of Rascal." He gave a nod at Beatrice's camper. "Maybe my neighbor."

Bishop sighed. Remembering that he once felt like Vince after his wife and family had left him and he'd been accused of defrauding people. Coming to Mississippi gave him a new perspective on life and then, he met Kathy and had a good reason to begin again. He was glad. He loved his house on Indian Creek so long as Kathy was with him.

"That's your business, Vince. However, I'd be careful about taking that last step if I were you. It's not something you can look at and change. It's permanent. Who knows what the next day will bring?"

The man agreed. That's why he was still hanging around, somebody wanted him to give a talk and somebody wanted to hear what he had to say. It gave him a psychological lift and was still giving it.

As if to underline that point, a nice looking lady, probably in her forties, came walking along the camp ground drive. Bishop saw her as did Vincent. She wore a pair of jeans cut off well above her knees, and a blouse that was tied under breasts. And, Bishop could tell from the wiggle in her blouse that she wasn't wearing a bra. Her brown hair was tied back in a ponytail and she was smiling as if she didn't have a care in the world.

"Vince," she called and waved when she came closer.

He stood briefly and waved back with a smile. "Jennifer," he said. "Didn't see you last week."

"Out of town," she said. "I'm back now. I'll see you this week if you're around."

"Yeah. I'll be around." He gave her a big smile which she returned.

She walked on, even began humming.

Beatrice watched her from her doorway. "Bitch," she said under her breath. "Sleeping with half the men in the camp. Her husband should have killed her."

Beatrice was jealous of the woman for good reason. Jennifer seemed to be more familiar with Vince than she preferred. She'd seen them both at the wash house at times, laughing and talking. And, she had a notion that they didn't stay in the wash house while their clothes were washing.

"She'd better stay clear. Vince's my man," she whispered.

"Jennifer's headed for the convenience store around the corner," Vince said. "We run into each other in the wash house over there now and then. That's where we first got to know each other. She makes me laugh, something I don't do much of these days." He pointed toward a small, white block house some distance away, where the people in the camp ground washed and dried their clothes.

"Laughing's a good thing. Looks like she's interested," Bishop said. "The way she was smiling at you."

Vince laughed. "Her husband left her. Caught her with some guy awhile back." He told Bishop Jennifer's last name as a matter of course, Cooley.

"Her camper is a couple of pads from the wash house." Vince pointed. "She has her eyes on an older guy who lives in Del Mar but keeps his camper here, a divorcee. She says he's interested but is taking his time. She's not sleeping with him, she says. I don't know if she's running a game on him or what. I doubt she's playing me. I've told her I'm not seriously interested in any woman for anything but the frolics she and I are having. I won't say those frolics aren't fun. They make me sleep better.

"While the Del Mar guy is trying to make up his mind, we've become ... what some people might call intimate ... friends. Even though I miss Carolyn desperately and stay depressed most of the time, I'm still a man and ... pardon my crudity, I still get horny. I don't always like it, but it comes along and not a damn thing I can do to get rid of it except what I do with Jennifer. She's not interested in me for anything long term, like my neighbor Beatrice is, but she does like a little ... exercise with me once in a while and I need it to keep from going crazy. Keeps me from having to go out for it, if you know what I mean. Cheaper too. Safer, so far." He gave a nervous laugh.

Bishop said he did know, adding a slight chuckle of his own. He wondered why Vince didn't ... exercise ... with his neighbor if she was interested. *Sounds like she is. Most likely doesn't fit a blouse like the Jennifer woman. Men do like a little wiggle to check out.*

As if he'd heard Bishop's thought, he said, "Beatrice wants to get serious. I don't have any interest in getting serious with anybody. As far as I'm concerned, I'm still married and except for my occasional *doings* with Jennifer when I wash my clothes, I'm not ready to change how I feel."

Bishop figured he understood. Jennifer gave him the relief he needed without any strings. Beatrice would do the same, but hers would come with strings and Vince wasn't ready for that.

"Okay. Enough small talk," Bishop said, taking out the note pad he had in his brief case. "Did you kill Snapper Cornwall? You said you didn't and I know if you did, you'd deny it, but I want to ask anyway. See if your face shows anything."

Vince's face grimaced. "No. Like I said, I didn't kill the bastard. I'm not sorry somebody else did. I can't say I've ever met anybody I disliked more and I've represented plenty of clients who were about as obnoxious. Some people are born that way, I've always imagined. But they weren't obnoxious to me, just to the world. They treated me with respect because they needed me to save their asses. And they paid a fee which I took. The only thing I got from Snapper was criticisms which I hated, but I don't kill people for that."

Just grab them by the shirt and throw them down, Bishop thought as he recalled the tennis court incident.

"Where were you?" Bishop added the date and time Snapper was killed.

"I was here, under this tree I imagine. I sit here till I get tired of the day or I see people looking out their RV windows at me. Then, I take my sleeping pill and go inside to survive for another night."

"You think anybody saw you that night?"

"Frankly, I doubt it. Beatrice maybe. You can ask her before you go. For a while people did spy on me, wondering if I might be nuts, but I think they've given up now. I've been here some time now, doing nothing but sitting in this chair, vegetating. I can't imagine them still wondering about that crazy lawyer who lives in a trailer and sits under a chair till it's time to go to bed. I guess I was the topic of their conversations for a while after I'd moved in but things get old and people move on. Find a good television show to watch."

Bishop could sympathize with him but said nothing. He wasn't there as a friend. He was there to find a murderer.

"Who else might have killed him? Any ideas?" he asked. Often people knew or had a thought or two about it.

Vincent shook his head. "I'd guess anybody he'd known for some time, at least ten minutes, would be on the list, but I don't know anybody. I've … well, I had more or less resigned from the human world. I've been wearing blinders ever since."

"He was into investments, I understand," Bishop said. "The Taco Wagon Company. Any information about that? Any troubles there? Disgruntled investors?"

Money, Bishop had always believed, caused more murders than anything else. That and infidelity. Some people didn't take kindly to somebody moving in on their spouses, a killing offense. Bishop didn't try to include homicidal killings where killers acted irrationally because of their mental conditions, usually congenital.

Vince shook his head again. "I knew he was in investments but only a little about it. Nobody asked me for money. If they had they would have been disappointed. I think the two girls who help me with my talks, Cindy and Amy, must help him somehow. They hand out his brochures. You'll probably want to talk to them."

Bishop nodded and interrupted to say, "Yes. Ellen and I had a match against them in the tournament."

"Must have won. They're pretty good."

Bishop shook his head.

"Well, they put the brochures about Snapper's business beside the hats they also put out for my talks in case anybody wants to leave anything. People do leave money most of the time. I share it with the girls. They get the lion's share. It was their idea, the hats. Frankly, I don't give a rat's ass. As I said, the talks are my excuse to stay alive. I don't need much money. Costs almost nothing to live here."

"What kind of investments was he selling?" Bishop asked. He hadn't listened carefully when Ellen was talking about them. "Do you know?"

"I glanced at the brochure before I threw it away. I'm not interested in an investment. That's for people with a life. I don't have one. But, to answer your question, he was selling shares in the company, bonds actually, that yielded almost ten percent, the brochure said. Probably a high risk venture. The company was setting up street vendors and the like to sell tacos and other Mexican stuff out of a wagon styled after an old Conestoga wagon. All the vendors had to do was pay money for a franchise and they were in business. Snapper's investment company did everything else they needed. Turn-key franchise."

"Sounds interesting." That's what Bishop said when he didn't care or didn't have a legitimate response. "You have full names for the girls? Addresses?"

He stared a Bishop in thought for a couple of seconds then said, "I might. I think they gave them to me at one time in case I wanted to tell them anything. The La Jolla Light gives the locations of my talks in the paper although recently, I've used the hall at the Rec Center."

He left to go inside but returned right away holding a sheet of paper. He handed it to Bishop. "I copied their names and addresses and phone numbers on this paper. There are also email addresses. They share an apartment in La Jolla apparently. I've never been there. Nothing sexual between us. They haven't offered and I haven't asked. One of them, Cindy, I think, has maybe hinted, but I ignored it. I kind of like her for whatever that's worth. Not much, I think. Anything serious with a woman ended for me when my wife died."

It'll come back, Bishop thought. *Mine did when I met Kathy.*

Beatrice walked out just then and Bishop asked if she'd seen Vince the night Snapper was murdered. She confirmed that she had. He had been sitting where he was just then, under the tree, until around ten when he went inside his camper.

She said she watched Vince every night until he went inside his camper, knowing he was depressed and worrying about what he might do. She talked to him when she could, and invited him to dinner when she had prepared something good.

Seems a pleasant enough woman, Bishop thought, but knew two people only got serious with each other if there was some kind of, what people called, chemistry between them.

Bishop gave Rascal a scratch behind the ears and left the man under his tree to think about what he wanted to say in his next "talk." He wondered if the girls were at home. Vincent didn't know.

Bishop would call.

Chapter 9

After Bishop was out of sight, Beatrice came out of her camper again, ostensibly to look at her two rose bushes. In reality, she wanted to talk to Vince if he wanted somebody to talk to and she always prayed it'd be her. Evidently he didn't want anybody then, since he didn't make an effort to respond to her. He seemed content just to stare into space.

Before she went inside though, she did walk close enough to invite him to a dinner on her outside table that evening. "I found some steaks at the market. They look good. The butcher gave me an extra 'cause I shop there all the time."

Vince agreed just to get rid of her.

When he got depressed as he was then, having just talked to the man from the police about Carolyn, he didn't welcome familiarity with anybody.

So, they'd eat outside. Her choice and he didn't care. She liked for the neighbors to see her entertaining a man, especially Vince. All the ladies liked him, *especially that Jennifer slut. But* there a*in't no flies on me. I ain't dead yet and I don't sleep with any man just because they've got one of those hanging things they seem to think with.*

Vince didn't want to have dinner with her. She was always asking and he usually said "yes", as he had then, if he didn't have time to come up with an excuse, but he was never comfortable eating with another woman. It always seemed to him as if he was cheating on Carolyn. It was stupid, he admitted, but that's the way it was.

She's okay, he thought. *And, only an incompetent fool wouldn't know that she was interested. She practically tells me every time we're together. One of these times, I'm going to have to tell her. It's not fair to let her think there could ever be anything romantic between us. I wish there could be, but ...*

*****

From his car, Bishop called the first name Vince had given him. Cindy answered. They would be at home for another hour and sure, he could come over to ask them questions.

Bishop knew about where the apartment complex of the two girls was located, in a trendy looking building near down town La Jolla.

He drove there from Vincent's trailer pad. Cindy let him in.

"Come in," she said and recalling the tennis match, complimented him, saying, "You guys were too good for us."

"We just had a hot day. Ellen bailed us out of every tight spot. Everything we hit went in and you and Amy had one of those days you think about. When it can go wrong it does."

"Thank you." She showed him into their living room. Amy joined them.

"You're investigating Mr. Cornwall's murder, Snapper," Amy said.

He had told Cindy over the phone he was a special investigator for the San Diego police department and had a few questions for them.

"I am," he said and asked where they were when the murder took place. He knew their descriptions, both females, didn't match the description given by the witness who saw a young man running from the scene, but he also knew a female might disguise herself to look like a man so they weren't automatically excluded from his investigation.

Usually though, they do it with a cap or hat. The witness didn't say anything about a hat on the person he saw running away. Even so, I need to dot the "i's" and cross the "t's" of everything that's part of the investigation. And, the girls are within the scope of what I need to do to do that.

He was aware that young women likely knew young men and young men could be convinced to do young women a favor. He knew it was a big stretch to think anybody would kill somebody as a favor, but it was possible so he had to interview them.

"You think we killed him?" Cindy asked. Her hand went over her mouth as though embarrassed to have someone think they would have done it. Amy joined her with a shake of her head.

"No way," she said.

"I have to ask anybody who knew him or had anything to do with him," Bishop answered. "Police procedure."

"Oh. Well, we were here," Amy said.

"Alone?"

"Uh, yes. We had some dinner and watched a show on television."

He asked what show and received an answer. He'd later check and that show was on at the time Snapper was killed. That didn't clear them, just established that they knew what show was on.

He also asked if they had steady boyfriends. Neither said they did. He made a note. Later, Ellen would send someone out to ask the neighbors if they'd seen young men visiting. The neighbors would say they'd seen very few.

"I understand Snapper was, in effect, franchising street vendors. Selling tacos and the like out of a Taco Wagon," he said. "What part did you play? You were working for him, weren't you?"

Cindy looked at Amy, blank faced. "I … well, we had played tennis with Snapper a time or two. He asked us to talk to his manager, Mr. McNally, about having us recommend an investment in the company to people we knew who might be looking for a good investment. Other tennis players mostly, also clients and people we know. Everybody wants to make money. We don't know much about investments, but some of the people we talked to said the … what, the yield on the bonds the company was selling, was very good."

"Right," Bishop said. "I've heard that as well. Eight percent."

Bishop was told the manager's full name was Walter McNally.

"We play tennis with lots of rich people and we recommended the investment to them. I think Cindy just said, and you too, that the investment gives a good return. Snapper and Mr. McNally told us if anybody we recommend decides to invest, we'll get a kind of finder's fee," Amy said.

"We've made a few bucks that way," Cindy added. "As far as we know, nobody's lost anything."

"Did Vince invest?" he asked.

They shook their heads. Both said, "Not that we know of. I doubt it."

Cindy said, "For sure. I think he stays depressed a lot. Probably thinking about his wife. She died. I get the impression, he's not interested in much of anything."

He nodded and asked, "Did you send anybody to Snapper?"

They hadn't. The people who were interested, they'd send to McNally.

"How do you contact McNally?"

She gave him the phone number in the brochure and told Bishop where he lived. "He has a house in the Shores on the beach." She gave him the man's address.

Doing better than Snapper, Bishop thought. *At least as far as where he's living. But,* he reminded himself, Snapper *Cornwall didn't have to impress anybody. McNally does.*

"You've been there, I assume," Bishop said.

"Sure. He has parties now and then," Cindy said. "We're invited. We're the glamour, he says. We know some of the investors, the ones we brought in. Some are kind of flirty. Up in years, but they can apparently remember how things were, you know what I mean, when they were younger." She laughed.

Bishop gave the comment a laugh and asked, "Did Vince come to the parties?"

"Sometimes," Amy told him. "For sure, once. We invited him. He didn't say much at the time as I remember. Didn't mingle either. Just had a drink and left."

Bishop didn't blame him. *Drinking with people he didn't know or give a damn to know and warding off people trying to sell him something he didn't want. No free drink is worth that.*

Bishop wondered if any hanky-panky went on but knew it did. It always did at such parties. He didn't know if the girls participated but figured they might. He didn't ask. It wasn't relevant to what he was investigating.

"Did Snapper have any children?"

Amy frowned and shaking her head no, said, "I think … no, I'm wrong. I remember that he had a son from an earlier marriage. I'm not sure where he lives. We've never met the guy."

Something for Ellen's staff to track down, Bishop thought. *Probably won't have anything to add, but they'd have to be on my list. Snapper possibly would have talked to them about anybody who'd threatened him.*

He left them and after a bite at Harry's along the main drag in La Jolla, went back to his apartment and sent Ellen a report on what he'd been doing with a request to find Snapper's son. Calling McNally for an interview was next on his list.

Before he could do that, his phone rang. It was Ellen.

"I got your report," she said. "Good work."

Bishop was about to ask how she got that out of it. He thought it was pretty bland. Nobody said anything useful as far as he was concerned.

She continued. "You have to be at City Hall at four. The Mayor is having a press conference about Snapper Cornwall's murder. He wants us both there to answer questions. Okay?"

Bishop said he'd put on his better clothes and be there.

He was a few minutes early.

*****

The Mayor walked up to the microphones set up in front of his office. He was smiling but only a bit. After all this was a serious occasion. "I called this meeting to give you all an update on what we're doing to find the killer of Snapper. Charlie Cornwall was his name but he wanted us to call him by his nickname, Snaper. A fine man, one we'll have a hard time replacing. We'll miss you Snapper."

He never played tennis with the guy, Bishop thought. *And, apparently didn't know him well or he was a contributor to his campaigns and all his shortcomings took a back seat to that.*

After he'd said a few words, he introduced the Chief of Police, Ellen Wasserman, and the special deputy assigned to the case, Bishop

Bone. He talked a minute or two more about how Ellen and Bishop had investigated and solved the murder of Marc Flint, a couple of years earlier. And how both were threatened but those threats did nothing to stop their investigation and soon they found the murderer and he was convicted.

Both Ellen and Bishop stepped forward to shake the Mayor's hand and to look out at the assembled press corps with nods and smiles.

The Mayor went on to extoll the virtues of Snapper. How he was always there with a helping hand to anyone who needed him.

Money, Bishop thought with a smile that didn't make it to his face. *Snapper was there with the money, somebody else's money.*

The Mayor then talked about the many needs the man had supported and how he would be sorely missed.

"But, I'm confident that we have the best team possible investigating the case and that the murderer will be found and brought to justice soon."

He turned it over to the press for questions. They always had questions. They wanted a report on what had been done to date. They knew about the altercation between Vince and Snapper on the tennis court. They wanted to know what had been done about Vincent who might have later killed the man.

Bishop took the question and said that he'd interviewed Vince Valley and the two ladies who worked part time for Vince and for Snapper. He alluded to Snapper's investment activities and indicated that he intended to look into those activities since money was at the root of many crimes, including murder. But his investigation had just begun and he wasn't ready to point to a possible guilty party just yet or even suggest a real motive.

Ellen stepped forward and said about the same thing but embellished on what he'd said. "Bishop and I have many more people we'll be interviewing within the next few days. We will find the guilty party and get him before a judge very soon."

She knows how to play the press, Bishop thought. *I wouldn't think 'very soon' was on the list of terms I'd use for the murder investigation right now. Hell, I don't even have anybody I suspect yet.*

After a few more questions for their newspapers and radio/television stations, the conference ended. The Mayor thanked Bishop and Ellen. Ellen assured him that they'd bring in the guilty party as soon as possible. That brought a smile to the Mayor's face.

"Good. That'll stop the phone calls I've been getting," he said.

She must know something I don't, Bishop thought. *And, who in the hell would call about an arrogant shit like Snapper unless they're missing the money, somebody else's money, from what I've found so far, that he was handing out.*

As they left, Bishop told her his next call would be on Walter McNally, the man who managed Snapper's investment company.

"I'll say it again, money, more often than not, is at the heart of most murders," he told her.

He laughed to himself when he remembered something his grandmother had said, *Money is the root of all evil.* Not far from the truth, he told himself.

"Well, get moving. You heard the Mayor and my promise to being the guilty party to justice soon."

"Yeah, I heard. I'm just glad 'soon' doesn't have a fixed deadline."

She laughed and hurried away.

Bishop looked at his cellphone. It was too late, he decided, to call McNally. He'd call him first thing in the morning. He'd have bacon and eggs for dinner and do what Vince had been doing when he walked up, think.

*****

The next morning Bishop more or less invited himself over to interview the man who, surprisingly, seemed to be expecting him. McNally had readily told Bishop to come on over when he called.

"Saw you on television last night so I figured you'd be calling," McNally said. "I have to be on your list."

"You are."

Bishop was a bit surprised to be expected but not too. He'd more or less forgotten the news conference was being televised and recorded for radio news casts.

As always, the morning air was cool and it'd stay that way most of the day. Perfect tennis weather, Bishop reminded himself. La Jolla had that reputation. Except for a few hot days in July and August, it was always mild.

He drove from his apartment downtown to McNally's La Jolla Shores home on the beach. "Must have been doing a hell of a lot better than Snapper," he told himself.

Snapper's townhouse wasn't bad by any means, he knew. Had to be worth close to two million and close to everything without a hell of a lot of maintenance. What was required was most likely covered by the home owners association.

"Ellen said Snapper must have been rich. Inherited it, or got it somehow, some from his last wife," he said to himself as he drove. "Her house was on the beach, Ellen had said. He must have sold it. I guess I'd better talk to the wife's children, if she had any to see what had happened. One of them might have had enough of the way Snapper was spending their mother's money that they figured on inheriting someday, and decided to do something about it. Make sure he wouldn't spend any more. They'd sure as hell have a motive to kill him." He kicked himself for not thinking about it sooner. *I should have had them on my list. Even ahead of Vince or right with him.*

He called Ellen's number and left a message for someone to find out about the children. Also, check to see if there had been any controversy about the estate when the wife died.

He'd told her the day before, but as people do, he told her again where he was headed, to interview McNally. He'd give her a report later.

Chapter 10

Bishop parked in front of the single story home, a Cape Cod elevation with a parking garage along the street. *Good condition and decent elevation but nothing much to write home about*, Bishop thought. *But, it is on the beach. That makes it look like gold and is probably worth a hell of a lot.*

McNally answered the bell and immediately shoved out a hand with a big smile, like Bishop was a long lost friend. "Mr. Bone," he said. "Come on in. I'm having a cup of coffee. Won't you join me on the back patio. We can enjoy a cup and watch the surf while you ask me about Snapper."

Bishop took note of the man's appearance. He was almost six feet tall, large, with a jowly face and stomach that pushed at his belt.

Must entertain lots of investors, Bishop figured. *Acts like it and that's most likely how he came to have that stomach. Has to learn not to eat what he's feeding his guests. Couldn't have been the one the witness saw running away after Snapper was shot. I doubt he can remember the last time he ran anywhere. But, he could have hired someone to do it.*

Bishop followed him to the outside patio where the frothy surf was rolling onto the beach. A housekeeper brought a tray with coffee and the snack "fixins."

Looks like something, maybe some kind of melted cheese with bacon bits mixed in, Bishop thought. *Probably expensive.*

McNally explained that he was divorced and had to hire a housekeeper to keep him going.

"Now and then I think about hooking up with somebody, you know what I mean, but I decided it's easier to get along with one-nighters … and cheaper in the long run. No alimony to pay." He grinned.

Bishop nodded with a knowing smile. *Probably has to pay double for his one-nighters with a stomach like that. That life style is not for me. Never was. I prefer Kathy, full time.*

The surf looked almost like it could come all the way into the man's back yard but the yard was separated from the ocean by a deep stretch of sandy beach. Already a couple of people, a young man and his girl fiend,

Bishop assumed, were spreading a towel on the sand. They had surfboards. The sun over the house lit up the ocean further out and gave it a sunlight tint. A sail boat floated along further out.

As if hearing his thoughts, McNally said with a wave, "Used to be more sand, the beach, but the ocean's been rising of late."

"I've heard."

An older man jogged past at the edge of McNally's yard with his dog while Bishop poured himself a cup of coffee. He didn't need it but figured it was a friendly way to get the interview underway.

McNally looked at him as if to say, "Okay, what do you want to know?"

Bishop began. "You managed Snapper Cornwall's investments, I understand."

"I'm not sure about that. I think he may have had others, investments from brokerage houses, but nothing like the one I managed, the one we named the Taco Wagons Investment. It's a hands-on investment vehicle. We sell shares in the company to investors, bonds to be accurate, ... did anyway. I don't know exactly what we'll do in the future, now that Snapper is gone. We use the investors' money to buy what we need for the Taco Wagon business.

"We sell franchises to men mostly, some women, who want to be in business for themselves without having to put much money into it."

"That's the one I know about," Bishop said and asked if McNally would tell him how it worked. He knew something about the company's operation, but wanted to hear it from someone who knew it from the inside.

"I'll give you a quick overview. If you want more, ask and I'll elaborate."

He explained how it worked. He got to know "Snapper" when he was selling real estate. Snapper dabbled now and then in investment properties. He and Snapper got to talking over lunch one day and the idea for the Taco Wagons company came out of it.

They designed a wagon on wheels equipped with propane to heat the food they would sell on the street, tacos and burritos. It could be switched to electric if the franchisee preferred and it was available. The food offerings were deliberately kept simple. They'd also sell canned drinks. Easier than pouring something each time. The wagons would use a battery operated cooling unit for the food and drinks they kept overnight. If they had electrical on the street where they set up, they used it but it wasn't always available so they were set up to operate without it.

People loved to have their pictures taken beside the wagons, according to McNally.

"Made us feel good about the design."

He took out a file and spread photos of a taco wagon on the table for him to look at. Bishop agreed. Bishop had to admit that the wagon was charming to look at, like the real thing, a miniature Conestoga.

"I can imagine," Bishop said as he looked at the pictures. Cindy and Amy were in one shot. Snapper was standing beside them.

"Where is this Wagon now?" he asked McNally. He had in mind seeing it firsthand.

"Probably in Arizona. Somebody's franchise now. Making money. We don't keep them around."

Each wagon was built in China from their design with a canopy for the franchisee to stand under when they were servicing customers. Kept them out of the sun and heat, not to mention rain. The canopy was big enough to protect customers from the elements as well.

"Each wagon costs about twenty thousand to build. They're shipped directly to where a franchise is to be located."

The wagons would be left out overnight. They'd get permits from the cities where the wagons were located and where there were wide sidewalks and, if possible, electrical outlets to keep the batteries charged.

McNally pushed a button and the television came on. He played a video of a franchisee making a taco at his taco wagon. Bishop had to admit, it looked easy. And, the franchisee appeared relaxed, not under stress at all.

Damn, looks like a winner to me, Bishop thought as the video came to an end.

"We supply all the franchise holder needs, food stuffs and drinks and make a profit on it. We'd also provide all the maintenance needed to keep the wagons operable. All a franchisee holder has to do is call and we'll have a man out there to fix whatever needs fixing right away. A malfunctioning Wagon's not making money for anybody."

He paused to let Bishop nod.

McNally continued, "We sub everything out and have somebody in each town, where we have franchisees, ready to respond to calls. We have very little staff here. Me and Snapper were practically it. That keeps our overhead as low as possible and our dividends high for our investors."

"Sounds like a sound business plan," Bishop said.

"It is and it works! And the best part, everybody's happy!"

They used small towns for the wagons figuring the smaller town would be easier to deal with, easier to watch over the wagons at night to keep vandalism to a minimum.

"How's that working out?" Bishop asked.

"So far very good. We've only had one serious case since we began."

"I haven't seen any wagons in La Jolla," Bishop said.

The franchise wasn't active in California at present, McNally explained. They went to cities small enough to consider the money they'd get from permits to be worthwhile. They also had to find cities with sidewalks wide enough to accommodate the wagons. They hadn't found many in California that worked but they were always looking.

"Right now, we're in small towns in New Mexico, Arizona and Utah. When we get big enough with some clout, we'll expand into California. Right now though, we're working out the bugs in small towns that want our money and are willing to watch our wagons when they're closed for the night."

A typical wagon opened at ten or eleven in the morning for the lunch crowd and stayed open until a little after five to sell to hungry people on the way home, people too tired to cook. They had designed carrying boxes to hold the food in their cars without spilling it.

"Sounds like a winner," Bishop staid.

"So far. We sell a franchise for, five thousand down and five thousand every six months until we've recovered the construction costs ... for a wagon. Actually, we lease the wagon to a franchisee. We do everything necessary to get the franchisee going. All he has to do is show up where we unload the wagon and start selling tacos and the other foods and drinks."

Bishop said, "I see."

"Of course, we give them a crash course on how to operate the wagon, keeping it going, preparing the food, complete turn-key. They lease the wagons from us so if anybody wants to go out of business, all they have to do is call us to pick up the wagon or we lease it to another franchisee at the same location," McNally said.

He sighed and continued. "Once in a while, we run into a town that's very friendly but don't have wide enough sidewalks for a wagon. What we do there is use small hole in the wall, walk in places. People come inside to buy their tacos."

"Sounds simple," Bishop said. "I'm impressed."

"Our buyers are generally people who have retired but are not ready to spend their days in front of a TV or working in the yard. This way, they get out, get to talk to people, and make money. They're their own bosses. Some of 'em never enjoyed that luxury before."

"I can imagine. Any problems so far?"

McNally shook his head.

"I don't guess Snapper got to know any of the franchisees. I'm assuming you did all the selling and management."

He did. He had notified everyone in any business that dealt with the public about the new venture. And anybody with a referral received a fee. That was basically how they sold franchisees and investments.

"People like Cindy and Amy?" Bishop asked.

McNally nodded. "Right. They've sent me a couple. People they met playing tennis or ran into through their work. Mostly though they've referred investors to us. People who were interested in our bonds. They have great yields."

"What about Snapper? Did he bring in any buyers for the bonds? I've heard that he actually developed the idea for the Taco Wagon venture."

"Ah, well, that's what we say for the public. That gives the venture a little glamour. Important man, well known, creating something useful but he was primarily just the figure head. His name was what we needed. People knew him. Knew his name anyway. He didn't get into the business once we got everything worked out. Stuff I've told you about. He got paid for his referrals – he brought in a few - and as a board member. We have five. I'm a director as well. But, I've done all the hands-on work."

Brochure indicated Snapper was more than a figurehead. Reminds me of what somebody said, maybe Benjamin Franklin, believe none of what you hear and only half of what you see.

"Must get to be tedious, everything you have to do. Chief cook and bottle washer."

He laughed. "Some truth in that. Now and then it gets tedious, but I enjoy it for the most part and I have subs who do the actual work. People I call. One sub handles the food that goes out to the Wagons. Another any maintenance problems. I have people in all the states with Wagons collecting money from the franchisees – I like to call them Wagoneers - for the food and stuff we sell them. It's pretty much a cash business. Not enough money on each transaction, as a general rule, to warrant credit card use so we recommend cash."

"And, you set all that up, not Snapper, the man who created it all." Bishop said that tongue in cheek.

McNally looked at him as if he understood. He said, "Well, we both did some creating, I guess. And, uh, I … I'm not sure I remember who did what. Things were moving pretty fast when we were getting the business off the ground. You know how creative meetings go, give and take until all the problems are worked out."

"But everybody knows to call you now," Bishop said. "Now that Snapper is dead."

He nodded. "Too bad about Snapper, but I'll tell you, it makes me feel good to see happy people, enjoying themselves and making money at the same time. I don't mind some hands-on involvement. Keeps me from getting old. You know what they say. Keep your brain alive and it'll keep your body alive."

"Some truth in that," Bishop agreed. "So, I guess you've had no problems. No disgruntled franchisees wanting their money back. Investors … the same thing, Wanting to cash out."

"No, not yet. We're paying a good dividend. Taco Wagons is a cash business, a good one. We pay monthly dividends to investors. We use their money to buy more wagons. Right now, our Chinese supplier is stalling on the wagons. Wants more money, I think. I'm not going to give in. If they don't send more wagons this month, I'll find an alternate source. "

"I guess that's to be expected. Everybody wants more money."

"Yeah."

"Any other problems? Anybody upset with Cornwall? Anybody wanting to kill him?"

"Not a soul. I was shocked when I heard that he'd been shot. The man had the world by the tail and the world was enjoying it from all appearances. He was making money out of his name. I was too. And, everybody else too. It was one of those franchises that blossomed into a money machine."

"I've never had one," Bishop said.

"Well, I'd be happy to let you in on one," McNally smiled and said. "Give you a discount."

"No thanks. I'd be precluded. Conflict of interest," he fudged the truth a bit, but in reality, he just wasn't interested in selling tacos from a taco wagon, no matter how charming they looked. And, he wasn't interested in owning stock or bonds in the Taco Wagons company. No matter what McNally said, any investment carries a risk.

"Where's the closest one I could look at? If Chief Wasserman says I need to."

"Well, let me see. Driving from here. I guess you'd drive?"

"I would."

"Let me get a map. I can show you better on a map." He left and returned a minute later with a map of the US. He spread it out on the table in front of them.

"Okay. Beaver, Utah is a good place. Just north of the Arizona line. An easy drive for you from here. Weldon, Arizona might be better. Not far. Quartzsite too. Want another one or two?"

"No. A couple is enough. If the Chief wants me to, I'll drive over and take a look. I doubt she will."

"No reason to really. We've had no problems with any of our franchisees. It'd be a waste of taxpayer's money. Let me know if you're going to inspect one. I have to notify the franchisee and get his or her permission."

Permission, Bishop thought with a long look at McNally. *Road block is what I'd call it.*

"Some of our franchisees were well known before they retired and don't want to talk to anybody who might know them. Before they retired, some of 'em anyway, had offices and a staff of people ,,, hell, employees. Now, they make tacos. You can see how they might feel a bit sensitive. And, they don't want people bothering them while the business is open. You'd have to schedule a meeting for early in the morning or late evening. I'll have to do it actually. Schedule it."

"Yeah. I understand, I think, but I doubt I'd have known any of them and I wouldn't want to cause them any problems." Bishop said. "I'll let you know if I want to talk to a couple of franchisees."

McNally nodded. "I can't see how that'd help you solve Snapper's murder, but let me know what you decide. I still have to contact a franchisee to get their permission. That's in their franchise agreement."

"I will."

Bishop then looked hard at McNally before saying, "By the way, I just played tennis against Snapper in a tournament in La Jolla. He almost had a fight with his partner. He was belligerent throughout the match. Was he that way with everybody?"

McNally seemed surprised, "No, he wasn't. I always found him congenial and easy to get along with. Maybe his tennis partner did something to him. I heard about their argument."

"His partner just played as hard as he could. I don't see how that would have upset anybody."

"Well, I don't know what to tell you. I never saw that in Snapper. Have you talked to his partner? Maybe they had a problem going way back. It just came to a head while they were playing in the tournament. Both were probably under stress."

Bishop decided to let it go for then. "Maybe you're right. I'll see what I can find."

"Good idea. Wish I could help you, but I can't."

Bishop looked McNally in the eyes and asked, "Did you kill Snapper?"

McNally's mouth dropped open, his eyes widened as if in shock. "What? Kill my partner? No. Hell no! We worked together. He brought in investors. He was valuable to me … valuable to the company. I didn't kill him!"

"Did you pay somebody to do it?"

"Good God no, man! I just said. He was more valuable to be alive than dead. I wish he was sitting here now. Wish we were having a beer and talking about how the company's doing. I guess you're doing what you have to do, but I haven't killed anybody, and certainly not Snapper and I didn't hire anybody to do it. Based on what I've heard, you should be talking to his tennis partner."

I have talked to him. His neighbor saw him under the tree in front of his camper about the time Snapper was being shot.

Bishop figured he sounded sincere but was well aware that the man was a salesman, a huckster, capable of lying at the drop of a hat if it suited him. His report to Ellen would include what McNally said and his caveat about McNally's character.

As he got into his car, another thought crossed his mind. *Beatrice may love Valley. What about that? Damn. I've been going along with what she said. Hell, somebody in love would lie to save somebody they loved. I'd better keep an open mind.*

He kicked his butt for not thinking about that before then.

Chapter 11

Bishop drove back to the apartment and made his report. Ellen called thirty minutes later. He included his supposition about Beatrice.

"Boiling it all down, you didn't find out a thing that points to a damn soul, did you?" she asked. "However, I liked your suspicion about the neighbor lady. Good gossip, Bishop. I guess you've thought about a search of Vince's camper and all other places where he might have hidden the gun that killed Snapper."

He had thought about it but figured if Vince offered to let them search, and he had shot Snapper, he would have hidden the gun in a place no one could possibly find or he just threw the thing away. But, his suspicion would stay just that, a suspicion, until he had something concrete he could go on.

He answered her question. "Yeah. That's all it is, a suspicion. And, I didn't find a hell of a lot worth a damn. McNally more or less said Snapper was a figurehead but kind of admitted that he might have had something to do with creating the company and its operations. Practically everything the company does in support of its Taco Wagons is sub'ed out. All Snapper and McNally, now just McNally, had to do was read the monthly franchisee operational reports and bank statements, I assume, and tell another outfit to write checks to their suppliers. Pretty easy business. No stress. No conflicts. Just rake in the money.

"I wouldn't mind driving to Arizona or Utah and do a little investigation on site. No reason really, but I'd like to see what a Taco Wagon operator has to say about things. See if there might be a conflict nobody knows about. Could be somebody got pissed and took it out on Snapper who might not have known a conflict existed. Might have been something McNally did and blamed on Snapper. Snapper didn't know it and paid the ultimate price."

"I hear you but I think that's a stretch. Nobody's complaining. And, it appears anyway, the money keeps rolling in. No, a trip would be a waste of your time and the City's money. From what you've found out, this isn't one of those situations, as far as I can see, where people are getting screwed and one of them decided to get even."

"No. I guess you're right. It's unbelievable, the way it works, but it's a money making idea apparently. People on the go want to grab a taco and keep going. And, the Taco Wagons are charming. I have to admit. It's the new age, apparently," he said. "Eventually somebody will decide to horn in. Put out some push carts selling tacos and the rest. When that happens, Taco Wagons will not be making so much money. People will be turning in their leases. Then, somebody might have a reason to kill somebody."

"Maybe so, Bishop, maybe so and then, we'll have some conflicts, but for now, they're doing okay and we don't have any."

"New ventures do okay until the vultures see 'em and swoop in to get some."

"Yep. No doubt. Even so, I wish we had one around here. I'd use it."

"I guess." *Not me. I wouldn't buy anything from a street wagon. I figure I'd be dead by the next morning.*

"What's next?" she asked. "What do you have on your agenda?"

"All I have left I can do is interview the older children involved in Cornwall's life. I asked you to do some background research on his marriages and children."

"I did and I have something for you there," she said. "He married his first wife for money, evidently. But she got tired of him, according to her lawyer and he was a selfish bastard to boot so she got a divorce and he got a settlement. They had a son. He's a doctor someplace."

Ellen told him that Cornwall's second wife, Billie Talbert, was coming off a divorce when he showed up. She was too old to have children with him. But, she'd had three children with her prior husband but Ellen didn't know much anything about them or the divorce.

"The boy's name is George but he's the only one that showed up on our initial search. We're still looking for the girls.

She was going to use an outside investigator to find out more. She'd let Bishop know.

She did know something about Snapper's third wife. "He remarried the woman whose husband had invented something and made some money. Quite a bit in fact. Snapper moved in some years after her husband died. However, the husband had made sure no one would take his money. He assigned most of his royalty income to his son and daughter. His wife kept the house and refinanced it for the money she needed to survive. Snapper helped her there. I think he orchestrated the last refi, took a bunch and left."

"Anything else?" Bishop asked.

"Well, the widow was, according to the lawyer we talked to, border line demented and had been for some time when Snapper came on the scene. She was estranged from her children because they wanted to put her in a home. Old Snapper loved her just the way she was, don't you know, so she didn't go anyplace. A housekeeper took care of everything. She paid for it. The lawyer said Snapper wrote the checks."

"No doubt made sure some of the money ended up in his bank account."

"Probably. He was writing the checks."

The lawyer wasn't sure how Snapper made out when she died but thinks he did well. By then, Snapper had moved her affairs to another lawyer, one he selected, Ellen told him.

Bishop laughed. Ellen had emailed him the names, addresses and phone numbers, including the emails of all the children.

"You named lots of people who might have wanted the man dead, it seems," he told Ellen before hanging up. "I'll see if I can get one of them to say something that puts them at the top of the list."

"I won't hold my breath on that," she said.

"I still have to do it," he said.

*****

Bishop arranged to meet the son and daughter of Snapper's third wife the following morning at Harry's for breakfast. They had careers so breakfast was the only time they had to meet.

He had no trouble recognizing them when they came in together. Both were in dark, business suits. They weren't handsome or beautiful, but had a look of confidence about them. They resembled each other. Both had brown hair and brown eyes.

He waved them over and after introductions they sat down for coffee and ordered one of Harry's breakfasts.

He found out after introductions that the son, Garret, had a tax accounting practice and was well connected with major companies. The daughter, Margret, was in commercial real estate. Her firm did it all.

Strong family genetics, Bishop thought after listening to them. All had been born with ambition and the intelligence to back it up, like their father.

They knew about Snapper's death and knew him from his marriage to their mother. They came to realize that she was suffering from a form of dementia. Snapper played into that. He arranged refinancing of the home for her living expenses and managed her affairs.

"We think he skimmed some off each refi for himself," Garret said. "He most likely used that to buy the townhouse he owned when he was shot."

Margret agreed.

"We investigated him when he first began snooping around Mom," Margret said. "We figured he was just after her money."

"Had to be," Garret said.

They did some checking and found out that Snapper had received a lump sum to leave his second wife. Bishop knew that from what Ellen had said, but let them tell the story.

"He had enough money from his marriages and divorces to play the big wheel around town, contributing to politicians and worthy causes, all to get a name for himself. People thought he had money. They didn't know he'd been given money to get out of his wives' lives. And, he skimmed whatever he could, when he could."

"What happened to his son … from his first wife? I understand he's a doctor someplace," Bishop said. "Do you know?"

Margret answered, "Yes. We tracked him down when we began investigating Snapper. After we began to figure that Snapper was just after Mom's money. He's a plastic surgeon in Beverly Hills. Apparently very good. Jacques Cornwall is his name. We never met him but figured he wasn't a factor in what Snapper was doing."

"Probably used his mother's money to get through med school," Garret supposed.

"So, you decided Snapper was a crook," Bishop said.

"He was," both answered.

Garret said, "But we'd decided we no longer had any control over mother. I think we could have had her committed but we didn't want to humiliate her that way."

"And," Margret said. "Dad had already anticipated Mom's condition and transferred his property to us. She had the house and could reverse mortgage it as necessary to live. Of course, we would have jumped in if necessary to help Mom but old Snapper was always one refi ahead of us."

"Any thoughts about who might have wanted to kill him?" Bishop asked.

"Not us," Garret said. "Dad left her the house and although Snapper got some of it, off the refinances, it didn't impact us. And, Mom was too far gone for it to matter to her."

"How about the other children from the marriage before? Snapper's second wife?"

"We didn't find out much when we investigated. We were told by an attorney that the children were happy to get rid of him," Margret said. "He was paid money, we think, to leave but we never found out for sure. So, you may want to do your own investigating."

She's right. I probably should contact them to get their story if Ellen can find out where they are.

That was what Bishop discovered from the children of Snapper's third wife. Not much. He was a crook but Bishop already suspected that.

He went back to his temporary apartment and typed a report for Ellen. Basically he said he'd confirmed that Snapper was corrupt but they both pretty much already knew that so he'd found out nothing new. For certain, he'd developed no sure leads that pointed to the man's killer.

"We can tell the Mayor he was a crook but that wouldn't get us anyplace. Not after the Mayor went on record for the guy like he did during his news conference," Bishop told her during his subsequent phone call. "I'll call the children of Snapper's second wife as soon as you find out who they are and where they are."

She was working on it.

They agreed to have dinner together at Mr. A's, the old time restaurant in town that overlooked the harbor and planes landing at Lindberg Field, the San Diego airport.

"Well, Mr. Bone," she asked. "Where do we go from here?"

He smiled. "Damned if I know. I could refund some of the money you've paid me and go home. What do you think of that?"

"And leave me holding the bag? Not on your life. I need somebody to blame if we don't find the killer. You're it."

"Yeah. I kind of thought that was how it would come down."

"This is the real world, Bishop. Somebody has to take the blame and you're the best person for the job. You'll be gone. And, taking your guilt with you. I'll be here, still employed."

"Thanks. I guess I'd better do some more thinking."

"I guess you'd better," she said with a big smile. "But, for the record, if anybody can find the killer, you can."

"I wish I had your confidence in me."

*****

So, Bishop went back to his apartment that evening and did some thinking. He didn't have any evidence, so far, that pointed to any of the children as killers. He knew it was possible that one or the other of them harbored enough of a grudge to do it, but he didn't think it was a strong possibility, based on what he'd found to date.

"I'll contact the children of his second wife as soon as Ellen tells me about them," he said. "Who knows what they went through and what, if any, impact it had on them."

That's how he went to sleep, thinking about who else might have done it. He'd want to interview Snapper's Beverly Hills son, Jacques, to see if he had any thoughts. It was possible Snapper had maintained relations with the boy. Now a man with a successful medical practice.

Maybe the son didn't consider him an out and out crook. Or maybe he's a crook, like father, like son. So, he wouldn't give a shit what old Snapper was doing.

*****

He called the number he had for the son. After a verbal duel with the receptionist, he got through.

"Dr. Cornwall," a man with a deep voice said. "I understand you're a police officer investigating my father's murder."

Bishop agreed and explained that he wanted to meet with him for about thirty minutes to get background information on his dad.

"I don't know … wait a minute. You're in San Diego, right?"

He was.

"I'll be at Scripps Memorial Hospital in the morning giving a lecture on the perils and pitfalls of plastic surgery. Can you meet me there at ten. They have a coffee shop. We can talk there."

Bishop agreed.

*****

Bishop was waiting for Jacques Cornwall at the door to the cafeteria at ten when he walked up dressed in an expensive, dark suit. He was an inch or so shorter than Bishop, not handsome, but with a full head of hair and a very confident look.

They exchanged greetings and went inside. Got coffee and sat down.

"My father?" Jacques said. "What do you want to know. I was notified about his death. When his body is released, I'll take care of the burial. The least I can do."

Bishop nodded. "I'd like to know what kind of man he was. And, what kind of relationship you had with him."

Jacques laughed. "I had practically no relationship with him. Anybody who did probably paid for it in some way. My mother was disgusted with him. He was lazy, chased any woman with a decent set of tits and no stomach. Went around town acting like he was royalty using my mother's money. If he was facing any situation that had money in it, he tried to get some. Seemed dedicated to doing that. It was pathetic to watch."

"I like a man who tells it like it is," Bishop said with a smile.

"Might as well. I considered him worthless as a dad and as a husband. He was an embarrassment to me and my mother. Frankly, I think he may have had something wrong upstairs. I hope to hell I didn't inherit it."

"I understand," Bishop said.

"My mother put me through school. I buried her. He didn't even show up. To get rid of him, I think she gave him something to get him to divorce her. I heard her talking about it on the phone one day. She'd already given most of what she had to me. Before he could waste it being a big shot. I gave him his nickname, Snapper. He snapped up every loose dollar he saw whether it belonged to somebody else or not."

"Damn. That's consistent with what I knew of him the short time I knew him. Not the money part, but the extreme behavior. Overbearing and completely selfish." Bishop explained how he'd met Snapper at the tennis tournament.

"Sounds like him," Jacques said with a grimace. "I had to watch him play one time. My mother asked me to. I was surprised his opponent didn't hit him with his racquet. He cheated on every line call."

"He hadn't changed."

"People like that can't, I believe, professionally."

"Do you know of anybody who might have killed him?" Bishop asked.

"Anybody who knew him for more than thirty minutes would be on my list. But, to answer your question. I don't know of anyone specific. I didn't see the man after the divorce. I stayed close to my mother. I think he called a few times, wanting money. She might have given him some, just to shut him up."

A leech, Bishop concluded.

By then, they'd finished their coffees. "Anything else," Jacques asked.

Bishop couldn't think of anything else so they said goodbye. "If you do think of anything that might tell us who killed him, please call me"

He said he would.

Chapter 12

Ellen sent him the information he'd requested on the children of Cornwall's second wife. She'd had three with her first husband, a boy and two girls. None with Cornwall. She got a big divorce settlement from her husband. That probably was what attracted Cornwall, Ellen's report said.

The girls, Wilma and Jean, had married and were living in the east and doing well. Ellen said she'd send an investigator to interview them if Bishop needed more information and could show some relevance in an interview.

She urged him though, for the sake of money, to see if the son, George Talbert, could tell him what he needed to know. He lived and worked close to San Diego so Bishop had a relatively easy drive to meet with him.

George, Ellen's report said, was living in Orange County, in the small town of Placentia and managing a restaurant called Big Plates, Small Prices.

Bishop called George and arranged to meet him at the restaurant at three that afternoon, the least busy time for them.

*****

Bishop parked and went inside. It was a couple of minutes before three.

He saw a heavy set man in his late forties sitting at a stark table staring down at a cup of black coffee. He looked worn out, Bishop decided and figured that was the man he'd come to meet. He shoved out his hand and introduced himself as the Investigator for the San Diego police department who had called him. The man confirmed that he was indeed George Talbert.

Bishop told him why he was there, to investigate the death of Snapper Cornwall.

After hearing that, Talbert told Bishop with undisguised bitterness that Snapper had "screwed" his mother and indirectly him and his two sisters.

"Praise the Lord, my sisters are doing good. Fortunately, both were nice looking and married good. They send me a little money now and then. I need it."

George was married but only had one child, Barry. He was married and working part time at the restaurant while going to junior college. He wanted to be an electrical engineer. His wife worked. Bishop got that from Ellen's report.

George's younger sister and her two children had just visited a month or so ago. One of the things they all talked about when they were together was what Cornwall had done to them while he was married to their mother.

"When we saw what he was doing, taking Mom's money, we forced her to get rid of him," George said. "We didn't know that in their divorce settlement, she'd given him half of what Dad was leaving for us, almost four hundred thousand dollars. Mom loved the crooked bastard even after we showed her he was a leech and only wanted her money. She thought he looked like a movie star. The son of a bitch slept with any woman willing."

"You know that he was murdered," Bishop said.

"Uh huh. I heard," the man said. "I'd say good riddance. He was worthless. Playing the good life using our money. He deserved to be killed. I called him a few months ago. The owner of this place was looking for a partner and asked if I had any money. The bastard, Snapper, laughed at me when I asked him to give me some of what he'd stolen from Mom. Laughed and threw me out of his house."

"I don't imagine that set well," Bishop said as he made notes.

The man laughed. "You imagine right! It pissed me off! I was just asking for some of my money." He looked at a man in an apron who'd just appeared behind the counter from the kitchen.

"The owner," he told Bishop, swallowing a curse in the process. "Wants me to get back to work. I hope I helped you." He stood.

"You did. Thank you," Bishop told him.

That ended the meeting.

*****

Bishop emailed a report of all he'd learned to Ellen. In the report, he suggested that George Talbert as well as the other children, had motives to kill Cornwall but he doubted anybody could put any of them at the scene.

"Besides, the killer was apparently a young man according to our one witness. Talbert wasn't what I'd consider as young and he sure as hell isn't fit. Looks older than he probably is. I didn't interview his son, Barry. He's married, working part time and going to junior college, trying to become an engineer. Doesn't sound like he's a killer, but you never know."

He closed with, "I don't have anybody else to interview. Do you have any ideas? I'll be in San Diego in about two hours."

*****

By the time he'd crossed into San Diego, he was figuring it was time for him to wrap it up and go home. As far as he was concerned, anybody Snapper Cornwall knew could be a suspect. Not only that, his killing might be considered by some as a mercy killing. As in "good riddance."

This is one of those cases that flat out whipped my ass, Bishop thought. *Damnit to hell. Sooner or later, it had to happen.*

She called him twenty minutes later as he was exiting the freeway. "Why don't we meet at Bread and Cie around noon for a bite and discuss it?"

He agreed and changed his course to head in that direction. She was parking as he drove into the parking lot.

*****

They went inside, ordered their usual and sat outside to eat it.

"I can't believe you don't have any more leads," she said, smiling slightly, after he'd told her about the interview with Talbert. "I believe that guy, Snapper, was a sociopath. Classic case. Somebody should have looked good for it."

"Yeah. Should have. You're right, he was a sociopath. That was his own son's diagnosis. Medical talk. Rotten to the core is how I'd describe him. Lawyer's talk."

"Must have been tough watching your own dad stealing from his mother like he did," Ellen said.

"Had to be," Bishop explained. "You said somebody should have looked good for the murder, Ellen. Lots of people I've talked to had motives. Snapper as his son nicknamed him, stole from everybody. The man in Orange Country, George, was pretty bitter about it. As I said in my report, he actually asked Snapper for money and got laughed at."

"That must have been hard to take. That sure as hell would have made me want to kill the bastard, It's a hard case, Bishop. By now in a case, you usually have somebody you at least suspect for the killing," she said.

"Usually, yeah. All I know about this one is that everybody Snapper knew likely wanted him dead. I'd have to say that Vince Valley is still the most logical man for it, but I'm fairly sure he didn't do it. Besides, his neighbor says she saw him outside of his camper when Snapper was being shot. Maybe she was fudging, 'cause she likes him, maybe not. I don't know anybody else to interview. Nothing else I can do."

"And, you want to put in a bill and fly to Mississippi to be with your beavers? You're throwing in your hand. Hard for me to believe."

"Believe it, Ellen. I couldn't have said it better," he said. "Not much need to stay in the game with a pair of deuces, if that."

"Let us talk about it some, Bishop, before we fold. The Mayor won't like it," she said. "if you leave ... before he can fire you." She laughed.

"I bet. I don't like it either," Bishop said. "I'm not a quitter, you know that, but when you come to the end of the line, you get off the bus."

"If you're on a bus, which you're not. We know that somebody killed him and I'm betting a clue as to who that somebody is, is somewhere in what you've already found out," she said.

"Maybe so, but if there is, I don't see it," Bishop answered.

"It's not like he suddenly went bad and when he did, he went bad in front of somebody who was worse and killed him on the spot. You found out that much. He was probably born bad and got real good at it growing up."

"Yep. He was a nut for money. Somebody else's. He was movie star handsome and women were offering money to get him into their beds. From what I've heard, he didn't turn any of them down. It could be that he took money from a woman that we don't yet know about and somebody called and wanted it back. He refused and paid the price," Bishop said.

"It'd be nice if we knew that for sure." she said. "We'd have our killer."

"It would, but damned if I can find anything that shows me that is what happened. The investment thing he was fronting could be a possibility. There's big money in it. That would have gotten Snapper's attention, but I haven't found anyway he could have gotten into it. The company looks clean from what I know about it."

"Well, tell me about the company," Ellen said. "Maybe I'll see something you've missed. Maybe it's not clean."

"Okay. Snapper was little more than a figurehead in the Taco Wagons company, according to McNally. And, that's what it looks like to me. Big name up front gave the company instant credibility. Maybe Snapper did some of the creative thinking to set it up but I can't see that bothering anybody. All he did was help get a money making venture off the ground. He did bring in some investors and apparently some men and women who bought franchises. In my opinion, that made him more than the figurehead McNally calls him but so what?"

"I agree," Ellen interjected.

"Yeah. It's making money. Lots of people, sub- contractors mostly, are working hard to keep it making money. All McNally has to do is take over from Snapper and start selling bonds to investors and franchises to men and women who want to sell tacos from a wagon that looks something like an old Conestoga. At the moment, they don't have any Taco Wagons to lease to franchisees so the business is shut down. The Chinese want more money, according to McNally," Bishop said. "I don't see how that would have caused anybody to kill Snapper, however."

"It is interesting however. Based on what you've told me, without new franchises to make money to pay bond dividends, McNally probably doesn't want to sell more bonds," Ellen said.

"That's a good guess. Wrapping it up, I'll say that Snapper got paid for using his name to bring people into the company," Bishop said. "He was one of the directors and got paid for every meeting. He also got paid for every investor he brought in to buy a bond and every person he sent in to buy a franchise. It wouldn't be much of a push to say that somebody got tired of paying him for sitting on his butt. I'd look at McNally for that, but, on the other side of that coin, Snapper was bringing money into the company so why would you kill a man who's doing that?"

"You wouldn't," Ellen said. "Money is in the life's blood of the company? That raises an interesting question. Have to talked to an investor? They might know if something McNally was doing looked funny. Or if Snapper was."

Bishop shook his head. "I have names to call. Nothing hard about it. Asking what, if anything, they know. You could do it."

"But, you know what to ask. Except for what you've told me, I don't know enough to ask anything that'd make sense. I'd make a fool out of myself."

Bishop frowned and said, "Just to make you happy, Ellen, I'll call a couple of investors and see what they have to say. Who knows? Maybe there have been complaints and McNally's been covering 'em up. Or, maybe Snapper knew about the complaints and was killed to keep him from talking about it." He laughed and added, "Or, broadening my scope, he might have been killed because he wanted money not to talk about it.

"I still think it would be a good idea to send somebody to Utah or Arizona to watch a retired senior citizen make a taco for a hungry customer and ask if they've heard anything. Maybe they're pissed at having to eat their left-over tacos."

"We've covered that already, Bishop. The Mayor rejected the idea. And, I reject the idea. You haven't offered any evidence to support doing that."

"You may be right. The big money is in the bonds anyway. Somebody once told me. I may have told you. Money is the root of all evil. Killing Snapper would be evil. I'll call some investors and see if they know anything useful. If not, I'll admit the case has whipped me and I'll tell this town goodbye."

"We'll talk about it then. Okay," Ellen said.

"I think we've had the talk but listen, I did have a question for you. A couple of questions that'll need answering regardless of who's handling the case if it isn't closed. Can you run Jacques Cornwall through your computers. See if you come up with links to any bad guys or anything else that might put him under a shadow. While I'm pretty sure he wouldn't have shot his dad, he might have had a friend or friendly patient who would have. While you're at it, see if George Talbert has a record."

She agreed to do it.

"By the way," she said. "I had somebody call the junior college closest to Placentia and ask if Talbert's son was in school the night Cornwall was shot."

"You did. I was wondering about that. Good job. What'd you find out?"

"The records show that he signed into a class at the time Snapper was shot."

"Damn. I'm glad you checked. It was on my list but not a priority. Even so, I wanted to check it out. He was young and he might have had a gun."

"My thinking too," she said.

He finished his cappuccino. "Best in town."

Ellen agreed. "I'm always tempted to get a second."

Both laughed.

"Listen, Bishop, I know we've had this talk and that you're fed up with the case. Hell, I understand. You are tired of frustrations and want to go home. See your lady friend. The beavers, but please don't leave me hanging in the middle of this mess."

Bishop began shaking his head but Ellen didn't stop.

"I can't argue about that," She said, "Besides, it's beginning to look like this is one of those cases that goes unsolved until somebody on their death bed confesses to it. And, that will probably be long after we're gone. But, damn, Bishop, I hate to tell the Mayor that after he had that rosy press conference. Can't you hang in there with me a little longer. Maybe something will happen."

"Ellen, I'm sorry. I don't see any benefits to hanging around much longer. But, I'll turn over one more rock and have one more go at the Valley guy, Vince. Could Snapper was riding him and he snapped and shot him. I doubt it, but I'll talk to him after I talk to the bond investors. Unless I find something, I'll be handing in my police badge. Okay?"

Ellen's reply sounded glum. "He did attack old Snapper when we played."

"Yep, he did. Well, I'll show up at one of his so called talks. See if I can pick anything up that's useful. And, hang around afterward to … chat with him. Only for you, Ellen. Only for you."

"Thank you, Bishop. You know I'd do the same for you if it came up."

"I do."

*****

Kathy called later with some distressing news. It seemed that his fruit trees, about half, were dying, probably poisoned. He asked her to get the local nursery to test the soil to see what, if any, poison had been used.

"Probably Parsons. Revenge because I did what I was supposed to do for the bank on his loan. It was in default and he blamed me for the bank's decision to foreclose on his property."

He explained what he was talking about. Parson's father was a big shareholder in the bank so no one in the bank wanted to be the one to pull the plug on the big loan to his son.

"I thought we had an agreement about how Parsons was to bring the loan current. He was supposed to get his father to put up more money. Killing my trees like that makes me think the agreement isn't going as planned. I guess the father didn't go along with the agreement."

"More than I want to know, Bishop. But, I'll call you when I find out about the trees," she said.

"If it's poison, file a complaint with the Chief. He won't be able to do anything about it, unless he sends a team to search Parson's utility shed. Even then, there'll be no proof he actually used any poison they find to kill my trees."

She agreed to do it.

Bishop cursed and had an extra beer that night. There was little else he could do.

When I get back though, I'm going to have a talk with that bastard Parsons.

Chapter 13

Bishop, wearing khakis, his usual working clothes, took a seat near the rear of the Rec hall. It was half full when he arrived. The hat with the "donation cards" from Cindy and Amy were neatly placed on tables near the entry door. Beside the hats were the Taco Wagon brochures.

Vince was talking to them at the front and didn't notice Bishop walk in. He wasn't playing his guitar and wasn't singing that morning.

Vince was also dressed casually, short sleeve shirt and pants with tennis shoes for the talk. Ginny and Amy wore their informals as well, tennis shorts and pullover blouses. Both looked enthusiastically youthful, Bishop decided.

Youth adds a lot to the way somebody looks, he thought, recalling his look in the mirror that morning. *Lots of wrinkles.*

The hall was almost filled, Bishop noticed. Vince had told him he was drawing around a hundred "these days."

People must like his "common sense" talks. That's what Bishop called them after Vince gave him a run-down of some of his topics. That's what they seemed to be, a common sense look at today's problems and conflicts facing people.

Amy and Ginny found a seat and sat down, as Vince moved to the center of the room, signaling the start of the talk.

Be damned, Bishop thought. In the front row, along the aisle sat Beatrice, her hair done, wearing a nice frock and smiling nicely. *I wonder if Vince has seen her. Surely he has. Probably why she's smiling.*

"Where's your guitar?" a man at the rear shouted.

Vince laughed with a wave. "Not today."

As if to answer why, he looked at the hall full of people and said, "Today I'm going to talk about greed ... money in plain terms. How it's destroying what is left of our civilization. And, to be fair, maybe it's been underway since the beginning of time.

"In the old days, rich people or people in power, would empower expeditions to go into the undeveloped parts of the world and confiscate the undeveloped riches they found for the sponsors of the expeditions. After some production, the sponsors would sell them at great profit.

"They also brought back prisoners to serve families willing to pay for them. The rich did it because they had the power and resources to do it."

He went on to talk about the profits the rich made from the expeditions and how that made them richer and more powerful. And that made them greedy for more. And, soon, everyone who could was doing it.

"And, that's how it is today," Vince explained.

He elaborated and told them how some unscrupulous people with plenty of money and power hired others to find out what people wanted or needed and then, they'd hire people to make it and put it out there for the people to buy and use.

"Right now, we all want to be beautiful and live forever so the class of people who used to empower expeditions, now empower people to make potions and lotions we can slather all over our bodies to keep them looking young. We want our friends, and others we want to impress, to look at us and wish they could look as good as we do.

"And, what else? We want to live till we're at least a hundred and go out and play tennis while we're doing it. So, big Pharma hires people to make miracle drugs that theoretically make that possible. But, let me add this. If the miracle drugs don't or won't do that, they hire people to go on television and radio and swear by all that's holy that they do. If not, it's not their fault, but the fault of the user ... somehow.

"Some people think it's okay to sell drugs on the street. Why bother with a doctor's prescription. If there's pain, let there be pain medicine without wasting time seeing a doctor. They say that people are entitled to become addicted if that's the price they have to pay to eliminate pain.

"Everybody wants money and they don't give a damn how they get it or if they have to lie to get it, in the process. In this day and time of greed, lying or misrepresenting is part of the process of getting wealth and keeping it. Power isn't good unless it grows. And the more it grows, the more it's sought after.

"And, talking about greed, it's not just the rich and powerful who're greedy. Greed had filtered down to the lowest of us. When we go to sell our houses or anything we have of some value, we automatically want to get the most for it. Forget fairness, we want as much excess as we can get. Greed has become part of our way of life and we think nothing about it. It has become us. I talked about the Bible one time. Do you think the Bible supports greed? Hardly.

"But, let me get back to what I started with. As some wise person once said, power begets power. The people with the power that comes from money know all about begetting. And, politicians who want more power, most of them, make a beeline to people who've already taken power by hook or crook, and hold out their hands for some of the money that came with it.

"And, we all know what they say when they do. 'Give me some of yours and when I get elected, I'll give you some of mine.' They think nothing of trading the power of their office for the money the special interests have acquired."

He then moved on to talk about the perils of politics. How, once elected, those who made it possible, the special interests, controlled what the elected officials did. Almost always, the elected politicians have to do what those who got them elected want them to do. If not, they don't get re-elected.

"Most of the politicians get reelected, as we know, and each time they do, they pick up more power and with it, more money.

"As an aside, let me say this. Why in the world don't we put limits on how long a politician can stay in office and milk the office for all he or she can get? If we put limits on their terms, they probably won't do any more to solve our problems, but at least we can limit how much they get paid to serve the interests of the big dogs, the special interests with the money."

In his opinion, he told the men and women in the hall, that was why democracy had become stagnant. "That's why we're no longer a government of the people, for the people and by the people. It has become a government for the benefit of special interests, for the people who put up the money to get politicians to do special favors for their companies.

"The politicians only care about the needs and problems of the people if those needs coincide with the needs of the special interests. It happens now and then, but not often enough to preserve our democracy."

Beatrice was beaming, Bishop noticed. Vince's *alibi. Obviously in love. Of course she'd lie to protect him.* She even spontaneously applauded a couple of time. Vince noticed and smiled with a nod in her direction.

"As I said, it is imperative that we put limits on how long politicians can stay in office to serve the special interests of the people who put up the money to get them elected. How about a politician who will serve the interests of the people they're supposed to be serving, that'd be US." He said the last word loudly.

Then, he paused to let that sink in. As he did, he scanned the room and looked as many people as he could in the eyes.

Beatrice practically rose out of her chair when he looked at her.

"Sometimes it seems to me that we're only allowed to live because we serve the needs of the special interests. We get to buy the crap they put out for us or the services they tell us we can't live without. And, they give us jobs so we can pay for it."

Vince embellished on what he'd been saying, giving examples of the favors some politicians did for special interests, and how they were often exposed by men and women standing in the wings waiting for their turn to run for office. And, he went on to say that each time someone exposed a favor, a dozen others popped up under different banners to take their places.

He paused to admit he'd taken that description from literature. "Probably butchered it, but I wanted to make a point. I think the myth involved the sowing of dragon's teeth, but I liked the way I used it.

"Wrapping up, I'll say this. The supply of scams – I dare call them that. – of the special interests are endless and nobody wants to stop them because those doing the scamming are in control of the hen houses, the government. We stop one and more are invented as I just said. If one goes down, another pops up."

As was his usual practice, Vince stopped for people in the hall to ask questions. Most agreed with what he'd been saying. Like Vince, no one had any actual proof however so all they could do was speculate and bitch about what appeared to be rampart injustices everywhere.

Vince saw Bishop in back as he neared the end of the session. "I see the police department has sent someone to listen and report back, I presume, about my rabble rousing. Mr. Bone, did I advocate overthrowing the government?"

Bishop stood, as had the others who'd participated in the questioning part of the talk. "No, I just came to be educated. And, you didn't disappoint me." He smiled and sat down.

The meeting ended. Some people, including Beatrice, crowded around Vince at the front to have a private word. One lady, who had been to all of his talks, had worked up enough courage to ask him to dinner. He took her number with a smile and a hug. He told her he'd call if he could make it. He knew he wouldn't call.

Another lady wanted to know where he got his ideas for the talks. He told her they came to him in the night when he was trying to sleep.

Beatrice hugged him enthusiastically and whispered something in his ear. He drew back and stared at her for a second but caught himself and forced a smile. He leaned down and whispered something in her ear that brought a smile to her face.

Bishop correctly assumed she was telling him what she had prepared for them to eat that evening. He knew Vince preferred to eat whatever he could find in his refrigerator. And, he'd eat it standing up. *But, he most likely doesn't want to hurt the woman's feelings,* Bishop thought. *Who knows what he told her. Poor bastard.*

Beatrice left with an idyllic smile on her face so Bishop assumed Vince had agreed to eat dinner with her.

The attendees paused at the front of the hall to drop money in the hats left by the girls. Beatrice dropped in a ten dollar bill.

Ginny and Amy counted the money and picked up their hats and the Taco Wagon brochures. They no longer went through the charade about the division of contributions. They took two thirds and left a third for Vince who shared his with the Rec Department as "rent" for the hall.

Ginny and Amy left, speaking to Bishop as they did. When they were gone and the hall was empty except for Vince, Bishop went to the front to speak to him.

"Good talk," Bishop told him. "Based on what you were saying, I wouldn't be surprised to find you dead in your camper one day."

Vince's eye brows raised. "You could be right, especially if I ever made the papers or television. I'm still below the radars of the interests I'm attacking. I guess you could say, I'm attacking them. Really, I'm just talking about what I've been seeing most of my life and it's getting worse all the time. Democracy is being tarnished if not destroyed, by the influence of greed and power. However, I think greed is the force behind the power."

Bishop shrugged. "I quit worrying about politics and all that comes with it, years ago. I came to the conclusion that I couldn't change anything so why frustrate myself trying to change it or talking about it. I'm glad people like you still care enough to tackle it. Maybe you can do some good."

"Right now, it's keeping me alive," He told Bishop.

"Yeah. I understand. Keep it up. I saw Beatrice sitting in the front row," Bishop added.

He shrugged. "Yes. It was her first time to come to one of my talks. I guess you saw how much she seemed to enjoy what I was saying."

"I did."

"She invited me to lunch today. I've told her I don't much care for dinners. I thought that may get me free of her interest in feeding me but it didn't. She just switched to lunch. We have to sit outside where God and everybody can see us. I think she wants people to see that she can still attract a man. Unfortunately, I'm not the man she needs."

He sighed. "I hate to do it, but I'm just going to have to tell her. Damn, I dread it."

"I don't envy you that," Bishop told him. "I got lucky and found somebody I related to when I got over my divorce." He was thinking of Kathy.

"Good for you. I can tell you I'd rather have a root canal without Novocain than having to eat with her. We probably have nothing in common. But I hate to hurt her feelings. She lost her husband and I think she's looking at me as a replacement. Sooner or later though, I'll tell her but I keep putting it off."

"Can't say that I blame you. As I said, you're in a hard situation. Living that close. You'd still have to see her every day."

"Yep. That's a problem. I bet you didn't come to hear me talk about the corrupting power of the special interests or my problems with Beatrice. So, why'd you come?" he asked Bishop.

"No slight intended, but as I said, years ago I quit giving a damn about what goes on in the world. I take care of what happens in my world and let the rest of the world take care of what's happening in its."

"Wish I could," he said. "The greed and corruption eats at me. I'm glad I have a way to speak out."

"But, why did I come?" Bishop began answering his earlier question. "I came to talk about Snapper and you. Snapper was probably one of those people you were talking about in some ways. Somebody with ill-gotten power who wanted more. More money and consequently more power. He liked being the big dog around town, I gather. He enjoyed having politicians like the Mayor jump around."

"No doubt," Vince said. "I wasn't really thinking about him, well consciously anyway, but you're right. I could have been. He wasn't one of those outfits with special interest looking for favors, but in his own way, he was just as bad. So, maybe subconsciously he was on my mind."

"Officially speaking, I figure you might have decided getting rid of him was one thing you could do to fight the greed you say seems to be slowly creeping into our daily lives."

He shook his head. "Think what you want, Mr. Bone but I didn't kill the man. Hell, I don't even have a gun. Never have. Search my camper if you like. I'm not sorry somebody did, but you'll have to look elsewhere for his killer. Maybe somebody didn't like what he was and what he did. From what I saw and what I've heard, he had nothing he'd earned by himself, but wanted us to think he was big shit. I've heard that he ... I'll say it like I heard it. He stole money from the women he'd married.

Pretty low in my opinion. He was a selfish man. He had no respect for anybody."

"He helped develop the Taco Wagons business venture, I understand," Bishop said. "He got … still gets, I guess, his estate gets money from that."

"Yes, you're right. Amy told me the Taco Wagons thing was a money maker. I understood Snapper was skimming bucks off the top of what came in. Finder fees for letting them use his name."

Bishop nodded and asked, "You aren't an investor, are you? In the Taco Wagons company?"

He laughed. "Hell, I've been on the verge of joining my late wife since she died. I gave most of what I had to my children. If somebody hadn't asked me to give a talk, I'd have already joined my wife. At night when I'm in bed trying to sleep, I wish I had joined her. But, even if I had some extra money, I sure as hell wouldn't be investing it in some kind of wagon that sells tacos to people in a hurry."

"So, killing him wouldn't have been a problem for you. You could have."

The man looked hard at Bishop, frowned and said, "I guess I have to agree with you. I could have. I wouldn't have had anything to lose. But, I've just never thought about killing him or anybody else. It wasn't me, Mr. Bone. I didn't do it."

I don't think you did either, Bishop thought. *Probably a decent lawyer in his day. Too damn bad his wife died.*

"The police department is paying me to find out who did. Have you had any thoughts about who might have done it?" Bishop asked.

"I've thought about it as you can imagine. Like everybody else. Human nature. But I don't have any ideas. I didn't know him well enough to know if he'd been fooling around with somebody else's wife or girlfriend. I doubt I would have cared if I had known. I had my wife and we were happily married. We let the rest of the world take care of itself."

But, you do tell people … in your people talks what should be changed to make life better, Bishop thought. Then, decided to tell him.

"So you say, but right now, every Saturday, you're talking about how the rest of the world is screwing up and what should be done to make it better."

He grinned. "I guess I am. With my wife gone, I've let my mind wander. These talks are what my mind finds in its travels. You know what they say. Talk's cheap. But if I can light a fire, so be it. I'd have done some good. However, I'm not one of those guys who'll do it. I just talk about it."

Lots of us do that, just talk about it.

I guess I'd better ask him about Beatrice.

"Vince," Bishop said. "I think it's fair to say that Beatrice loves you. Hell, she practically clapped at every word you said and you've said as much. I've reported what she said about seeing you the night Snapper was killed. Some people think she might have been lying out of love for you when she said she saw you sitting under the tree when Snapper died. How do you answer that?"

"I can't. I'd say you're right. She likely is in love with me. That's a problem I'll have to deal with. If she's lying about seeing me, I can't do anything about that. I was under the tree. I didn't kill Snapper. I've never had a gun. You can search my camper anytime you want."

Bishop thanked him and left.

Chapter 14

After Bishop left, he met Ellen at one of the tennis courts to rally and get some exercise. They had agreed some days earlier that both needed exercise to work off the stress that had built up from the frustrations they'd experienced during the case.

As people do when they are rallying, they talked back and forth. Mostly, he told her what Vince had said about Beatrice being in love with him and how therefore, she might have lied about seeing him the night Snapper was killed.

"Ain't a damn thing we can do, is there? If she's lying, we're stuck with it for now," Ellen said.

He agreed. "Well, I'm keeping an open mind. If I see anything, I'll pounce on it. But, I really doubt he killed Snapper."

"Let me know. As far as I'm concerned, Vince still looks good for Snapper's murder, especially if you throw out his alibi."

He agreed on the face of it, notwithstanding his gut feeling which went the other way.

After almost an hour, they went to Starbucks for cappuccinos and a pastry. They talked more about Snapper's murder and the lack of progress they'd had in finding his killer. He reported what Vince had told him after his "people's talk" at the rec hall.

"He denied killing Snapper. I asked him directly. Frankly, I believe him. Now, I'll interview a couple of investors like I promised. And, if I don't find something worth a damn from them, I'll recommend that you save some money and send me home."

"Uh huh. The Mayor called me last night to see if we were close to making an arrest. I told him the truth. We don't even have a suspect."

"And, no hope of one as it now stands. However, see if Vince has ever bought a gun. He'd have to have registered it, wouldn't he?"

He would and she'd check and let him know.

"That doesn't mean one of his clients didn't give him one," she said.

"Yeah. I thought of that too," Bishop said.

But, she promised to check Vince's registration.

They wouldn't find anything.

As they were sipping the last of their cappuccinos she said, "Let me know what the investors say."

"I will," Bishop told her. "I told you the investors were my last gasp. If I don't find something, I'm going home."

She grimaced. "This may be the case that neither of us could crack," she said.

"It's looking like that. I wake up at night thinking about how I haven't found shit."

"Yeah, I've noticed," she said, shaking her head with a look of dismay on her face.

He answered her with a decided nod.

*****

While Bishop and Ellen were rallying on the tennis courts, Vince went back to the camp ground to have lunch with Beatrice as he had reluctantly agreed. She already had the BBQ set up with coals and paper under them.

"I was waiting for you to light it," she said proudly. "BBQing on the grill is man's work. When you get it going, I'll bring out the strip steaks. We'll have steak for lunch instead of dinner."

Damnit, Vince thought but said, "Sounds like it'll be good." He walked over and lit the newspapers to get the grill going. Soon, the coals began to burn and heat the grill.

She brought out a platter with the steak strips, set them down and put her arms around Vince for an intimate hug. Others in the camp ground were outside doing one thing or another and saw them.

She enjoyed that. *They can't lord it over me today,* she thought. *I've got me one, by God.*

She had heard that some of the ladies were feeling sorry that she had to live alone. And, that bothered her. But not today. She had a younger man, somebody they all wished they had in their beds. And, she hoped Vince would be in hers soon.

He did the grilling and when the steaks were done, he told Beatrice, "They're done." He left them inside the BBQ to keep warm while they ate the salads Beatrice had brought out.

She poured the red wine she'd bought for the occasion. They touched their glasses together and took sips. The wine was very good, both said.

Expensive, Vince noted. *Poor woman. I just have to tell her. I just wish there were other men around she could attract. She's not bad looking, not bad at all. And, she's got good sense. Unfortunately, I'm worthless as a man to any woman just now for anything serious. I should tell her what Bishop said about her alibi but hell, she'd deny it anyway.*

A second later, his relationship with Jennifer popped into his thoughts. *She's just fun and games*, he told himself. *I'm worthless, but I have the same damn instincts as any other man. Man hasn't evolved a hell of a lot.*

I wish I could get over Carolyn's death, but it just hangs on. I can't get her out of my mind. Hell, I don't want to get over it.

One day when Beatrice isn't cooking for me, I'll lay it on her. Damn, I dread it. That'll be a blow to her. I wonder how she'll accept it. I may have to move my camper to another camp ground.

That's what I'm going to do. I have to. I don't think I could stand looking at her every day knowing I'd just crushed her dream of having another man to share her life. Where in the hell is there another camp ground I can move to. I could do that and not tell her anything. Just tell her I want to be close to whatever the new camp ground is close to. I'll look for one close to the beach.

It pleased him to think there was a way out of his dilemma. However, Jennifer popped back into his thoughts. He couldn't escape the fact that he needed a woman now and then.

I need to solve both problems. How in the hell can I do that? I think I'm between the rock and the hard spot people talk about.

*****

Bishop went back to his apartment after his break with Ellen and called two investors from the list McNally had given him. They agreed to meet him at the Cottage the next morning for breakfast.

They seemed eager to talk about the Taco Wagons company. During his brief conversation with the men, neither mentioned having any problems with their investments.

I think I'm barking up the wrong tree. Somebody killed the bastard. Why can't I find him ... or her? He could have pissed off some woman who didn't know what a con man he was when he made his move. She found out and when he laughed at her, she shot him. As good a story as any. But, where is the woman? Did she disguise herself when she did.

Who can I ask? Hell, now and then people tell their secrets to their neighbors! Maybe they can give me the facts I'm missing. I've never been so frustrated.

That would be his job for the next day even though he'd told Ellen his interviews with the investors was all he was going to do.

Checking with the neighbors is something I should have done anyway. That's assuming the investors don't give me a better lead I can leave with Ellen.

He called Kathy to see how she was doing. She was fine. His remaining trees were thriving.

He told her how much he was missing her.

"I want you home," she said. "I'm lonely."

"If I don't have a break through very soon, I'll be turning in my badge and catching the next flight home. I'm accomplishing nothing and I'm going crazy without you."

Before hanging up, they talked some more about what they'd do when they were next together.

"Hell, not only am I missing Kathy, I still have the Dalton problem to solve. Maybe they've worked it out. Dalton's daddy may have stepped in with some money."

He knew that was wishful thinking. If they had worked it out, he'd have been told or asked for an opinion. He cursed at the thought that it was still on the stove, brewing. That thought didn't tell him the mix of the brew and what it could mean to him. But, he'd find out.

Chapter 15

Bishop was drinking his first cup of coffee at an outside table in front of the Cottage when two elderly men walked through the latticed entry of the popular café, one street off La Jolla's main drag. They were talking together and smiling. Life was good.

The cafe was always busy, even during the week so Bishop grabbed a table when he got there. Breakfast offerings on the menu were for sophisticated eaters of which Bishop wasn't. He'd order a plain plate of fried eggs and toast.

Denny's does it right, he said to himself with a chuckle that didn't see the light of day.

Bishop waved them over. Both wore jogging attire and both were several pounds over what their doctors undoubtedly could accept during their annual physicals. Their stomachs overlapped the tops of the jogging pants so Bishop couldn't see the strings belts that held them up. *Too many bagels.*

He stood and greeted them. Fred Hillman and Larry Friedman, they gave as their names and extended their hands according to the local custom when greeting someone. Bishop did the same and gave his name too even though they knew him from his call. Fred looked to be a few years younger than Larry and in better physical condition. He also seemed more relaxed.

The two men were apparently known to the restaurant since the waitress gave them a smiling "Good morning" brought coffee and creamers right away.

Bishop gave them his story, how he was working for Chief Wasserman on the Snapper Cornwall murder. "I assume you know him since you're investors in the Taco Wagon venture he started and headed."

They agreed. Fred said, "Snapper held a couple of investor get togethers at the Beach and Tennis Club for us. We met everybody, Snapper and Walter McNally, the main man. Also, we met a couple of girls too, maybe they were included for decoration. Didn't hurt a bit. Snapper liked 'em young, we heard. Who doesn't?" He laughed.

"Mostly, we went on about how happy we were with the money we were getting from the investment."

Both men were soft spoken and seemed very comfortable and at ease like they had no troubles and never had had any.

Unlike some of us, Bishop thought. *Nice to meet people like that. Where in the hell do they come from? Maybe they were born rich and kept it. It's the people who get money after having to fight for it that don't always keep it.*

They gave their breakfast orders to the waitress. Fred and Larry ordered the sophisticated breakfasts with all sorts of strange looking things in the eggs as Bishop had supposed. He didn't want his eggs mixed with things that should be kept in salads, so he stayed with his usual.

"Just curious," Bishop said. "What was your impression of the man?"

Both men drew in deep breaths. Larry answered, "I think you could say we thought he was over-doing his friendly act but otherwise, he seemed okay. Very nice even. We'd heard that he could be … bitchy playing tennis but we never played with him. I've also heard some stories about his marriage habits. They say he liked to get married and get some money out of it. Usually the children objected to his carrying-ons and forced their mother to divorce him. He was a good looking guy and that kind stays in trouble with women. That's what I've heard anyway. He acted like he was born into wealth and it seemed to wear well on him."

When people want you to invest, they arrange to be nice to a fault and I don't think it hurts if you look like you and money are close friends, Bishop thought but said, "I was witness to some of what you're talking about in a tennis tournament I was just in. His partner got pissed and left in the final set, defaulting the match to me and my partner."

Fred shook his head. "Well, I had an invitation to play with him one time and I flatly refused."

"So, how'd you get involved in his investment?" Bishop asked.

Fred said. "I was at a party and heard Snapper talking about it to some people. I didn't like the man – I don't think many people did – but he was known as a big hitter so I listened and liked what he was saying about the company, The Taco Wagon thing. Good idea too. The bonds he was talking about had a great return, eight percent, and I had some money laying around making nothing. I knew Larry and talked to him about investing. We decided to give it a shot. I put in twenty thousand and …" He looked at Larry and asked, "You put in more didn't you. What, fifty? We figured it wouldn't kill us if we lost some of it."

Larry agreed. "I put in fifty. Been getting four hundred dollar return every month."

"I've been pleased with my return," Fred said.

"No problems?" Bishop asked.

Both men said, "Not a one. It's been a real money maker."

The conversation digressed into a discussion about comparable investments. This one had only a modest investment fee which both men also liked.

Larry said he'd heard about the Taco Wagons investment opportunity when he overheard Cindy – he'd known her from something around town - talking about it over coffee at a Rec Center event. She referred him to Snapper and McNally. McNally was the one who handled the paper work when he bought his bonds.

Fred said about the same thing. McNally and the company attorney took care of the paper work when he bought his bonds.

Breakfasts were brought, with fresh coffee, and they began eating.

"I guess lots of people have invested," Bishop said between bites.

They shook their heads. "Some we know. Some we don't. We haven't heard anybody complain if that's where you're going," Fred said. "We get out checks regularly."

"I understand the franchises are not sold in California because of the sidewalks. They need wide sidewalks for the Taco Wagons," Bishop said.

"That's what they told us too. I understand that they have guys running around small towns, searching for wide sidewalks and a friendly city government. They need electrical outlets because they want to leave the Taco Wagons out at night but they can run on gas and batteries if need be. In exchange for permits and an annual fee, the cities send patrols past the Wagons at night to make sure they're there the next morning," Larry said.

"Sounds like the best of all worlds. The small towns have an additional source of revenues and seniors – they tell me mostly seniors buy the franchisees – have something profitable to do," Bishop said

The two men agreed and talked about how they got bored sometimes and often looked for something new to do.

"I don't think I could do it, work a wagon like they're talking about, but it sounds like fun," Fred said. "Selling tacos on the street. Kind of exciting. I've never done that sort of thing, you know, deal directly with the public. But, I don't want to move out of La Jolla, even if I did want to do it. And, hell, my wife would divorce me if I even suggested moving. She looks at La Jolla as being next door to heaven." He punctuated that with a chuckle.

Bishop also laughed. "I can understand that. Who wants to move from La Jolla. Most people I know want to move here."

The waitress came by to ask if they wanted anything else. All of them said no but waved their cups for a coffee warm up. She left a check which Bishop picked up.

"But, I've seen pictures of the Taco Wagons," Bishop said. "They look charming."

They agreed.

Fred said McNally had one in La Jolla at one time but he hadn't seen it lately. They were told it had been shipped to a franchisee.

By then, they'd finished eating and were having the last of their coffee.

"I travel a lot," Fred said. "I love Bryce Canyon. When I heard there was a Taco Wagon in Kanab, I thought I'd take a detour by there and see one in action."

"How was it?" Bishop asked.

"I never made it. McNally says we have to contact the franchisee ahead of time and I wasn't sure when I would be there so I haven't done it. McNally said Sundays are good days. That way we don't interfere with their business. I can understand that they don't want people asking questions during business hours. All of them, as I understand it, are one man businesses. So, I've never followed through on it."

Larry said he'd never been curious and had never cared to see a Wagon in action. Like Fred, all he cared about were the monthly checks. "His wife loves them too," he laughed.

"You ever meet with McNally again? Privately. After you got into the Taco Wagon thing?" Bishop asked.

"I've seen him at the investor parties. Actually, as a matter of fact," Larry said, "I'm meeting with him today. A private meeting. Lunch at the Beach and Tennis club. He wants to talk to me about putting more money in. Fred's already told him no.

"All of us get together, have drinks, party food and talk about our investment. We're all happy if you want to know."

Bishop gave that a nod.

Fred added, "Hell, I was lucky to have twenty to invest. Wish I did have more. I could use the income."

"Couldn't we all?" Bishop said.

That pretty much wrapped up the meeting. Bishop paid the check since he'd invited them. They went one way and he headed to the car Ellen had provided. He had an hour before his meeting with the neighbor who lived on Snapper's left side. He figured to meet the right side lady afterward.

*****

He drove around La Jolla to see how it had changed. *Not much. The stores all look like they sell only the most expensive or exclusive stuff and none looked like they were hurting for business.*

At the appointed time, he rang the doorbell of the unit next to Snapper. It belonged to Marina Ballanger, a divorcee. She had bought the townhouse with some of the money she received from her wealthy husband in the divorce settlement. He wanted to take up with a woman thirty years younger than he was and was willing to pay Mariana for the priviledge. Like most marriages between older men and younger women, it would only last twelve months or so. And, he'd end up paying her off as well. Not that it mattered, he had plenty of money.

It was the culture for some in La Jolla. Live it up if you could. You only live once and if you have the money, live that one time big. In La Jolla, that was the order of the day in most circles.

A nice looking lady, well dressed in tennis togs, and physically fit, answered the door. "You must be Bishop Bone," she said with what he took to be an inviting smile.

Bishop figured she'd used some of her divorce money to get herself in good shape. *Probably works out every day. Most likely made an appointment with a plastic surgeon as soon as the first divorce check cleared. Face lift and boob job. Looks good though. Both. But, so does Kathy and I'm not looking for a change, even a short time change.*

Bishop answered, "I am." He added a smiling hug. She had indicated that was what she was looking for and responded with a big smile and outstretched arms. Behind her stood another lady, not as good looking or in as good a shape but she was smiling also.

Either her divorce check wasn't as big or she is living off what her deceased husband left her and she has nothing to prove and no needs to be met.

Mariana turned and introduced her. "This is Linda Marshall, the neighbor on the other side of Snapper. We talk and figured you could see us both at the same time."

Damn considerate, he thought. *Saves me having to do my thing twice.*

He and Linda exchanged handshakes. No hug.

He thanked Mariana for being so astute and thoughtful for inviting Linda.

She showed Bishop into the living room where he sat down. "Is it too early for wine?" she asked. It was eleven.

Bishop thought about it for a moment. He knew if he agreed to the wine, he'd be sipping the paint stripping red most people in La Jolla seemed to love, so he begged off and took coffee instead. She had one of those machines that ground the coffee beans for each cup so it wasn't a problem and it'd be fresh.

The ladies would take wine.

Mariana brought the coffee and sat down with her glass of wine. Linda was already nursing a glass.

"I'll tell you up front, these units are well constructed. Double walls with the best insulation. I could play drums in here and my next door neighbor wouldn't be able to hear a thing."

"So, you didn't hear what Snapper Cornwall did or said?" Bishop said, assuming that was why she told him that.

"Not much. We call him Snapper like everybody else in town. We did see some things. Heard a few things. You want to know that?" Mariana asked.

"Please."

After sipping from her glass, Mariana looked at Linda and led off. "Snapper liked 'em young. Very few ever came back a second time. Don't know if he didn't like 'em or if they didn't like him. Some stayed the night but most left after an hour or so. We could see from our windows. Didn't they, Linda? Leave after an hour."

"That's right. They didn't stay long," Linda said. She also sipped.

"Must have been paying them," Bishop supposed.

"We don't know," Linda said. "You're probably right though. I can't imagine them coming by for an hour for nothing. He wasn't a bad looking man, damned good lookin' really, but he was getting too old to be chased after for sex. You can find plenty of that on the beach or at the Tennis Club. Just smile and go without a bra and they line up. At least for Mariana." She smiled and did a little wiggle.

Bishop laughed to himself. *No bra.*

Mariana laughed and shook her head. She added, "He would have had to offer a ring to get them to stay longer than they did. That's my guess."

Linda said. "Two girls did come by more than one time. I don't know how he handled that. Probably one of those things where he watched. I've heard people talk about that."

Bishop nodded. He'd heard the same.

"Anyway, one he called Cindy and the other he called Amy when he was telling them goodbye. He'd walk to their car with them now and then. They seemed on good terms."

I'm glad these ladies don't live next to me, Bishop thought. *Old Snapper didn't have a lick of privacy, double walls notwithstanding. I'll have to talk to the girls about what went on. I know it wasn't about sex.*

He didn't bother to tell Linda and Mariana that Ginny and Amy were kind of business associates. Bringing investors into the Taco Wagon deal for a fee was their motivation for coming by, not something extracurricular.

So, the neighbors don't know a hell of a lot. Snapper liked young girls but so do lots of men. He most likely paid for the services they provided and liked variety.

"Did you hear or see anything the night he was shot?" he asked.

Mariana said, "I thought I heard a shot but I couldn't be sure. I was in back getting ready for bed. Just before I heard the shot, I heard a car drive up and figured it was Snapper's. His motor sounded big if you know what I mean. He usually parked out front. Evidently didn't want to take the time to park in the garage and come up in the elevator."

"Me too," Linda said. "I probably heard the shot even though I didn't know it at the time. And, I just heard the one car. Snapper's most likely. He was the only one who parked in front."

So, whoever shot him must have been waiting. When he drove up, the shooter came up from wherever he was hiding to shoot him. Then, he walked away to wherever he'd left his car. Probably where the wallet was found. Minimum noise. No neighbors alarmed. Premeditated.

He thanked them for their time and information and left.

"Come back when you have more time." Mariana said. "It's always wine time in my house."

He smiled, gave her a goodbye hug, and left.

He drove back to his apartment and emailed a report to Ellen who phoned a few minutes later.

"All we get are dead ends," she said, exasperated. "You got any more ideas?

"I'm going to talk to Cindy and Amy. They're the two girls we played tennis against in the tournament. They're on the string I've been pulling. I'm still on the short end of my assignment as a detective."

"I remember them and I'm aware you're doing me a favor and I damn well appreciate it, Bishop. You're doing things I just don't have the time or skills to do."

"You're my friend, Ellen," Bishop said and continued his discussion about Amy and Cindy. "They're involved somehow and may know something. They came to Snapper's townhouse a few times according to the neighbors. Could be he said something relevant. Anyway, it's worth asking. Won't take that much time."

"You said that in your report."

"I wasn't sure you'd read it thoroughly."

"I did. I read everything you send. I'm always hoping you'll say something I can tell the Mayor."

"Good. You wouldn't happen to have their phone numbers would you? I can probably get them from Vince but I figured you might have gotten them during the tournament. In case you had a scheduling problem or something."

She had their numbers and promised to email them to him. "I hope to hell you find out something useful. I'm tired of sending the Mayor these reports with nothing in them but bullshit."

"If I keep getting what I've been getting, I'll be turning in my badge," he said. *Right now, unless I find something damn compelling, I'm still headed back to Indian Creek ... and Kathy.*

He thought about that for a second or two. *Hell, my soul lives in Lawton. Kathy is my soul, but can I leave my old friend hanging out here? Damnit!*

"A couple more like you've been sending and the Mayor'll be asking for mine. I'll have to put the kids on the street with one of those signs asking for money."

"Not likely, Ellen."

She laughed. "No, not while my old man is working. But, shake something loose for me."

"Shaking over here boss."

Chapter 16

Cindy's number was first on the list Ellen had emailed so he called her first. She didn't answer so he called Amy who did answer.

He explained why he was calling. He was looking for anything that might point to who'd killed Snapper. And, he'd been told that they visited Snapper's townhouse a number of times.

"We did. I figured you might call, after you showed up at Vince's people talk Saturday and stayed, we assumed, to ask him questions about Snapper."

"I did and now, I'd like to talk to you and Ginny about the man. I think you or somebody told me you share an apartment."

They did. And, she and Cindy would be home that evening. They usually finished dinner around eight. He'd be there at eight. She gave him their address, an apartment complex on La Jolla Blvd.

Doing well then, he thought. La Jolla was considered the high rent district in San Diego, and that extended to apartments as well as homes.

So, for the rest of the afternoon, he did what Vince said he did between talks, he sat and thought. But, except for going home, nothing enlightening about the case came into his mind.

Here's what I have, he thought. *I'm talking about a man with reasonably good look, no, unreasonably good looks, I have to admit that. He used money he'd extracted from his ex-wives to make a big shot out of himself. A man about town that well to do people had on their lists to invite to parties and ask for his help with worthy causes. Yeah. Let's all help the poor people. Except for the Taco Wagons thing, the investment he had something to do with, but maybe more figurehead than anything worthwhile. Apparently, he had never worked or if he did, nobody knows what he did.*

He was a selfish, arrogant bastard as far as what I saw when we played tennis together. And, the people who knew him don't disagree.

And somebody killed him. Obviously premeditated and there are no unequivocally obvious suspects. Well, no one I can believe did it. Vince Valley had a motive, but he doesn't strike me as a killer even if his neighbor, Beatrice, might have fudged the truth about seeing him the night Snapper was killed.

Taco Wagons looks to be a success but I'm not sure Snapper did much of anything to make that happen. Apparently not according to McNally if I believe what he said. At any rate, there are no pissed off investors I can find and I can't talk to a franchisee. But, I can't find a reason to kill him over Taco Wagons.

No children, his or his ex-wives, look good for his murder. All his ex-wives are dead anyway. Still waiting for Ellen's police report on Jacques Cornwall. He didn't have much of a motive that I can see, though. But, ignorance is bliss. Who knows what I'll find out when I get Ellen's report. I sure as hell don't want to drive to Beverly Hills to ask him anymore questions..

I still haven't closed the door on George Talbert. George is another string. Do I pull it or let Ellen. He has to be on the list of probables, he reminded himself. Snapper laughed at him. *I don't doubt that Talbert hated the guy, but did he have the get up and go to kill him.*

Something bothered me or had bothered me when I was focusing on him. What the hell was it? I had a thought but let it slip away. Now, I can't remember what it was.

"Think, Bone," he said.

Okay, In any case, Talbert didn't fit the description of the killer. His son probably did fit the description but he had an alibi. He was in class. The boy is married and wants to be an engineer. Would he jeopardize his life to take revenge for his father?

"I wouldn't have, if my dad asked me to kill somebody," Bishop said. "So, what bothered me about Talbert? I think it was important but who knows."

He assessed where he was in the case and what else, if anything, he could do before talking to Ellen again.

Cindy and Amy might be my last shot to find a decent lead. If I strike out there, I guess I'll go home. Damn, I want to see Kathy anyway. I miss her. Ellen'll just have to understand.

*****

Fortuitously, Kathy called about his dead fruit trees after he'd finished his "thinking."

"The nursery guy smelled of the dirt I brought him to test," Kathy told him. "He said he didn't need to send it anyplace. It was roundup. Extra strength. Because of the smell. Somebody just poured it around your trees. When they ran out, they must have left and didn't come back. Or, maybe they heard a car coming. That's most likely why only five trees were killed."

"Parsons either did it or sent somebody to do it," Bishop said. "No way in hell will I ever be able to prove it one way or another."

"Anything else you want me to do, Sweetheart?"

"Hmm. Well, yes. Call the security company and have them put in a camera that covers the orchard. Have them rig it so the video will be available for a week. One or the other of us should be able to look at it within a week. Don't you think?"

She did.

"And, have the nursery replace the dead trees. Get some good sized ones," Bishop told her.

"He suggested as much. I told him I'd ask you. I'll tell him to go ahead."

"Good."

"When are you coming home?" she asked.

"Damned if I know but I wish I were there now. I'd give you a big hug and start kissing you. I've been missing you.

"Ellen knows I'm on the last legs of this investigation. I just have one more string to pull. Maybe two. If I don't find something on one of them, my next stop is Indian Creek. I miss our talks on the back porch."

"I feel the same way," she said. "You said you're close to finishing. Do you have somebody you think did it?"

"Hell no! I haven't found a damn thing worthwhile. I have a couple of inteviews lined up. After that, I don't have a thing else to do. I can revisit a couple of things but nothing looks very promising. I dread telling Ellen. I don't often fail, but this time looks like I'll be doing just that."

She was sorry he hadn't found the murderer, but was very happy to hear that he'd likely be coming home. "I've been missing our times together too. I feel alive when we're together."

"Me too. I think of you day and night, sweetheart," he said. "You're my raison d'étre."

"I'm always glad to hear it," she said.

That's how they left it.

He got ready for his interviews of Cindy and Amy.

*****

Amy let him in and offered wine. She had a glass. Cindy a step behind her also had a glass. They'd finished dinner and were having after dinner wine.

He declined. He just wanted information not wine that he knew he was afraid he wouldn't like. If they'd offered a gin and tonic, he might have taken one.

So, he sat down and asked his questions. "His neighbors said you were at his townhome several times." He laughed. "They thought you were having some kind of sexual liaison."

They both laughed hard. "That's a joke," Cindy said. "He'd have been at the bottom of my liaison list if I had one. It was strictly about business, our visits. Talking about people who'd said they wanted to invest in Taco Wagons."

"We'd give him names and phone numbers. He said McNally would call them," Amy added.

"I figured as much. However, I'm hoping he said something to you during your visits that might point to his killer. So, tell me anything you know about Snapper or anything he said. I'm running out of people to ask."

I've run out of people to ask. Hell, Talbert's still on my list ... or Ellen's.

They looked at each with blank stares. Cindy said, "I don't think we know anything about who might have killed him. All we ever talked about were people who'd said they were interested in buying bonds in his Taco Wagons company. Like Amy said, we'd give him the names and what we knew about them. We'd have a glass of wine while we did it and then, we'd leave. He never said anything about anybody, frankly. He was barely what you'd call friendly. I think he could put it on, but he never did with us. He considered us hired hands"

Amy agreed. "We first met the guy on the tennis courts. He was talking to somebody on the phone about Taco Wagons. When he hung up, he saw us standing there and told us about it. Put some glamour with it that time."

Cindy smiled and added, "He told us if we brought in investors, we'd get a fee. So, when anybody came along at the office who looked like he might be interested, I'd tell him and Amy did the same. We gave out brochures at work. You did too, didn't you Amy?"

She did.

"We didn't get many," Amy said. "But we've enjoyed the fees from the ones we did bring in. And, the ones who bought in say they appreciate the tip."

Cindy agreed. "They're all happy with the money they're getting. Nobody's complaining or anything."

"So, no reason for an investor to shoot the man?" Bishop said.

"None at all," Amy said.

Same story I've been getting from everybody, damn it to hell. I'm getting nowhere. Wasting my time and the City's money. I guess I'll have to leave the damn case with Ellen.

Responding to his questions, they told him Snapper never talked about his son Jacques or George Talbert."

Getting nowhere, Bone. Spinning my wheels and wasting everybody's time.

"Okay," he said with a sigh. "What do you know about Taco Wagons." *Might as well wind it up and go get a glass of decent wine someplace.*

Amy more or less told him what he'd already been told by McNally. The investors put in money for bonds and McNally used it to buy Taco Wagons made in China for the franchisees, usually older men but sometimes women, looking for something to do to keep from being bored and to make some money.

Cindy said, "Usually they set up in small towns willing to make a place for the Wagons and keep a look out for vandalism. So far, last time we talked to Snapper, it has worked. Most of the time, the franchisees have to move from a large town where they lived to the small town where the Wagons could be placed."

Yeah, I know all that.

"And, Snapper said no one had complained about anything. The men and women making the tacos and stuff were doing well. Making money," Amy said. "We were asked to be part of the opening ceremony here in La Jolla. We go to the meetings the company has."

I know that too.

She pointed to the picture Bishop had already seen. Both girls were standing beside a Taco Wagon with Snapper and McNally and some others. All were smiling.

Cindy said, "Wait a minute. I have to go back some. Vincent complained about Taco Wagons. Kind of complained."

Damn. Maybe I'm finding out something at last.

She explained. "He went with us to one of the investor parties held by McNally at his beach house. We invited him. Snapper said we could bring a guest. I think any guest was a possible investor. Not that Vincent was. He came just to get out. Didn't stay long."

"What was his complaint?" Bishop asked.

"We talked about the party after his next "peoples" talk. He said he wouldn't trust McNally with a dime of his money. He said McNally struck him as a crook," Cindy said.

Amy added, "He didn't like Snapper either and said so. He said, birds of a feather stick together." She laughed.

Yeah. Not much in that.

"Lawyers get to be cynical after practicing for a while," Bishop said. "We meet plenty of crooks or people who would be if the temptation were great enough."

"That's about what he said," Amy said. "He said he didn't have any money to invest anyway, but if he did, he said he wouldn't put it in the Taco Wagons thing."

"I doubt I would either. But, you haven't heard anybody else complain have you? Like investors? Or people who bought a franchise." Bishop asked.

"Not a one," Cindy said. "We never had much contact with anybody other than taking names and giving them to Snapper."

"And, you never saw anything suspicious going on?" Bishop asked.

They both shook their heads.

Bishop wound up the meeting saying, "Whoever shot Snapper must have had a reason. It's beginning to look like a hired job. Almost impossible to solve cases like that. Any guesses about who Snapper might have pi… uh, irritated enough for them to hire somebody to shoot him?" He was going to say "pissed."

Both women shook their heads. Their faces were puzzled frowns.

Bishop sighed. *Son of a bitch. A dead end. All dead ends. A man nobody liked that somebody killed and not a suspect in sight. Vince didn't like either man and more or less said Snapper and McNally looked like crooks.*

He thanked them for their time and told them "Goodnight."

It was too late to call Kathy so poured himself a glass of wine from the apartment refrigerator and emailed another report to Ellen. In the report, he sidestepped giving her a final notice by asking for a few days off to check on a problem in Mississippi. He mostly wanted to be with Kathy but didn't get into that.

Ellen called the next morning and told him to go ahead. "But right now, Bishop, you're still all I've got investigating the murder. Without you, I'm hanging in the wind. Do what you have to do down there and get back. Okay? But, I'm thinking like you. We need to wind this thing up with or without a killer."

"I hear you. I'm tired of chasing the wind."

Chapter 17

Kathy picked him up at the airport. After a hug and kiss, she drove him home with a stop at his orchard for a look at the security camera she'd had installed to watch over his trees.

"It will come on if anybody walks into its range. See," she pointed at the camera. Their car had triggered the camera light to come on. "It's taking pictures of us right now and sending them back to the security office. You'll have a video also, on your unit, in the house."

"I bet when that light comes on, anybody wanting to pour round-up on my trees will start running," he said.

"They'd have to be drunk to stand in the light knowing they are being video-taped," she agreed.

He looked at each new tree that had been set out to replace the dead ones. "They all look healthy." The old ones did too, the ones that had not been poisoned.

"Are you going to do anything?" she asked, pointing at the trees.

"I don't know. I want Parsons to know that I know. I may call him. Nothing I can do legally that'd make sense. Without proof, I can't point a finger at anybody. It could have been anybody even though I know it was Parsons. I'll let you know if I do anything."

He told her he was going to be there for only a few days. He had to go back and wrap up his investigation.

"Not much more I can do," he said. "Been a hard case."

"I was hoping for more time," she said.

"I wish, sweetheart, I wish. I'll tell you what I'm facing. The case is dead as far as I'm concerned, but the Chief says she needs me so I'll go back for a few more days. Right now, it looks like one of those cases that'll never be solved. I hate it, but I've done all I can do. She knows it too, but she's in charge and doesn't want to admit we didn't find the killer."

He told her how the Mayor had gone out on a limb to promise a quick resolution of the case. And, on that limb were Bishop and the Chief.

Kathy said she understood.

*****

They enjoyed a glass of wine from the back porch and watched the beavers working in their pond across the Creek.

They relaxed some more before going out for dinner. He took her to a steak place that only used locally raised beef. It was delicious.

The next day, he checked in with his bank clients in particular the bank with the Parson's loan.

"Nothing happening," Garman said. "He said his father would buy that 500 acres you told us about and bring the loan current but he's been dragging his feet. Stalling. And the President is telling me to give him a little more time."

"Everybody's hoping the cotton market will turn around, I suspect," Bishop said.

"That's what I think too. The old man says he's going to buy the land. He cursed me when I called him. I've called him twice already. I've called his son half a dozen times. Both of 'em give me the run around and I report it to the President who shrugs and tells me to give them another week."

"I think you have to file a default," Bishop said.

"I told the President that the last time I reported. He said give 'em a couple more days. I always take that to mean a week. If they don't bring in some money by the end of this week, I'm filing. I'll tell the President after I've filed it. I think he'll approve. He'll have me to blame if the Parsons complain, which I'm sure they will."

"I wouldn't call Dalton or his dad and tell them. I'd just do it. If you call, they'll give you some bullshit double talk," Bishop told him.

He agreed.

"I'd like to hear what Dalton says when he finds out."

"You might. He's bad mouthed you every time I've called. If I boil his bull shit down, I'd say he blames you for the cotton downturn."

Bishop laughed and thought, *Yeah and the son of a bitch killed five of my fruit trees too.*

*****

He called Ellen to see if she had any news on Snapper's murder. She didn't.

"The Mayor called me. Wants to know when I'm going to charge somebody."

"What'd you tell him? When hell freezes over."

"Not quite. I told him you had some business to take care but would be back in a few days turning over more rocks."

"Thanks. You should have told him I haven't found a damn thing and I don't have any more rocks to turn over."

"I'll save that for the next time you give up," she said.

"I haven't given up, Ellen. I just can't find any reason to plug away and spend your money."

"Hurry back," she said.

She just doesn't want to face it. I'm resigning.

*****

Two days later, Bishop's phone rang. It was the senior Parsons and he was fit to be tied; barely understandable. "You worthless piece of dog shit, Bone. You pushed the bank into foreclosing on my son's business!"

"You think like your son, out of your ass hole," Bishop replied. "And, you're just as full of shit as he is. No wonder you both just as screwed up. I haven't pushed the bank into doing anything. As I understand it, the regulators took note of the loan on the bank's list of defaults. Since it's a high dollar loan, they want the bank to do something about it. So, the bank filed the notice of default to get you and your son off your asses."

"Bullshit. The bank would give my boy some leeway if it wasn't for you. That's what I've been told and I believe it!"

Bishop laughed ruefully to himself. No doubt. Nobody wants to offend the old man with his bank shares. So, it's easy to point the finger at me. Hell, if the shoe fits wear it. I guess it fits me. And I get paid to wear the damn shoe.

"Well, I guess you'd better hop around and do what your son and his lawyer said you were going to do when we had that meeting. Looks like you're going to have to put up or shut up."

He heard the old man cursing as he hung up.

He added a few curses of his own. There was nothing to be gained in calling Garman. He knew the game.

They paid me a fee to handle the default when it came up. That gave them the right to blame it all on me. I take the heat when nobody else will. Well, it's what I do for a living. If it were easy, anybody could do it. Good thing I've got a cast iron stomach.

He and Kathy had their usual late afternoon happy hour on the back porch of Bishop's cabin. He told her about the senior Parson's call.

"Blowing off steam at me because the bank won't extend the loan to his son. A loan he instigated. The cotton market is in the ditch and nobody's using the servicing facilities. Big loan. Millions. The old man has the money to take care of the loan but he'd rather the bank be inconvenienced than him."

"What's going to happen?"

"The bank is foreclosing finally. I imagine his Dad will step up to the plate very soon. Otherwise, the Parsons will have a foreclosure on their record not to mention a loss of money and their service facilities. I should add something else. A loss of face. I suspect that's what been driving both Parsons to stall hoping the market would bail them out and they could say, 'I told you so.'"

"And, the whole thing will have been your fault," Kathy said with a laugh.

"That's about it."

"And, they had their little revenge by killing some of your fruit trees," she said.

"That's what I think. Most likely sent one of their hands down here to do it. Probably laugh about it over their afternoon bourbon over ice."

"Well, if they do it again, you'll have a video tape of it."

"And, I'll sure as hell file charges," Bishop said.

They had barbecued steaks for dinner and afterwards watched something on PBS and went to bed early. She went to work the next morning and Bishop looked at his grass and decided it needed cutting. It had been awhile. Most of his land was covered in trees and shrubs and vines but about 4 acres of it was in grass partly shaded by giant old Pines and Oaks. And, that grass needed cutting from time to time.

He uncovered his riding mower and checked the gas and oil. When he pulled out the oil stick, he saw something move behind the seat.

"What the hell!" It was a big cotton mouth moccasin and it was trying to coil to strike. Bishop backed off and went in search of a long stick. By the time he'd returned, the snake had slid off the mower and was making for the woods.

Bishop caught it in an opening and finished it off. "Damn," he cursed. In all his years in Mississippi, that was the first time he'd been face to face with a snake that big and that dangerous.

"I guess the poor bastard was chasing something that hopped on top of the lawnmower to escape. Then, I came along and it got defensive. And, I got defensive in response. End of snake."

He breathed a sigh of relief and got the mower ready to cut grass.

About an hour into the job, he stopped for a swig of water and cranked up again. Something caught his eye in the woods but he couldn't see anything so he whirled the mower around and began cutting grass from around an old pine. He was making a turn when he heard a crack and automatically turned towards it. As he did, a bullet struck the left side steering lever and careened off.

"Son of a bitch!"

He ducked down behind the instrument dash and a second shot hit the rear of his seat and made a furor through it. He managed to maneuver the lawn mower into a thicket of wild huckleberries that had grown around a huge oak. A third shot hit the tree. But, by that time, Bishop was on the ground, safely behind the lawnmower.

A minute later, he heard a car leaving.

He stood to see if he could see anything but only heard the sound of the car leaving.

"Somebody was trying to get rid of me," he said. "And, I have a pretty good idea who it was."

One of the Parsons. *Probably the old man.*

He called Chief Jenkins who came out with a couple of deputies to inspect the lawn mower and to dig the bullet from the tree. Considering the distance between the shooter and the lawn mower, they concluded the shooter had used a rifle.

"Sure as hell, somebody was trying to keep you from cutting your grass," Jenkins said. "Must have felt sorry for you riding around in that heat. Damn near got you."

Bishop replied with a half laugh. "Damn near did," he said. "If it hadn't been for that steering lever, the first one would have hit me in the chest. I ducked away from the second one."

"Damned if you don't piss people off, Bishop. Is that a natural talent or do you have to work for it?" Jenkins asked.

"I'm not sure,"

"Any ideas?" Jenkins asked when they were finished looking over the mower.

"If I were a betting man, I'd be looking at the Parsons. I imagine they'll come up with alibis but they are the only people I know for sure that I've pissed off this week."

Jenkins would check them out and indeed they claimed they were nowhere close to Lawson or Bone's cottage.

"I think I'm going to throw down the gauntlet and see if they'll pick it up," Bishop told Jenkins.

"How're you gonna do that?"

Bishop told him.

"They probably won't go for it, but I wish you luck," Jenkins said. "You may end up on your back … permanently, if it blows up."

"I may, but I'd rather be the moving party than sitting on my ass, dodging bullets and waitin' for the next one."

"As long as you're good at dodging, you're okay."

Bishop laughed but inside, he agreed with the Chief. *It could be risky.*

*****

Bishop dialed the number he had for Dalton Parsons, the son.

"Hello," the son said.

"You're letting your old man fight your battles for you. I didn't take you to be a coward but I guess you are. Little boy. Letting your daddy take up for you."

"Fuck you, old man. What the fuck 're you talking about?"

Bishop gave him a blow by blow of the senior's call and how somebody had tried to shoot him on the lawn mower. He threw in the killing of his fruit trees.

"Dad said he'd called. Okay by me if he called you. You're crazy if you think he took a shot at you! Stupid! And, killing your fuckin' worthless damn fruit trees! Good God! You must have shit for brains."

"At least I have brains," Bishop said. "More'n I can say for you or your Pa!"

"You're fuckin' around with his money and mine. He has a right to be pissed at you. As far as we're concerned, the world will be a better place when you're sleeping under a slab. I doubt anybody will bother to put flowers on top of you when somebody finally kills your ass."

"Talk's cheap on the phone. Why don't we do our talking face to face?"

"Any time. Any place! Ass hole. You name it!"

"You live high on the hog in a house at the Barnett Reservoir, I believe. Why don't we meet up there and see who blinks first."

He was talking about the Ross Barnett Reservoir on the Pearl River in north Mississippi. The 33,000-acre lake was the state's largest drinking water source and had 105 miles of shoreline. The Natchez Trace Parkway bordered one part. People with means built houses overlooking the lake. Bishop had heard that both Parsons had homes along the shore of the lake.

"You bastard. I'll beat your ass till you piss in your pants," Dalton said.

"Damn. You're real tough on the phone, Parsons. I can't wait to see how tough you are when you're standing in front of me." Bishop knew the man was younger than he was and he obviously worked out regularly. He recalled that from the way he filled his shirt at the meetings they'd had at the bank.

But, muscles don't mean much, without guts, Bishop thought and I'm betting he doesn't have any guts. His old man has probably run interference for him all his life. Sounds like I'm going to find out. One way or the other, I have to stop their threats. If he beats the hell out of me, that should satisfy them. If I'm the last one standing, that'll let 'em know I'm not to be messed with.

"There's a little park just as you drive into the rec area of the reservoir. I'll be waiting for you," Dalton said. "Pick your time."

Bishop told him he'd be there the next morning around ten thirty. That'd give him time to drive up.

He called Chief Jenkins and told him what he was doing and why.

"I hope it works," the Chief said. "Sometimes you test my resolve, Bishop. If you weren't right more times than you're wrong, I wouldn't put up with you. Fishing in your pond and the Creek wouldn't be worth it. One of these days, somebody might mistake me for you."

Bishop laughed to himself. He and the Chief didn't look alike at all.

Jenkins often came out and fished in the beaver pond off the banks of Indian Creek in front of Bishop's cabin. He always caught a good "mess" to take home, a little boney but fresh with a good taste.

"Good luck with it. I think you're gonna need it," Jenkins said. "Let me know, when you get ambulatory if you end up in the hospital."

"Yeah."

Chapter 18

At almost ten thirty, Bishop got out of his car in the recreational area of the small park overlooking the reservoir. He'd parked a short distance from where he Dalton had agreed to meet and settle their differences. He saw Dalton standing in an open area at the edge of the woods, fidgeting.

He motioned for Bishop to come on! His face was a vicious snarl. There was nothing in his hands, nothing like a gun. That gave Bishop some relief. A man to man resolution of their dispute had to be better than trying to dodge bullets or replant fruit trees. And, he felt comfortable going man to man with him even if Dalton was bigger.

Bishop nodded and hurried toward him. As he neared, the man moved a bit and adopted a fighting stance. "You're gonna need some dental work, old man," he shouted.

"We'll see who'll need the work," Bishop shouted back.

Dalton shifted left another pace or two and did a little jog, jabbing out with his left hand.

Back in the woods, some forty feet away, unknown to Bishop, the senior Dalton lay on the ground with his rifle trained on him as it had been since he got out of his car. He'd already focused his scope in on where his son had been standing, about where Bishop would end up.

He'd come to the park with his son earlier. Their plan was to shoot Bishop and take his body to the Delta and bury it in the rich Delta cotton ground, never to be found.

When Bishop was a couple of strides away from the son and getting revved up to do battle, the old man took careful aim and cocked the rifle. As he slipped his finger into the trigger guard, he felt something metal touch the back of his head.

"Move a muscle and you're a dead man," Chief Jenkins told him. "Right now, I have you for attempted murder. Squeeze that trigger and its murder in front of a police officer. Think you can get away with that? That'd take more money than you have."

The old man sighed with a curse and hesitated like he was thinking about it, but did take his hand away from the trigger guard. He rolled over to see Chief Jenkins pointing his Glock automatic at his head.

"A trick. You and that bastard, Bone, tricked us," he said.

"Call it what you will. I'm arresting you and your son. I imagine you'll be spending time in Parchman," the Chief said. He knew their attorneys would work hard to see that they didn't, but he felt good saying it. "I understand you can pay protection money up there to get safe conditions. The lifers love new arrivals."

Parchman was the name of the Mississippi State prison in the northern part of the state, near the Tennessee state line. Most people who'd been there or had somebody there knew it was a rough place to spend time.

While Jenkins and the senior Parsons were having an understanding, his son and Bishop were facing off. The son kept glancing into the woods. Bishop wasn't surprised. He kind of figured they might try an ambush. That's why he'd asked the Chief to get there an hour earlier and take a position in the most likely place a sniper would wait for his shot.

Jenkins got to the reservoir around eight thirty and after giving the place a good inspection; picked the location he did and waited. The Parsons came in the same car. They talked. The son pointed to an open space at the edge of the park ground. The father nodded.

When Jenkins saw where the boy would likely stand and wait for Bishop, he knew about where the old man would set up to take his shot. So, he took a position behind a tree a couple of feet away to wait.

The father took a scoped rifle from the trunk of the car and went into the woods near where Jenkins waited. He found a place where he'd have a clear shot and lay down to wait for Bishop to show up.

Thirty minutes later, Bishop drove up, got out of his jeep and walked toward the junior Dalton waiting to do battle with him.

Bishop was relying on Jenkins to stay alive and Dalton was relying on his dad to make sure Bone didn't.

As he drew within a foot or two of the son, Bishop thought he heard talk coming from the woods but wasn't sure. The ambient sounds from the road and the reservoir blanked most other sounds.

Bishop assumed Jenkins and the father were having an understanding in the woods. *I hope that's what I'm hearing.*

Assuming that's what he was hearing, Bishop told the son, "Your dad won't be firing his rifle. So, if you want to settle this man to man, now's the time."

Dalton's lips formed a "what."

About that time, his dad emerged from the woods walking, slumped shouldered, in front of Chief Jenkins who was holding the old man's rifle in one hand and pointing his Glock in his other hand at the man's back.

"You were right Bishop," Jenkins called out. "One of these days I'll learn not to doubt you."

When Bishop had told him what he had in mind, Jenkins had laughed and said, "That's … well, I'll just say it. That's stupid. No way in hell will the Parsons try anything like that. Hell, man, they're practically royalty in this state. You can come up with some real time wasters, Bishop."

Bishop disagreed. "Money is a powerful motivator. People kill for it."

"No way. They're not that greedy," Jenkins had said. But just then he was having to eat his words.

Jenkins looked at Bishop and shook his head. "I wouldn't have believed it."

Bishop nodded, looked at Dalton and said, "This is it. Put up or shut up. Take your best shot." He added a gesture with his fists.

Dalton looked at his Dad, all grim faced, then at Bishop. Suddenly, he lashed out with a big right hand hoping to catch Bishop by surprise. But, that was not to be. Bishop was waiting. He blocked the shot with his left arm and hit him in the face with his right fist. The blow staggered Dalton and before he could right himself, Bishop was all over him, hitting him with lefts and rights, driving him to his knees. The son leaned forward and Bishop took a step forward to finish him off.

"That's enough," his father shouted, then softly said, "Enough. Quit hitting him. You got us. Damn carpet bagger from California. Probably one of those weirdos that live on the beach and smoke pot all day. Give it up son! Bastard!" He looked at Bishop when he said that.

Complying, the only thing that made sense anyway, Dalton just rolled over, giving up.

Jenkins called his deputy to bring the van to the park. The deputy had dropped the Chief in the park and had driven some distance away to wait for the Chief's call. He loaded both Parsons in the back of the van and drove them to Lawson where they would be charged and put in jail to wait for their attorneys to arrange bail and get ready for a trial.

During his drive back, Bishop called Kathy to let her know he was safe and what had happened. Knowing she'd object, he hadn't told her everything he was going to do. Just that he was going to meet with the son and see if he could work things out.

In fact, until he saw Jenkins bring Dalton's father out of the woods, he wasn't completely sure Jenkins would even be there. He knew if he wasn't, it would likely be a short day for him if the Parson's did what he expected. They had already tried when he was on his lawn mower, he figured. But, when he wasn't shot right away, he knew the Chief was out there backing him up like he always did.

*****

Lawyers, high priced and well known in legal and political circles, got involved in their defense immediately. They appeared for both Parsons, got bail and both were released pending their trial.

The decisions were no surprise to Bishop. Politics often made its way into court rooms in all states. *Somebody, even judges, have an eye out for higher positions.*

Bishop got a call from the old man's lawyer the same day. "Can we talk, Bishop, off the record. Lawyer to lawyer."

"Talk," Bishop said.

"Just between us," the lawyer said.

"You got it." Bishop just about knew what was coming next.

"You've been inconvenienced. I understand that. My client understands it as well. Actually, I'm speaking for both men now."

"I figured as much," Bishop said.

"What would it take to cover your troubles?"

Bishop laughed to himself. *Typical.* "So, your clients want me to drop the charges including their attempt to shoot me while I was cutting my grass. No one has been charged with that but we have a bullet and now that we have a rifle, I imagine there'll be no trouble matching the bullet to the old man's rifle."

"I think all mistakes by Mr. Parsons have been discussed. That's basically it. My clients just want to take care of all complaints that have been filed or might be filed in the future and get on with their lives."

"This whole damned disaster started because your clients were trying to avoid responsibility for a loan the bank made the son," Bishop answered.

"Mr. Parsons has said as much. I'm telling you that to let you know they are serious."

"Well, before I can do anything, I'll have to discuss it with Chief Jenkins, off the record, but I want that loan paid off."

"My client says he's willing to bring his son's loan current and reduce the principle as required to satisfy the bank. In addition, they'll pledge additional property to the bank as collateral for the loan when it gets re-written, assuming we can reach some kind of compromise on the attempted murder charge."

Bishop said he'd get back to him.

He called Jenkins and told him about the offer. Jenkins said he didn't care one way or the other. "Do what suits you, Bishop. You're the one who could've got killed. I know you want the bank loan taken care of."

"That's right. I'm not into revenge in this case. It started with a bad loan. If I can get that settled, that will satisfy any feelings I have for revenge and my obligations to the bank. My tussle with the boy at the reservoir satisfied my need to get physical with them."

"What you say makes sense and probably saves everybody a hell of a lot of time and money. Lord knows how long the lawyers would drag the trial out."

Bishop thanked him and called Garman and told him what the Parsons were willing to do. Garman said he'd have to call him back.

He talked to the President of the bank who, like Bishop, only wanted the loan to be current and paying as agreed.

With that understanding, Bishop called the lawyer and told him once the loan was current to the bank's satisfaction, he'd drop all charges. The Parsons also agreed to pay Bishop's regular fee for all the work he'd done. That was a plus. Bishop demanded that as part of the settlement but didn't figure to get it.

The settlement the Parsons up and made the bank happy. Even so, Bishop kept his new security camera in place.

He and Kathy had dinner out to celebrate. Chief Jenkins and his wife joined them.

Bishop was feeling pretty good about things the next morning. He enjoyed coffee with Kathy on the back porch and listened to the birds greet the new day. The beavers were already up and working.

Then, his phone rang. It was Ellen.

"You sitting down?" she asked.

"I am."

"Well, when are you coming back to finish your work?"

"Tomorrow? But I don't think I have any more work, do I? Don't we have an agreement to let me resign?"

"I'll answer you this way, Bishop. You've got another murder to solve," she said. "Vincent Valley, you know, Vince, has been ... killed. Hit over the head with something. From the shape of the cavity in his head, the lab people say it looks like somebody used a hammer."

"Damn! Son of a bitch. I was hoping you'd solved the case when I saw it was you on the phone. I could resign with dignity."

"Don't I wish," she said.

"Either a different killer or somebody wanting us to think it was," Bishop said.

"I had the same thought. Or, whoever killed Snapper threw away the gun they used to kill him and had to use a hammer on Vince."

"But, big question is why? What did Vince do to piss anybody off?" Bishop asked.

"Same question I asked. Nobody liked Snapper, but from what we know, everybody liked Vince. From what you've said, the man was one depression away from being laid to rest next to his wife."

"Yep. I agree with you."

Somebody answered Vince's wish, I guess, Bishop thought. *Probably prematurely I'm betting.*

He told her he'd take the first flight out of Lawson and be in San Diego mid-afternoon. "I don't know what I can do, but I'll take a look at it."

Ellen was happy he was coming back. "I am still shorthanded and the Mayor keeps calling me. And the drug epidemic hasn't diminished. Little towns around San Diego are also catching hell. Drug dealers are shooting each other now."

"Glad I don't have that problem to deal with," Bishop said.

"I wish I didn't."

"Yeah. I imagine the media people keep calling the Mayor. They want something they can sell to the public," Bishop said.

"I don't imagine, I know it. And I know he's fed up with it. Talks like he's going to retire."

"I bet. Being Mayor can't be much fun with the shit hittin' the fan like it has been."

"It's been hitting mine as well," she said. "Daily."

"Well, if anybody walks in and confesses, call me and I'll cancel my flight," he told her.

"The next time I have a walk-in confession will be my first."

"I get you."

At least I'll have one more evening with Kathy.

She had listened to his telephone call and knew what had happened.

"No resignation?" she asked.

He shook his head.

They enjoyed their last night together.

She took him to the airport the next morning and he was back in San Diego that afternoon. And, he didn't have a single idea who might have killed Vince and likewise still didn't really have a clue about who killed Snapper. He cursed to himself.

After I ask questions at the trailer park, I'll see Cindy and Amy. They might have an idea about it. They were closer to Vince than they were to Snapper. Maybe somebody had been heckling him ... threatening. Hell, maybe he'd attacked somebody in one of his people talks. Don't I wish it'd be that simple?

Somebody from Ellen's office picked him up and took him to the apartment. His car was already there. He threw his bag on the bed and went to work.

*****

He drove to the trailer park where Vince's camper was parked to begin his new investigation. Snapper's murder was a lost cause anyway, he and Ellen had decided unless he could connect them.

They both hoped for that and just behind that hope was a silent prayer that one person killed both men. And, both knew that hoping and praying would get them nowhere. So, Bishop went to work.

The autopsy report told him that Vince had died between 8 and 9 the night before his body was discovered. The next morning, Beatrice found him in the chair he sat in under the tree in front of his camper. She screamed and a neighbor came to see why and called the police when she saw Vince's body.

After the police came, they gave Beatrice permission to take Rascal into her camper.

The dog had begun to bark around the time the autopsy said he'd died but that didn't alarm anybody. At that time, people had finished their dinners and were watching television. And, everybody in the park knew Rascal barked all the time when he wanted to get outside to do his business and for some reason, Vince couldn't or wouldn't let him out. He'd quit when Vince would do what he wanted.

Two people in the park had seen Vince sitting in his chair earlier that evening, apparently reading since he had a book in his hands. No one noticed anything happening in that area after they had gone inside for the evening.

A man in an apartment down the street told the police he'd heard a car crank up nearby and leave also about the time Vince was killed. He didn't see anything however.

Another man outside the park told the police that he saw a man hurrying along the sidewalk, away from the camp ground, about that time, a man he hadn't seen before. "A heavyset man" was the only description he could give. He also heard a car drive away soon after.

When Bishop read that, he immediately thought of McNally.

Jennifer also said she saw Vince in his chair that evening, like he was asleep, when she went to wash her clothes in the camps wash house. She still seemed in shock when Bishop interviewed her.

"I know you and Vince were having what I'd call an affair," he said. "Was it serious?" He knew what Vince had said but wanted Jennifer's assessment of it.

Her, red rimmed, brown eyes looked into Bishop's as she answered. "He told me up front he was still missing his wife. We could have sex, he said, if I wanted to, but that was all. So, I accepted that. If he had wanted anything serious, I'd have jumped at it though. We enjoyed it, the sex, but that's all."

"That's basically what he told me as well," Bishop said.

"I've been trying to get serious with a man older than Vince. He lives in Del Mar but keeps his camper here. I haven't ... slept with him and he hasn't pushed it. I don't know if it'll ever turn into anything but we go out every week for something ... dinner or a play or movie. He seems to like me, but it stops there."

She chuckled and added, "Beatrice, his next door neighbor ... actually, she found his body ... anyway, Beatrice told me to quit trying to 'take Vince from her.' I told her I wasn't. I let her know that she should talk to Vincent if she had any problems that involved me. Besides, I didn't think she had any claim to Vince as far as I knew. I told her that too.

I don't know what came of it. We didn't talk anymore after that and Vince and I kept seeing each other, usually when he had to wash his clothes. He'd put them into the washer and I'd invite him to my camper for coffee. We never drank anything. Just … you know."

Bishop shook his head. He knew what she was hinting. They did what most men and women often did when they were together, gave in to their instincts.

"I'm asking if you killed Vince?" Bishop asked. "Jealously? Anger? Disappointment?"

She stared at him as if he'd thrown cold water in her face. "Me? Kill Vince? Why would I do that? He and I were helping each other out, if you were just listening. I needed him and he needed me. Hell no, I didn't. Anything else you want to know? I've got things to do."

"Could I look at your tool chest?"

The question seemed to puzzle her. "Sure. Why do you want to do that?"

"Just checking," he said.

She showed him an old red tool holder under a seat in her camper. It held the usual tools including a hammer. He stared at the hammer. "Mind if I take this?"

After a hesitations, she said it was okay. "Why do you want that? I haven't used it. My husband did now and then."

He told her Vince might have been killed by a hammer. "Probably was. Forensics will check it for blood."

She shrugged. "Bring it back. Might come a time when I want to drive a nail in the wall … or hit a nosey policeman over the head."

He responded with a half laugh and said he would.

A check by Forensics would yield nothing and he'd bring it back and leave it on her front stoop.

He next went to see Beatrice, hoping she'd recovered enough to talk. When he walked up, she was sitting outside, at her outside table, holding Vince's dog. It was clear from her reddened face and teary eyes that she'd been crying. Even then, tears were running down her face.

"Beatrice," Bishop said. "Are you able to talk about it?"

She nodded and petted the dog. "I found him, you know. He'd been out there all night, in that chair, all alone, dead. I couldn't believe it. I loved him, you know. I loved ..." She let the thought lapse.

Bishop said he understood.

"I was ... I almost died when I saw him," Beatrice said. "We were going to get married. I just know we were. He had to get over his wife. Poor man. I was helping him. We were together all the time. I don't know what I'm going to do. I feel like dying."

"Did you hear anything?" Bishop asked.

She was having her dinner when it happened, she figured, and didn't hear anything. She was watching a travel show on PBS and wasn't paying attention to what was happening outside.

"Didn't you look outside when you locked up for the night?"

She shook her head and sniffed. After wiping her nose she said, "Ordinarily I would have but by the time the show was over, I was tired and ready for bed. God, I wish I had. He might have still been alive. Maybe I could have saved him." She began crying. "Rascal was barking during my show, but he stopped. I reckon that was when ,,, it happened." She whipped her nose on the apron she wore.

"I think he was dead. The autopsy report said he died instantly when he was hit."

She shook her head. "Thank you. I appreciate knowing that."

"Have you seen anybody strange around his camper or in the park, lately?"

"No, I haven't. I haven't seen anybody I didn't know, around."

Probably thinking about Jennifer, Bishop thought.

"Had he said anything about being threatened? Was anybody mad at him? Do you know?"

She seemed puzzled. "I … no … not as far as I know. We talked all the time, but he never said anything like that. Mostly we talked about what he might say at his next talk. I think the talks were the only thing keeping him … alive. I tried …" She let the thought drop.

He said he understood and thanked her.

"I praise the Lord I have Rascal," she told him as he left. "He reminds me of Vince."

He didn't say anything to her about Jennifer. It didn't seem relevant and he was sure it'd upset her. She was obviously jealous of the younger woman.

He wanted to ask about her hammer but figured she was on the verge of a nervous breakdown so he didn't. Likewise, he didn't ask if she'd killed the man she so desperately wanted.

Probably'd faint if I did. Woman was living in a dream world as far as Vince was concerned. He wasn't interested in Beatrice. No woman really. Jennifer was a way he got physical relief from his instincts. Poor woman, he thought of Beatrice. *It'll take a while for her to get over it, I bet.*

He emailed Ellen a report. The bottom line said, "Still only dead ends. Frustration is still the order of the day. Maybe you should give the case to a junior member of your staff. He couldn't do any worse."

She sent back an email saying, "Forget it. You're my man. Just do what you're good at. Shaking trees and turning over rocks. Nobody does it better."

He cursed but knew he'd be until he found the killer or killers or the Mayor decided he'd had enough of him.

Chapter 19

He called Amy and Cindy and got Amy. She was understandably upset and said Cindy was as well. Amy had no idea who might have killed Vince but agreed to meet with him that evening to talk about it if he wanted to.

From what she said, I doubt they'll know anything. Probably a waste of time to see them. But my call may trigger something in their memories that'll give me a lead. They're the only place I can go right now.

*****

Ellen called him later in the day. "Your report on Beatrice and Jennifer was a downer. You still haven't come up with anything worth a damn." she said. Raising hell with him helped relieve her frustrations. Bishop understood that and just let it wash over him like a passing wind.

"Not a thing, Just what I emailed you. My guess is that the killer hit Vince over the head and was probably going to get into his camper, maybe take his computer, who knows, but the dog was barking and most likely scared him away. That's speculation but it makes sense," he said.

"I didn't find his computer when I searched his camper. I'll have to have another look. If the killer didn't take it, it has to be someplace. Vince kept notes, the two girls who helped him told me one time. Most people like that, like me as well, keep their notes on their computers."

"Damn, Bishop, find me something. I'm getting calls from the Mayor every day. Partly to ask why we haven't found a killer for Snapper and now Vince Valley. He's also concerned about the killings going on in the drug world. Hell, I'm up to my ass hole in problems. One of my paid informants tells me a new bunch has come on the drug scene. That's what's causing the killings. Nobody knows who the new guys are or where they're from. It's a war they say."

She went on to say that while they don't have as many drug deals to contend with, they have more shootings and killings. She wouldn't mind the drug dealers shooting each other if they didn't do it in public and hit innocent bystanders.

"But, drug sales are way down, from what I'm hearing. However, there are lots of emergency room visits from people who have a drug habit and can't buy a fix."

"Be damned," Bishop said. "Maybe the war will help some people break their habits."

"Could be. What's that saying about an ill wind?"

"It's an ill wind that blows nobody good," Bishop said. "Is that close?"

"Close enough. If the war forces people to break their habits, it might be a good thing."

"I'm sorry about your drug war, Ellen. I know you must be catching hell from all over, but I'm out here busting my butt to find a killer for you. By the way, did you do the search on Snapper's son, Jacques?" Bishop asked.

"Let me get my file," she said and put him on hold.

I'm damn glad I don't have her problems. Hunting a killer is bad enough. At least there's only one person I have to find. Who knows who she has to find in her drug war problem. People getting killed so dealers can sell people a drug to make 'em forget their problems. What a world.

"We did," she said after a short wait. "He's well known and highly respected. His clients and patients are movie stars and people from Vegas and the like. People who not only want a face lift, they want a new face. Nothing illegal as far as we could find out. He commands top dollar for his work. Of course, has no record or any record of complaints against him. Clean."

"It'd be too much to ask if he did have a record. But, could be somebody wanting a new face without enough money to pay for it, might have been willing to do him a favor. As in get rid of a corrupt father for a reduced fee or as a gratuity."

"Could be. But, finding that person would be like looking for a needle in a haystack. A big haystack. I don't think anybody would admit to it and how could we force them?" Ellen asked.

May be out of state as well, Bishop thought.

He agreed with her assessment. "So, we have a possibility but no way to make it more."

"That's about it," she said.

"But, Jacques is another name we can throw at the Mayor."

"I have already. I think he's beginning to get the picture. This is an impossible case. Lots of loose ends, none pointing to anybody."

"Well said," Bishop said. "I want to have another look at George Talbert. I doubt I'll find anything but I figure he hated Snapper. He had a reason to kill him too. Something bugged me about him. I don't remember what."

"Do it then. I don't suppose he's young, like our witness said."

"No but one step at a time."

"Right. I forgot. You're the methodical one. What else are you going to do? I assume you'll talk to Amy and Cindy about Vince's death. I doubt it, but they may have killed him for some reason. Who knows what drives people. But, the way this case is going, you probably won't find a damn thing. I was going to talk to them if you hadn't made it back. You want me there?"

"If you want to come, you can but I don't think I'll need you. I know both girls. I'll be asking what Vince was doing just before he was killed. My guess is there might be a connection to the Taco Wagons. He at least knew Snapper. Vince might have said something that scared the guy who'd killed Snapper and that guy might have decided to make sure Vince didn't tell anybody,"

"I suppose. Speculation's not getting us anyplace though. Try to find something worthwhile. Okay? Do the interviews and keep me informed. The Mayor will be calling," she said.

"I can imagine. I'm glad my badge doesn't qualify me for such calls."

"I'm working on that."

He laughed.

*****

Bishop's first question to Cindy and Amy was, "What was Vince doing just before he was killed?"

Amy looked at him and asked, "You mean what was he talking about at the Rec Center? His people talks?"

Bishop shook his head. "Start with that but mostly, I want to know what he was talking about with you and Cindy. Was he bitching about anything?"

"Oh," she said, "He never ... you know, bitched. He did say his next talk was going to be about politics. He'd hinted at it before in his talks, but he said he wanted to hit it hard. The way big money has bought into politics for their special interests. He said we no longer had the democracy our forefathers envisioned when they founded this country. Back then, everyone had a vote and the vote counted. Now a days, he was saying, it's just an exercise, the voting."

Cindy chimed in, "He said special interests fund a candidate's campaign. Sometimes funding more than one candidate. Then, regardless of which one wins, they still control what they do. They tell them how to vote. The regular voters have little to say about it."

"Bishop said, "Might be right. That's probably why nothing gets done in the country anymore. He give any names?"

"No. Just generalized. That's what he was doing with us when we were just talking. He said that all our politicians do is vote for whatever the special interests that got them elected to office tell them to vote for. No names though."

"And that was what his next talk was going to be about?" Bishop asked.

Amy said, "Yes."

"Did he ever have threatening hecklers. People who'd come up afterwards and make threats?" He was thinking a special interest group or somebody who was paid to do their dirty work might have decided to put a stop to Vincent's "scurrilous" suggestions.

Both women shook their heads not. Cindy added, "He didn't have many hecklers at the talks. Now and then somebody would say something, objecting to what he was saying, but it was never threatening. Most of the people at the talks were well educated, more listeners than hecklers."

"I don't guess the subject of his upcoming talks was reported in the newspapers?"

They shook their heads. "His talks were rarely reported, not even afterwards. Now and then, a reporter would run a story about him and feature one position or another. Just brief summaries, nothing in detail."

"Did he ever say anything about anybody threatening him about anything?"

"Not that he told us," Amy said.

"Uh, he wasn't going to talk about it, but one day he said something about the Taco Wagons investment," Cindy said. "A friend, maybe an ex-client, had asked him for a legal opinion, he told us."

Ah, a connection. "Did he say what he told the friend?"

She shook her head. "It had just happened, I think. A week or so ago. I don't even know if he had had time to do anything. He said he told the guy he didn't know enough to make a legal comment but would look into it. He told us again that he didn't much like the McNally guy. I guess he knew he'd have to talk to McNally. He said McNally looked and sounded too much like a con man to trust him. But, he said he wouldn't tell his client anything until he had more than his opinion to rely on. "

Damn, maybe I've stumbled onto something. "Did he ever find anything more than his opinion?" Bishop asked.

"Not as far as we know. As I said, I just got the impression he was going to see McNally but he never said if he did."

Both women shook their heads.

Amy said, "He might have something on his computer. He put everything he did or thought about on his computer."

Bishop said, "I figured he might. Problem there though. I can't find his computer. The guy who killed him might have taken it, but I kind of doubt it. That little dog of his would have been all over him. And, nobody heard the dog squeal like he would have if anybody had hit him. He just barked awhile before he quit. About as long as it took for somebody to bash Vincent in the head and look in the door before getting the hell out of the park."

Could be somebody gave the dog a bite of something sweet to shut him up long enough to get inside and take the computer. But, I'd better take a closer look. That damn computer might answer a lot of my questions.

"He said something about his computer one time. Like it wasn't booting up like it should," Amy said. "Maybe he took it to a shop."

"He did!" Cindy agreed. "I remember that too."

So, it might not have been in his camper for the killer to take. That'd be a break!

"Any idea where he might have taken it?" Bishop asked.

She shook her head. "Not a clue, but he was careful about his computer. He took care of business. So, it would have been someplace he trusted."

Bishop saw Cindy wiping tears from her eyes.

"I couldn't help but notice your tears. Did you and Vincent have anything going?" Bishop asked.

"A little, I guess. Nothing serious, you know. But we'd gone out to dinner. Did it a couple of times. I enjoyed his company. He had interesting things to say. And, he was witty. He made me laugh."

Amy looked at her. "I didn't know, Cindy. Why didn't you tell me?"

Cindy shrugged. "He was older and I wasn't sure if anything would come of it. He never made ... well, suggestions, if you know what I mean. We just talked."

She looked at Amy and added, "One night, he was so sweet, I thought he might be getting serious."

"What?" Amy asked.

"We were at the dinner table, waiting for dessert. He always liked a dessert. Anyway, he looked into my eyes with a slight smile, and reached over and put his hand over mine and gave it a gentle squeeze. I turned to putty. If he'd said lets go to mine, I wouldn't have argued, but he didn't. That was the last time we went out. He got killed right after it. I cried."

Bishop nodded. He understood how she felt.

"I imagine he was about to get serious," he said.

Cindy nodded. A tear rolled down her cheek. "I thought that too."

"I'll be. That's a surprise. I'd never have guessed," Amy said. "I guess he was the 'friend' you said you were going out with." She laughed.

Cindy wiped her tear and shook her head. "I thought that was the best way to handle it. Saying he was a friend. In reality, though, nothing ever happened between us. And, well, I don't think he'd gotten over his wife's death even though it had been years since she'd died."

Amy agreed with that assessment.

"If you think of anything else, let me know," Bishop said.

He left.

Guess I'd better see McNally. He was on Bishop's list anyway. *Vince might have talked to him on behalf of his client. Gotta find that computer. It'd have his notes.*

*****

He called from his car. McNally answered on the first ring. *Hoping I have money to invest in Taco Wagons no doubt.*

He identified himself to McNally and asked if he could drop by in a few minutes. "I have a couple of questions I want to run past you and I'd rather not get into in over the phone. These days, you don't know who's listening in."

"Hell, if it's that sensitive, come on over. You know where I live I guess. I'll be here."

Fifteen minutes later he was knocking on McNally's door. The housekeeper let him in and showed him to the back where McNally was sitting, watching the surf rolling up the beach at the back of his yard, wine glass in hand. He wore a comfortable jogging outfit. His stomach tested the waist line but it was holding.

He stood as they exchanged greetings and handshakes. "Wine?" he asked with a wave of his glass. "Beer?" "De caf?"

Bishop accepted a cup of decaffeinated coffee. The housekeeper who'd waited, left to get him a cup, cream but no sugar. Bishop had read that sugar was bad for his health so he'd pretty much given it up. He wanted to be around to enjoy Kathy as long as he could.

McNally gestured toward a chair and sat down himself. Bishop took the chair.

What a way to live. Surf breaking in your back yard.

A young woman jogged past with her dog on a leash. Another wasn't too far behind her, also with a dog who ran a couple of strides in front.

"Nice huh," McNally said, waving toward the beach. "Used to be more beach but this global warming thing everybody's talking about has caused the ocean to rise. Hell, next year the ocean may be up to my back door."

Bishop agreed.

"Okay, fire away," McNally said with a gesture. "The question."

Before he could, the housekeeper returned with a mug of coffee for Bishop. He thanked her.

"Freshly perked," McNally said.

Bishop shook his head and smiled. He had one of those machines in his creek cottage. Each cup was also freshly perked.

"You know, of course, that Vince Valley was just murdered," Bishop said.

"Read about it in the Light."

"He came to see you, I understand. Maybe he called. His associates just said he contacted you about the Taco Wagons investments. Wanted information. Can you tell me what you talked about? His associates gave me the gist."

Cindy and Amy hadn't said anything but McNally wouldn't know that. He figured putting it like he had would encourage McNally to be more forthcoming.

McNally frowned like he was wondering what to say. After a drink of wine, he said, "It was a phone call. Simple enough. Valley said he had a client who had heard about the investment and had asked him for an opinion."

"What'd you tell him? I want to hear it from you. His associates might not have gotten it all. I understand he didn't think much of it, just to be up front with you."

"I don't think he said exactly that. He just said he was always suspicious of anything that sounded as good as our brochures said the investment was." He stared at Bishop a moment before adding, "Well, I'll tell you he did come right out and say he didn't trust anybody selling such investments either. He didn't exactly call me a crook, but I'm pretty sure that's what he was hinting at. So, I guess you're right. He didn't think much of it."

"How'd you handle it? What'd you tell him?"

"Hell, I told him the investment was a good one. Not a damn thing crooked about it and I wasn't a crook either. I'd been in business a long time and no one had ever accused me of being a crook. I told him I resented the implications of his remarks."

"How'd he take that?"

"He gave me one of those attorney, half laughs, like lawyers do to make you think they're superior and know more than you do. When they do that, it makes me want to hit 'em up side the head."

Bishop nodded without responding but thought. *Somebody did. Was it you?*

He asked, "Did you?"

"No. Definitely no. I've never killed anybody. No reason to start now. Why would I?"

"He didn't like you. You said. Accused you of being a crook."

"Not much motivation in that. I've been accused of worse and I just let it roll off my back."

Bishop wondered if he had an alibi but decided to wait on that question.

Without responding to what McNally had said, Bishop looked hard at the man and asked. "So, what happened next? I assume he didn't hang up on you and you didn't hang up on him. He was, bottom line, representing a potential investor."

McNally shook his head. "That he was. Besides, I've been in this business long enough to have developed a thick skin."

"I'd guess you'd need one."

"That's right. Anyway, I told him we had almost a thousand franchisees out selling tacos and other Mexican foods on the streets of small towns all over the west. None in California and I told him why. No wide sidewalks."

"I imagine he wanted to talk to one," Bishop said. *I did.*

"That's what he said. I recited a number of small towns where we have franchisees with Wagons. I told him to pick a town and I'd call our franchisee and see if I could set up an appointment."

"Did he?"

"He said he'd talk to his client and get back to me."

Most likely had to talk to his client to see if he wanted to pay for the trip. It'd take a day's drive and probably one night on the road.

"Did he?"

"No. Next thing I heard, he had been killed."

"Based on what you've said and what I've heard others say, I'd say the investments in the company are in the multimillions by now."

"Yes, We've done well and the investors are happy. They like the monthly checks we're sending out. Right now, I'm held up from selling anymore franchises, my decision, until I get another shipment of Taco Wagons from China. I'm expecting a shipment in a week or so, maybe longer. Then, I can sell more franchises and more bonds. I don't want to sell bonds unless we have Taco Wagons selling tacos. We need the income to pay interest on our bonds."

Bishop said he had heard that.

McNally's face showed surprise but he continued, "Snapper had been handling that end of the business, the investors. A lot of it, I should say. Quite a few people contacted him because of his name. Everybody in town knew him. He'd sell both, the franchises and the investments but more of the bonds than the Wagons. I tell you, he could dish out the bullshit when it suited him. People may not have liked him but they sure liked the yields on our bonds. And, people like the franchises as well. The Taco Wagons were … charming and they all made money.

"Right now, I'm trying to get my head around all Snapper was doing because I have to do everything now. The money from a lot of the franchisees and most of the bond investors came from him. Our lawyer handled the paperwork. I took care of payments due vendors and bond holders. Day to day stuff. Management things."

"I thought Snapper was just a figure head."

"He was that for the most part but he set up the company, the way it worked and brought me into it as a kind of grunt. Lately though, I've been subcontracting out almost all of the grunt work."

"So, with Snapper dead, you're having to take over what he had been doing," Bishop said. "Or go out of business."

"I plan to keep going. People interested in buying bonds and any franchises that Snapper had been working on, have my name and end up here. I'll process them as soon as the next shipment of wagons gets here from China. After that …" He shrugged. "As of now, I can't sell franchises without Taco Wagons to lease. And, I can't sell bonds, as I said, because I need franchisees selling Tacos for money to pay dividends on the bonds. So, if you'll excuse my French, I'm up shit creek just now."

"Figureheads don't usually get involved in a business."

McNally shrugged. "Well, he did."

"Okay. If anybody contacts you about buying anything, ask if Vince Valley was their attorney. I'd like to tie up that loose end."

He agreed.

McNally gave him the card of the attorney Snapper recommended to set up the corporation with authority to sell bonds. And, he had no objections if Bishop contacted the attorney.

Bishop didn't finish his coffee. It had gotten cold while they talked.

Before Bishop left, he decided it was alibi time so he asked, "I need to know where you were the night Vince Valley was killed." He added a date and time. He also told him a witness had seen a heavy set man leaving the area at the time Vince was killed.

"Not me. I didn't do it. No reason to. I barely knew the man. He was a little pushy, but he was a lawyer. Hell, they're all pushy. Let me see where I was."

Bishop had a little internal laugh at that.

McNally left to get his calendar. When he returned, he showed the calendar to Bishop and said, "I was here. Just me and the housekeeper. She has a room over the garage." He called her in and told Bishop to ask her. He did.

She glanced at McNally who showed nothing and then told Bishop, "Mr. McNally was here as far as I know that night, at the time you said."

"How do you know? It was after dinner. Do you watch television together?" Bishop asked with just a touch of sarcasm.

She gave an embarrassed laugh and said, "No. But I served dinner and I didn't hear his car go out afterward."

"Does he always park it in the garage?" Bishop asked.

"Usually," she said after a hesitation and another glance at McNally. She thought he'd parked it in the garage when he came home that afternoon but when pressed by Bishop admitted that she couldn't swear to it. He'd walked in through the garage door and she had heard the garage door close so she'd assumed he'd parked in the garage.

That was as far as Bishop could get with that. He'd ask Ellen to send somebody to talk to the neighbors to see if they heard a car leave that evening before the time Vince was killed. If they had, it wouldn't be compelling in court, but it would point to McNally with the witness's description of a "heavy set" man leaving the camp area.

Bishop asked to see his work area before he left. He wanted to examine McNally's tools, in particular his hammer.

McNally showed him the peg board where everything was hanging. The hammer was there. Bishop put it in the plastic bag he'd brought for Ellen's lab to examine.

The lab report would say that the hammer was new and showed no blood. McNally had said as much. "All my tools are fairly new. I don't use them. I have them for emergencies and hire my work out."

Bishop didn't figure calling McNally's carpenter or plumber to verify his statement would be worthwhile. How would they know what he did with his tools and they had their own? However, McNally's "new hammer" statement left everything up in the air. That plus the housekeeper's uncertainty about McNally's presence in the house that evening open McNally up to some suspicion.

But, what the hell can I do about it. It's just hanging there. No way to do anything with it. However, he reminded himself, *the witness did report a "heavy set" person in the campground area the night Vince was killed. McNally was heavy set even if he may have had an alibi and even if, he says, he had no reason to kill him. I don't know what Vince may have found out and what he may have accused McNally of doing. He'll stay on my list for now.*

He thanked the housekeeper on his way out and thanked McNally for taking the time to see him.

"No problem," McNally said. "I had nothing else to do but sit here and watch the surf. When I get more Taco Wagons from China, I'll be back in business."

Bishop wished him well.

Chapter 20

Bishop went back to his apartment and sent Ellen an email report of his meeting. In the report, he indicated his surprise at McNally's revelation. He had thought McNally had set everything up and that Snapper Cornwall was just collecting a fee for the use of his name. That was what he thought McNally had told him initially. But McNally was now saying that Snapper was bringing in investors and people who wanted to buy a franchise.

Snapper was definitely not a figurehead in my book. Which story was the right one? And, why did McNally change his story? Sure as hell makes me suspicious.

Ellen called.

"Do you believe what McNally said? I thought he was using Snapper to make his Taco Wagons business look legitimate," she said. "Big name out front."

"Yeah, I did too. That's what he told me the first time we talked. But, I have to admit that Snapper was slick enough to set it up as a neat way to let McNally make him money. He apparently brought in investors and people who wanted to buy a franchise. At least that's what McNally said."

She scoffed. "You think Snapper was that savvy? I know he could swindle lonely old ladies, but investors and people who want to sell tacos out of wagons in small towns. Hard to believe."

"Wagoneers, McNally calls 'em. But, I agree with you. McNally might be running a game for some reason. Or. It could be my snooping around has spooked him somehow. So, he decided to back pedal. I can't see how or why just now, but if he's spooked, he'd gotta be hiding something. Now, I've got my eyes on him."

"I'm glad. Maybe we seeing some daylight."

"Next thing in my list is the attorney for the company. I want to see what he says. I'll get back to you. I also want to run McNally's story past the two young women who were involved. See what they have to say about it."

"Keep me posted. This thing is getting complicated."

"I'd say."

"Glad you're back."

"Wish I could say the same."

"By the way, I'm interviewing people to take over your position and a couple of extras the Mayor thinks we need. The drug problems have him worried. His first term, I don't mind saying, we had it all pretty much under control. We had informants and we were bringing in the dealers. Reduced drugs sales."

"So, what happened?" Bishop asked.

"I wish I knew. Six months after he was re-elected, a drug war started up. Competition cropped up and dealers began to shoot each other. We were looking at an epidemic. Drugs being sold everywhere. Dealers fighting for corners. The Mayor said if it had happened before the election, he never would have been re-elected. Now, it's getting so bad, he's even talking about retirement. The City Council is encouraging him to. All the councilmen want to take his place."

"Doesn't sound good for him."

"Not a bit. And, what he catches from them, I'm catching from him."

"I'm sorry for all of you. I'm not sorry you're interviewing people though. That puts me on borrowed time. How is that coming?"

In addition to the Mayor wanting to kick me out to make him look good.

"I've made one offer to a guy in Santa Ana. He's thinking about it. I'll be making another offer next week, I think."

"So, I may be prematurely on my way out," Bishop said. *Not prematurely in my book. I'll cry all the way to the airport. I've never had such a frustrating case.*

"Well, it's a fact that things are heatin' up," Ellen told him with grimness in every word. " The City Council has been bitching about your lack of progress. They're blaming it on the Mayor who, of course, is blaming it on me, now publically. Hell, I may be on the way out too."

"I'm sorry Ellen. I have to admit that it's all my fault. I've failed you and the Mayor. Everybody is right. I'm not making any progress." He said all that tongue in cheek. He knew he'd done the best he could do.

"I hope the Santa Ana guy takes your offer. I hope the other guys you're after do too. I can't do anything about your drug problem and I haven't done much good about the City's two front page murders. All I've done is take the City's money but … I've just had a thought."

He heard her loud sigh. "I didn't mean I was blaming you for anything, Bishop. I know what you're doing. And I know you're doing the best that can be done. You always do but it's a tough case. You know and I know it. Some others don't know shit and they're bitching. I can take the heat. If I couldn't, I wouldn't be here. But, hell no, as far as I'm concerned, you stay till I get a new guy up to speed."

"Thanks, Ellen but here's my thought. Consider it carefully. I have two loose ends to tie up. One is George Talbert if I can remember what bothered me about my interview with him. I have to get out my notes and see if anything jogs my memory. Anyway, that's one loose end.

"The second loose end is the Taco Wagons franchisees. I know we both agree that things look like they're running smoothly. Bond holders are getting paid regularly and on time. Nothing looks amiss, but suppose this. Suppose McNally had told the franchisees the Wagons cost more than he had thought. Now, they owe an additional payment of five thousand dollars. Or, suppose this. Suppose McNally told them their supplies were going up by some percent. They may be locked in to the price they're charging for tacos so now, all of a sudden they're getting less money than they were anticipating.

"Most of those franchisees probably gave up decent homes in decent cities, hell, La Jolla for example, to make a home in some one horse town, selling tacos on a street corner. I doubt it set well with their wives, … spouses in the first place. Now, having to face not getting the money they were promised, might be more than they can accept.

"Could be one or the other of the franchisees, one with a short fuse, stood all he could stand, he couldn't stands no more so he gets out his pistol and shoots old Snapper, thinking he's running the show." He laughed at his butchered phrase. Ellen did too. It was something he'd heard but didn't remember where.

He added, "And, that's why McNally all of a sudden is backing away from Snapper as a figure head to keep from getting shot himself. See what I'm getting at?"

Ellen was silent for a few seconds then said, "I do, Bishop. I guess that's why you always get your man when you take a case. You keep digging until you come up with something that makes sense. What do you propose?"

"I will pay. Yeah, I'll pay one of your new hires, before he's on your payroll. I want somebody out of the traffic academy or just out of orientation to drive to Weldon, Arizona. McNally told me they had a Taco Wagon working there. I'll brief the guy or girl but basically I want whoever goes, to buy a taco and talk to the franchisee about business. Ask if he's had or is having any trouble with the company. If so, what kind."

"Okay. I like it. You're basing that on McNally backing away from Snapper being a figurehead."

"Kind of. Mostly though, I'm back into looking into the franchisees. No other option in this case. I want to check it out before I get out."

"I get you and I agree. It's our, yeah, mine too, our last gasp."

"I'll send a guy over to check a franchisee out. He'll call and tell me what he found out. I may have some follow up questions or I may want our man, my man, to drive to Beaver, Utah or Quartzsite, north of Weldon and talk to the franchisee there. Those are the places McNally said they had franchisees."

"I thought you said McNally had to get permission from their franchisee before you could interview them," Ellen said.

"Yeah, but I don't intend asking him. As far as anybody knows, my man or woman is just somebody off the street buying a taco. Not somebody the City of San Diego or Bishop Bone has sent to ask questions."

"Good plan. If asked, your envoy can give a phony name and even say he or she is just driving through. That'll keep McNally from raising hell with the City."

Bishop continued. "And, by me paying the envoy, there'll be no connection with the City. Just cut my pay."

"That could work. I'd delay putting a guy on the force. Tell him we have an undercover assignment for 'em. Better yet, you tell them that. They'd be working for you."

"We understand each other, Ellen. We'll see if McNally's change of position about Snapper has anything to do with the business. We'll see if he's trying to put some distance between him and some funny doings. That may also be why he's not leasing any Taco Wagons out at the moment. He's afraid he could be next."

"I see what you're getting at, Bishop. He's just an innocent employee."

"Just that, Ellen. Anyway, I want to tie a knot in that string before I go back to Mississippi. And tie one in the Talbert knot if I can remember what bothered me about him."

Ellen was silent for a few more seconds before saying, "Okay. I agree. I'll send you somebody we are going to hire. What you do is up to you. You get me?"

"The City's not involved. If a law suit hits, it'll hit me."

"Sad but true, Bishop. This is the real world. I have a duty to protect my employer and that's the City."

"No problem. Frankly, I'm not worried. I'm willing to take the chance. I can defend myself and I have no doubt that I'll win."

More bullshit Bone. I hope I'm right.

"You'll get a call tomorrow," she said and hung up.

Before hanging up, Bishop asked her to send somebody out to talk to McNally's neighbors to see if anybody could remember hearing or seeing anything the night Vince was killed.

They wouldn't, but it was a "t" Bishop wanted crossing.

About mid-day the next day, Bishop got a call from a young man about ready to enter the police academy to prep himself for the San Diego police force.

"Raoul Martinez," he told Bishop his name. "Chief Wasserman said I was to call you. She said she didn't know why but you were on assignment and might want me for a job."

They agreed to meet at the nearest Denny's for lunch. Bishop figured it best to meet there instead of the apartment leased by the San Diego police department. This would be Bishop's gig from start to finish.

Over lunch, Bishop explained how he was working undercover, on his own, and needed Raoul to do job for him. Raoul told him he and his wife had just driven out to San Diego from Abilene, Texas. He'd answered an ad by the police department and his wife had several job opportunities.

He said, "My dad gave me his old car for the trip. Mine was on its last legs. His isn't much better but it made it okay."

"Good," Bishop then said what was on his mind. "You'll be reporting to me and only me on this job. This has nothing to do with the City. I just need someone bright to do a little investigating for me for a loose end I'm looking at and I heard you're waiting to be hired by the City so I thought you might be available for a few bucks."

Raoul's face lit up. "I am. Money's tight. And, I've got a few days, I understand, before they can put me on."

Raoul's thoughts were jumping up and down. What Bishop was saying about an undercover job sounded important. He asked what it was. Bishop repeated what he'd told Ellen about driving to Weldon, Arizona and possibly to Beaver, Utah depending on what he found out in Weldon.

"Probably not Beaver," Bishop said. "That's too far a drive, but, you could drive to Quartzsite if you get anything in Weldon that suggests a trip to Quartzsite."

"I've made notes," Raoul said. "I'll look at my maps when I get home."

"Good idea. When you get to Weldon, you'll have to go to the city hall and find out where the Taco Wagons guy has set up. I understand they had to have a license to do business in Weldon so the City Hall will know the business location. Will your car make it?"

"It got us out here. It should be okay. I'll baby it along."

"You have a credit card? If not, I'll give you cash," Bishop said.

He had a card. "Dad paid it off last time. I owe him," Raoul said.

"Sometimes dads come in handy."

Bishop went on to tell him what to ask the franchisee and when he was finished, to make good notes and then call and tell him what the franchisee had said and his facial expression when he did.

"Sounds exciting. Can I tell my wife?"

"Sure but tell her not to tell anybody else until I give the go-ahead. It's very important that none of what you're about to do gets out. I'm looking at one murder, maybe two that could be linked to what you're going to do ... what you may find out. I don't want to tip off the murderer or someone who knows the murderer."

Sure as hell, if he tells her, she'll know somebody who knows McNally and my ass will be mud. So, he'd better tell her to keep her mouth shut.

Raoul said he understood. "We don't know anybody out here yet, anyway. But, I won't tell her until I get back."

Raoul couldn't resist a big smile. He felt important to be given a job like that even before he began work for the City.

"Well, as I said, what you find out could help solve the murders. I'd say it can't get any more important than that."

"When do I leave?"

"In the morning," Bishop told him.

After they'd finished lunch, Bishop sent him home to pack. He had given him a copy of the Taco Wagons' brochure to help him find the franchisee's wagon should he have difficulty.

Chapter 21

Bishop went back to the apartment to call the Taco Wagons company lawyer for an appointment. When the secretary got the lawyer on the line, Bishop told him why he was calling.

The lawyer, Reeder Boxman, said he understood and asked if he could come to his office to discuss it that afternoon. "Too much to talk about over the phone. And, I'd guess you'll have questions," he said.

Bishop agreed and said he'd be right there.

They met in the lawyer's conference room.

Boxman more or less confirmed to Bishop what McNally had already told him. McNally and Snapper showed up one day with a request to form a corporation entitled, Taco Wagons. They wanted stock issued and authority to sell bonds. He didn't know which one was the moving force behind its creation.

"Nobody told me and I didn't ask." Boxman said. "I didn't think it was important to what I'd been asked to do."

Bishop agreed.

McNally was named the Executive Vice President and Snapper the President. The lawyer was appointed the Secretary/Treasurer by the men. He logged in all the bond holders and signed all monthly checks to them. McNally was his contact with the operational end of the company. Boxman would only write the checks when McNally told him to write them.

Boxman did everything they asked, so long as it was legal and within the scope of his appointed office. He took care of the paperwork to sell bonds to investors. He had a list of the bond holders and volunteered to Bishop how many there were.

"Bond sales have slacked up a bit lately, but they've sold in the neighborhood of fourteen million dollars worth. The bond holders get monthly checks equal to eight percent of what they invested."

Bishop asked and was told that Boxman didn't get into anything to do with the franchisees. That was done, as he understood it, by McNally himself. He didn't know how the company got buyers for the franchisees but from what he'd heard, the word about selling tacos from a taco wagon had gotten around in various states.

"People from all over are leasing the Taco Wagons, according to Mr. McNally," he said. "I heard Mr. McNally telling Mr. Cornwall one time that they had well over a thousand Taco Wagons in various states, maybe five. I'm not sure about that. In small towns from what they were saying. Apparently, they are selling more every month. Leasing, I guess is how they're handling it."

McNally had told Bishop that sales were held up because they were waiting on a shipment of wagons from China but Bishop didn't think it relevant to get into that with Boxman.

The attorney knew very little about the business itself, the day to day stuff. Subcontractors handled all of that.

Bishop had asked him.

"I think McNally told Mr. Cornwall that the company was getting something over a hundred thousand dollars a week from the wagons, net after expenses. Everybody called him Snapper. He seemed to prefer it.

He didn't say what the gross was but he did say that he expected their income to increase as they worked the bugs out of their system. That'd net the company around half a million a month. Probably more now. They don't tell me."

"Pretty good," Bishop said. *Looks like they're making enough to pay the bond dividends.*

"They've been good clients. Always paid on time. Corporate checks. Always signed by Mr. McNally. They've been easy to get along with. I only saw Snapper, the one time. After that, I dealt with McNally. I understand that Snapper was killed recently. I think you said that's one of the reasons why you're here. Investigating."

"That's right," Bishop said and added that he was also investigating the death of Vince Valley.

Boxman said he didn't know Mr. Valley and asked. "Do you know if Snapper's death will do anything to hurt the business?"

Bishop told him he didn't know. He'd have to talk to McNally for that kind of information.

Bishop thanked him and left. He returned to his apartment and emailed Ellen a report of his meeting. She didn't call, apparently satisfied.

I didn't really find out anything new from Boxman. Some details about the company and its bond holders, insider information. Interesting stuff about the number of franchisees. Sounds like they're doing okay.

From what he told me, I'd say McNally was the day to day manager of the company. But, mostly, it seems to me, he used other people, including Boxman, to do the actual work. No surprise. Most managers do that. Delegate the work and get paid. That's the way most businesses work.

I'm betting Snapper WAS a figurehead, just sending potential investors to McNally. That's all, I'm betting, that he ever did. Maybe he also sent him a few franchisees too if somebody showed up.

Afterwards, he called Cindy to see what she knew who developed the plan for Taco Wagons and any other details about how it came into being. He wanted to nail down the extent of Snapper's involvement. Did he create the company plan or not?

"I don't know much about anything to do with the company or the business, Bishop. The first time we met, Snapper said we'd get a finder's fee for every investor we brought into the Taco Wagons Company. The company was already in business by that time. He said I was to bring people interested in investing in the company or interested in a franchise to him. He'd take care of it after that. I never asked who was doing what. All I know is that when me and Amy brought in somebody to invest in the company, buy bonds, we'd get a fee. We rarely dealt with anybody wanting a franchise. In fact, I can't recall any. Snapper said most of those people called McNally directly."

"Hmm," Bishop said. "I'm curious about who started the venture? Was it Snapper or McNally? McNally wants to be ambiguous about it. And, that makes me suspicious. Sounds like he's setting himself up as an innocent party if anything goes wrong. Could be he sees trouble down the road."

She had no idea. They were given brochures to hand out at Vince's talks and any other place they went to or had an interest in, as in their work places.

After they ended their conversation, Bishop cursed to himself. *One damn frustration after another. I'm beginning to think it smells funny though. But, I don't have a clue as to how or why. Gut feeling. Like Vince, anything that sounds that good, makes me suspicious especially with McNally apparently back peddling on Snapper.*

Everybody involved is making money. If it weren't for that, I'd suspect it was a scam. But what kind would it be?

I can't wait to hear what Raoul finds out. I should'a done it earlier. I may kick my butt for not doing it.

Just to cover himself on Raoul's bootlegged visit to a Taco Wagons franchisee, and to protect her, he sent Ellen a report "suggesting" a visit to one of the franchisees to check how they were doing. If the Mayor approved, it'd be a legitimate trip. Otherwise, he'd have to find a way to report what, if anything, Raoul found out but Ellen would be out of it.

After he sent the email, he had a beer to relax and said, "I'll do what Vince did … think."

I don't have anything to do but wait. I'll look at my Talbert file tomorrow to see if I can remember what bothered me about it. Then, I'll wait for Raoul to call. Could be I'll be on a plane to Mississippi in a couple of days, if I'm wrong about the Taco Wagons business or the Mayor needs a scapegoat to cover his political butt.

If I am gone because Raoul couldn't find anything wrong, I imagine Ellen will take a day's leave to laugh until she cries. My gut feeling will have bit me in the back side. But, I won't hear a thing. I'll be in Mississippi nursing my bruised ego. I guess that's what happens when you run out of logical options. You take chances and if you lose, you look like a stupid fool.

*****

 Ellen called when he was mid-way through his beer. She acted like she knew nothing about Raoul. That's how she and Bishop had agreed to treat it. That would keep her out of it.

In response to his suggestion that someone check out a franchisee, she said, somewhat tongue in cheek, "If I do, the Mayor will bitch that Bishop Bone is looking for some way to drag out his investigation. He's the only one complaining about Taco Wagons."

"Vince was skeptical about the company and he ended up dead," Bishop said, playing along.

"Hardly skeptical. His client asked for an opinion. So, he had to ask questions and obviously did. If all you had to do was drive out to Indio or someplace close, I'd say do it, but two days of your expensive time and a night in a hotel, I'm not so eager to explain that expense to the auditors."

She let out a noisy breath of air. "Tell you what Bishop, just because it's you, I'll pass your request on to the Mayor. He's tied up in budget meetings at the moment, so when he gets free, I'll meet with him and see what he says. If he says okay, you can drive to Arizona and look at some poor bastard making tacos for passers-by."

By that time, Raoul should have already interviewed the Weldon franchisee. If he didn't find out anything useful and the Mayor says no to my request, I'll tell Ellen I've done all I can do and resign. I'll catch the next flight to Mississippi. Hell, maybe not quite. I need to find Vince's computer and have a look at that. Damned if I hadn't forgotten about that in the heat of sending Raoul to Arizona. Where in the hell did it get to? I need to find the computer before I waste time looking at Talbot's file. Probably nothing in it that'll help anyway.

Wait a minute. Wait a damn minute. I think I do remember now. The thought just popped into his thoughts.

Damn. I'm getting slow. It wasn't about Talbert. It was about Talbert's son! He had an alibi. That's what bothered me. His alibi. He'd signed in for a class the night Snapper was killed. What if he didn't sign in? His alibi would be nothing.

That's not to say he shot Snapper, just that his alibi might not be as tight as I'd assumed. I need to check the sign-in procedures. Most likely a waste of time. But, it's a lose end. If they have procedures, they must have a way to make sure they're followed.

But, that was my poor battered brain thought and it passed through too damn fast for me to catch it. I'll take another look at that as soon as I find Vince's computer.

Ellen had said she'd call him the next day or so or, as soon as she could get to the Mayor. Could be sooner. That was okay with him. The case had become a game at that point anyway.

Hell, if Raoul doesn't find something, I'm out of here anyway. I may leave in the middle of the night. I'll email my thought about Talbert's son.

He got out of bed the next morning thinking about Raoul being on his way and about Vince's computer. Had the killer taken it somehow, giving Rascal something to stop the barking or had Vince put it in a shop for service?

Chapter 22

Bishop checked under the brick in the flower bed Beatrice had told him about, where Vince left his spare key. The dog wasn't barking so he assumed he was either dead or Beatrice had made peace with him.

I'll find out. Hopefully she has him. I guess it's a him.

There was no key, but the brick had been recently disturbed so he went to Beatrice's camper and asked her if she had it. The little dog immediately came to the screened door and began barking.

Answers that question.

The woman showed up at her camper door right away, smiling tiredly and greeted him. The redness was gone from her eyes. He asked if she had the key. "I need to look for Vincent's computer."

She picked it up from the table by the door and handed it to him.

"I took Vince's food out of his refrigerator and pantry and used it. Some of it anyway. Kept it from spoiling and smelling up his camper. He didn't have much. Never bought more than he needed to get through the week."

Wasn't ever sure he'd get past the week.

"Good idea," Bishop said, adding, "I'll bring it back." He waved the key.

"Oh," she said. "I don't know if it's important to you but his son and daughter came by. They're going to probate his estate. They said they would sell his camper as soon as they got the court's approval. They're paying the rental for the space."

"Yeah. This will most likely be the last time I'll have to come by here anyway. But, since there's an on-going criminal investigation, I expect selling the camper will have to wait until that's wrapped up. They get permission to sell it. They shouldn't have any trouble selling it in any case."

"You want me to tell them?" she asked.

He shook his head. "Their lawyer will find out."

She shook her head and went inside her camper with the dog, Rascal. He seemed contented as far as Bishop could tell.

Once inside the small camper, Bishop checked Vince's table where he'd kept his computer. Usually, a man kept his useful cards on the desk, stuck to the wall or in the desk drawer. He couldn't find a card for a computer service business anyplace.

After a quick and unsuccessful look around the small trailer, he returned the key to the neighbor. When she came to the door, she was still holding Vince's small dog. Tears were rolling down her face again.

She looks like Vince said he felt, most of the time.

She said, "I'm sorry, Mr. Bone." She wiped at the tears. "I can't stop crying. I reckon maybe I was too old for Vince, but I loved him. He was a dear man. I fell in love with him when I watched him sitting under his tree, all depressed. I wished I could have helped him but he kept trying to tell me I couldn't. He just had to get over it … his wife dying like she did. Seeing you just now brought it all back. … I wanted to take care of him."

Bishop told her he understood how she felt and what Vince had been going through. "He told me once that neighbors like you helped pull him through the bad times he was having after his wife died." He stretched the truth, but felt it was worth it to make the lady feel better about herself.

Her face lit up. She smiled. "Did Vince say that?" Then, the smile faded away.

"Yes, he did. He said he was going to tell you but I guess he didn't have time before he was killed."

"Oh, thank you, Mr. Bone. God bless you for telling me. I can't tell you how it makes me feel. I just can't tell you." She looked away as if thinking about something then, slowly said, "I … didn't think he … liked me. I'm so pleased … what you said."

Bishop assumed she was remembering Jennifer. He was glad he hadn't mentioned her. *Best to let sleeping dogs lie,* he thought.

He said he was glad to tell her, "But, let me ask you something."

He asked her if the trailer park used anyone in particular to service their computers. Most people, even people in campgrounds, had computers. The Internet had all but replaced mailing letters through the post office, it seemed. People were using emails to communicate just then.

They didn't, as far as she knew, but there was a kind of rec hall with numbers on a cork board along one wall. She showed him where it was. He thanked her.

Bishop found a card on the board and called the number. He identified himself with his credentials and asked if the guy who'd answered had Vincent Valley's computer. The man checked and said he didn't.

"Damn," Bishop cursed after he'd punched off. "I know he had a computer. The girls said so and his mouse was on the little table where he worked. Ah!"

He had a revelation.

His office. They must have used a computer service. He'd naturally have taken the computer to that place!

He called Vince's old office and told the secretary who'd answered his call who he was and what he wanted. She asked him to wait and came back on. "We use an outfit called, Your Computer Service." She gave him the number and the address.

He called, identified himself, and sure enough, they had Vince's computer and it was ready. He told them he'd be by in a few minutes to pick it up.

They hadn't been sure what they were going to do with it. They'd heard that Vince had been killed. "Usually, there's somebody to call, but nobody answered his phone. We figured we'd have to sell it eventually," the service technician told him. "We weren't sure how to do that, legally." The computer had a bug that they cleaned out. It had been slowing the computer's operations.

Bishop picked it up, thanked him and took the computer back to his apartment to check his files. The technician gave him Vince's password.

He booted it up, went to "Files" and searched for "Notes" and "Talks." He found both but the files only contained ideas for talks at the Rec Hall. He broadened his search and found a file entitled "Taco Wagons."

A man's name, Arty Baker, and a phone number were the first entry. *The client who'd asked about the Taco Wagons investment,* Bishop assumed. He'd call him.

Vince had also summarized his meeting with McNally in another file. Most of what was in that file Bishop knew from what McNally had told him, but Vince did have personal comments which Bishop found telling. Vince was suspicious of the investment according to those notes and was going to ask his client to either drive to one of the small towns in Arizona that had Taco Wagons on the street or ask for authority from Baker to go himself to check them out. There was no indication he'd done either.

He found nothing else of interest about Taco Wagons on the computer. He'd turn it over to Ellen when he was finished investigating the murder.

He called Baker to see what else Vince might have shared with him.

"Mr. Baker," he said and identified himself as a temporary member of the San Diego police department. He told him why he'd called.

"I don't think I can help you," the man told him. "I don't know anything that I think could help you."

Baker went on to tell Bishop how he'd asked Vince, his attorney at one time, for an opinion about the investment and Vince said he'd look into it. Next thing he heard was that Vince had been killed. Vince had suggested during a phone call that a trip to a Taco Wagons franchisee might be worthwhile but he was killed before he could recommend one so no decision had been reached.

Another damned frustration.

"What have you decided to do about investing?" Bishop asked.

"Without Vince's recommendation, I declined. It looked good, good yield, but I don't know anything about it so I told that guy, McNally, who's been handling it since the other guy, Snapper Cornwall, was killed, no."

"What'd he say?"

"He gave me the song and dance about how well the venture was doing. How many investors and franchisees they had. Expansion into Europe was being talked about. He said my investment would be sound and would likely go up in value. He said I could talk to their attorney and to the bank if I wanted more information."

"Typical of a salesman," Bishop said. "He gave me the rosy as well but I'd have to see a Taco Wagon, maybe more than one, before I'd put money into it. Talk to the franchisees to see what they thought. What they may have heard. I prefer securities sold by named investment companies."

Baker did too and said, "You know how things work in this country, maybe all countries. Something comes out and is a big success. The word gets out and everybody and his brother want to get in on the act. If the Taco Wagons is a big success, as McNally said it was going to be, maybe is already, next thing you know some outfit will start selling push carts that sell tacos. They won't need wide sidewalks. That means they could expand into California. The big market state. Next thing to happen, the Taco Wagons investors would be getting smaller checks because the franchisees wouldn't be selling as much. The investors could be left holding the bag. So, instead of the bonds increasing in value, they'd decrease."

"So true," Bishop agreed. He'd thought the same thing.

He asked how he knew Snapper Cornwall and was told they'd met at a La Jolla beach party. "He was charming up the hostess, talking about the investment, suggesting that she might want to put some of her ex-husband's money in it. Later in the evening, I asked him about it. It sounded too good to be true but I thought it was worth looking into. I called Vince to see what he could find out. As I said, when he got killed, I dropped the idea totally."

Bishop thanked him.

He sent Ellen another report and asked if she wanted lunch. She did and met him at his favorite watering hole, Bread and Cie.

196

She had one of their delicious BLTs and he had his usual. Both had cappuccinos.

They talked about the case. First though, she gave him the gist of her talk with the Mayor about Bishop's suggestion that he wanted to drive to Arizona to see a Taco Wagon in action and talk to a franchisee. "When he called to talk to me about my staffing requirements I took the opportunity to ask him about a police visit - you - to one of Snapper's franchisees."

"What'd he say, tell Bone to go to hell?"

She laughed. "No. But in short, he said he didn't see that a trip was warranted based on what we'd discovered so far. We'd said that no one was complaining about anything. And, McNally was agreeable to letting you talk to a franchisee. He said our time and money would be better spent here, looking for the reason somebody killed Snapper Cornwall and Vince Valley."

He only agreed to call a franchisee and ask if he'd see me.

She looked at him and added. "I didn't argue with him Bishop. It's not like you have somebody putting up road blocks between us and a franchisee. I don't want to get into what … you're doing on your own. Okay? But I sure as hell want to hear what you hear as soon as you hear anything. We don't know shit as yet about who might have killed either man. And, I don't see how talking to some guy who's selling tacos out of a wagon is going to help us. You understand what I'm saying. I'm curious and I'm skeptical and I'll admit that you have a good track record on your gut feelings. It's about time that they showed some promise."

"Yeah. Hell, I agree. I've been hitting brick walls ever since I got here. But, I imagine things my gut feelings set in motion are close to happening," Bishop said.

By his reckoning, Raoul should have been close to Weldon by then. He glanced at his watch and did a quick calculation. *If he left early, as I bet he did, he should be approaching Weldon by now.*

"The Mayor kind of suggested that we find another ball of twine with more ravels to pull. He wants the cases solved and closed with a big press conference. He keeps his eye on the next election."

Bishop laughed. "Yeah. No doubt. Or, he wants the twine I've been pulling to be put back in a box and then, I imagine he wants me to give the box back to you. As in, get another investigator."

"He may have said that as well. Suggested it anyway," she said with a smile.

"Is that your suggestion as well?" he asked.

"No. You keep finding things. Not much, but things. I still don't see a killer but I bet you'll find something eventually that may lead to the killer. Keep at it another week. Then, we'll look at it. You're still within the budget I set up for you."

"So long as I don't drive to Arizona."

She laughed and winked. "Right, but let me know if anybody calls you from Arizona."

He promised.

*****

After lunch, he sat down in a comfortable chair in his apartment and thought about what he could do next. He had the thought about Talbert's son, but it was just a loose nut to tighten. After thirty minutes of evaluating what he'd done and what he could do next, he came up empty.

Hell, maybe it's time to rattle some cages. Yeah, but. whose? McNally's housekeeper, Lucile seemed a bit vague ... maybe more than a bit. Was she covering for that bastard? But what can I find out? Even if McNally was out at the time Vince was killed, that wouldn't prove he did it. And, hell, I have to agree with the Mayor and Ellen. What is there to kill about? The Taco Wagons company is making money, paying its investors ... or looks like it is.

But, Vince was at least suggesting a look see. He wasn't convinced. I wish he'd have said something about why. But, why was Snapper killed? Did he know something? Hmm. Could be a different killer altogether. The witnesses seem to be saying that. Snapper was killed by a young man. The only decent report on Vince has a heavy set man leaving the scene.

I don't know a damn thing when you get right down to it.

He thought about that and came up with a list of people he could look at while he was waiting for Raoul.

There's Jacques? Why would he do it? Kill his dad! Revenge? Could be.

The children of the third wife. They didn't seem upset, really. Both were doing well financially. Not them.

The second wife, Billie Talbert with three children. Old Snapper screwed them royally. The girls did okay. They married well. But the son, George, didn't do well at all. He got screwed good. Lost money. But, he doesn't fit the description the witness gave of the man he saw hurrying away. Young and energetic. But, ... he had a son. Would the boy have killed Snapper for his dad? Would be a bit of a push, but its possible. Its been done before. The boy lost money too. His dad's. But, he had that alibi I wondered about. He'd signed into a class at the time Snapper was killed. Hmm, or did he? It's time to look at that alibi, I think.

Anybody else? Cindy and Amy? Why? Snapper hadn't done anything to them that I know. They had no money on the table. And, they were making money on the investors they brought in.

Vince would have been a strong possibility as the killer, but why? No money was involved. He was killed before he could make a statement but Snapper was already dead. Having his feathers ruffled during a tennis match? Would Vince kill about that? Not likely as far as what I know about him. He didn't seem the type to let that bother him enough to kill over it. Besides, he had his revenge when he walked off in the middle of the final set.

Who else?

Hell, that's it except for Talbert's son.

Well, what do I do? Check the son's alibi or tell Ellen I don't have shit and haul my ass back to MS and Kathy. Tempting. Very tempting.

He decided to sleep on it.

It was nearing time for bed. Bishop looked at his cell phone. "Damn, Raoul should have been there by now."

His phone rang. Raoul's name showed on the screen. "Raoul," he answered. "What do you know?"

"Uh, I don't know anything, Mr. Bone. I'm just leaving Yuma. Had a flat this side of town and had to be towed in. Dad didn't have a spare. Who has flats these days?"

Bishop thought, *you did and the Mayor's getting ready to run me out of town on a rail and maybe demand restitution of what Ellen's been paying me.*

Raoul continued, "Finally got a new tire and I'm headed to Weldon now."

From the time, he'd have to spend the night in Weldon and track down a Taco Wagon in the morning, Bishop figured. *I can't do anything about it now. It's happened. Have to live with it.*

Raoul apologized and agreed that he'd stay in a motel and go to city hall first thing to find the location of the Taco Wagon in town.

"Call me as soon as you've talked to the franchisee," Bishop told him.

He apologized again and agreed. "I'll be at city hall when the doors open."

That was how they left it.

If it can go wrong, it will go wrong, he thought, laughed to himself with another thought. *And, when it does, it usually hits me in the face. That's the way this damn case has been going. One of these days, something's going to happen that makes sense.*

"Yeah, when?" he asked himself. He had to fight off a depression.

Chapter 23

He'd call Kathy later that evening, knowing it would help stave off his depression. He knew she wanted him home as much as he wanted to be home with her. Damn, he missed her. Missed being able to relax on his back porch with her. Somebody he could be himself with.

He never got tired of looking at the beavers across Indian Creek with a beer and Kathy. That was fun and made life worthwhile. He remembered Vince's neighbor, Beatrice. Poor misguided woman. Before he met Kathy, that might have been him, remembering his married life, his wife and children. He'd lost it all but Kathy saved his life.

She made it whole again.

But first, he called his bank clients. Get the work out of the way first. Fortunately, none were in dire straits. Nothing urgent that needed his attention. He had half wished they had cases for him. That'd give him an excuse to turn in his badge. He cursed.

It wasn't quite time to call Kathy. He had to wait until she had finished work at the library. When it was time, he called.

She answered on the first ring.

"Well, Bishop, how do you stand with your cases?" she asked. "I'd like for you to be here. You're like my sunshine. Without you, every day is like a cloudy day, threatening rain."

"I feel the same way."

He gave her a rundown on where his investigations stood on both murders, hoping it wouldn't be boring. Part of that was what he had Raoul doing.

"I first thought both men were killed by the same person. And, that may still be right. They had the Taco Wagons investment in common. Vince, not as much so, but there is a connection. It's possible he was going to investigate the business for a client who was interested in buying bonds in the company. I can't imagine what reason anybody involved in the investments would have to kill Snapper but I have a guy in Arizona following up a hunch I have. Ellen calls it one of my gut feelings."

"I know about those," she said. "You go into another world."

"Yeah, I guess I do. Well, it's possible that Snapper and Vince were killed by different people. And, that's the most likely scenario. And, right now, I don't have a clue as to why either man was killed. I'm hoping we only have one killer but things aren't usually that simple."

"No," she said. "Your cases are always complicated, Bishop. I think that's why Chief Wasserman asks for your help."

"Maybe, but this time she not getting any," he said and explained what he was doing on the Snapper case, sending a man to Weldon to interview a franchisee to see if anybody was hiding anything. And, he told her his thought about the Talberts, the son's alibi.

"That maybe nothing, but I'll have to follow up if my Weldon thing is a waste as everybody around here seems to think it will be."

He told her how he was handling it, paying for it himself.

"Sounds just like you, Bishop. I wish you luck."

"I could use some. I'm hoping the Weldon interview will give me a new look at the case. If McNally's been playing games, it should come out.

"If I find out that he has been putting the squeeze on their franchisees, I'll recommend that Ellen talk to the franchisees to see who might have been upset enough to kill Snapper, thinking he was responsible. They have a lot of 'em according to McNally, in the thousands, all over, but Ellen can handle that kind of leg work, interviewing them, as well as I can. Maybe better.

"I don't know what I can do about Vince's murder. It's possible, but, just that, possible that McNally might be implicated in that murder. Vince might have stumbled onto something when he was checking the Taco Wagons Company for a client. If so, that might have scared McNally enough to kill him. A witness saw a heavy set man near the camper grounds. That fits McNally's description. If all that comes together, it could be that I can be out of here, one way or the other in a couple of weeks."

"I don't know if I can stand it two weeks without you, but I'll do what I have to. Try to shorten it up, will you?" Kathy replied.

That was his goal. "I may just fold my tent anyway and tell Ellen I've done all I can do and come home. If all I have on my plate turns to you know what, I'll resign. She's hiring a guy to take my place anyway. I could be with you in a week, if I don't find something useful in the next day or two."

"I love you, Bishop. Don't forget that."

"I love you too, Kathy. Every day, I think of you and wish I were holding you close."

"Soon," she said. "Let's make it soon."

"Like I said, if I don't come up with something on the murders from what I have underway, it'll be very soon. I've been hanging on because Ellen doesn't have anybody else to turn to."

"I know this, Bishop, if anybody can find the killers, you can so I'm not going to get too excited about you coming home just yet."

He hoped she was right but the constant frustration of never finding anything this time had worn him down. He'd never been as boxed in as he had been on the two murders Ellen had given him to solve.

*****

After he hung up, he re-examined what he had he could do. There was still the one loose end he hadn't pulled. Talbert's son. His alibi.

Probably another waste, but while I'm waiting for Raoul, I'll pull it. Hell, it's the only thing I have that I can do.

He called Ellen at her home. He could have sent a report and a recommendation but he didn't think he had the patience to write a report and to wait for her response. He wanted a yes or no on what he wanted to do, right away. He wanted to check out the son's alibi and if that fell into place like he hoped, he wanted to be able to search for the gun that killed Snapper.

She listened until he stopped long enough for her to reply. She said, "Listen, Bishop, you may be right. Probably are … well, let me just say it's possible that you're right. Your instincts usually are on target. I guess that comes from being the cynical bastard you are."

"I've dealt with all kinds in my day, Ellen. Most of what I come up with when I'm chasing a murderer is based on what I've experienced and learned over the years."

"Okay, I'll give you that, but I don't see how I can let you storm in and terrorize people based on you cynical instincts, even if they're most likely right. See, I'm giving you a pat on the back."

"Well, a pat isn't your endorsement or approval."

"Get me a little proof, Bishop. No, just get me something that at least suggests you're right. I can hear our attorney standing in front of a judge saying, 'Your Honor, Bishop Bone's instincts tell us we should get a search warrant in case he finds anything that looks like he needs one.' We'd all get run out of town. Our attorneys just aren't going to embarrass themselves in front of a judge on your instincts."

Bishop sighed. "I guess you're right, Ellen. This case has been so damn frustrating with dead ends every place I've been, I get excited when I see a decent possibility or the least bit of daylight."

"I agree. Hell, I'm paying you a ton to find me a killer. I hate to throw water on your enthusiasm but I don't want to be sitting in depositions answering questions about why I didn't follow our usual procedures. Get me something our attorneys can use if the Talbert's hungry attorneys come after me when you're back in Mississippi looking at beavers."

"I guess you're right. I do get anxious to show some results for the money you're paying me. I forget that this is the litigious age. There's an attorney on every corner looking for a deep pocket to sue."

"I couldn't have said it better, Bishop. If I didn't watch my ass and the City's, I'd be down in Mississippi picking cotton and watching the beavers with you."

He laughed and didn't say anything for a few seconds. He had to think how he could make sure if the City got sued, they'd have something they could point at to show what he was doing, was logical and reasonable. Finally, he said, "Okay, suppose I can show you it was reasonably possible for Talbert's son to have shot Snapper, can we move ahead?"

"If you can show what you're talking about is true, reasonably true, not just some remote possibility, I'll give you the go ahead for a search warrant."

He thanked her, turned off his phone and made his plans for the next day. He dreaded the drive north but it would have been necessary anyway. He wanted to get there before mid-day when everybody was working.

He had an early Denny's breakfast, brushed his teeth, got gasoline and headed north. He had his phone so he could get Raoul's call. He assumed Raoul would call around noon or maybe earlier. That should give him time to check city hall for the location of the Taco Wagon, then find it and finally, ask the franchisee some questions between customers.

Because of Ellen's concerns, he was a bit anxious about Raoul's trip and his. But, he told himself, if nothing works the way I'm hoping, I'll clean the apartment, turn in my car and spend tomorrow night with Kathy. My replacement can solve both murders.

Hell, thinking like that, who gives a shit if it works? I'm at the point where one more failure gets me where I'd rather be anyway, in Lawton.

He knew he was just letting off steam. He'd stick with the case until he'd solved it or they shipped him back to Mississippi in a box.

*****

During the drive to Orange County, he turned his phone on to get Raoul's call. It didn't come so he turned it off when he reached the school that Talbert's son, Barry attended.

He parked, went into the Principal's office explained who he was and why he was there. The Principal, Washington Lederman, put him in a conference room and left to get the teacher he needed to see.

"I'll have him bring his attendance book," he told Bishop as he left.

A minute or so later, a tall, balding man with a stomach that sagged over his belt came in holding a loose leaf notebook. His face had the stoic look of many math professors he'd seen in his lifetime. *Damn theorems and equations killed their feelings,* he thought when he saw the man come through the door.

He introduced himself as Stuart Hatch, shook Bishop's hand, then pulled out a chair at the table where Bishop was sitting and sat down himself. He placed the notebook in front of him.

"Principal Lederman said you had a question about the attendance to my advanced calculus class," Hatch said and touched his notebook.

"I do," Bishop said. He gave him Barry Talbert's name and the date he was enquiring about, the date Snapper was shot and killed.

Hatch opened his notebook and flipped the page until he came to the date Bishop had asked about. "He signed in," he said and put his finger on Barry's signature. He pushed the notebook toward Bishop who looked at Barry's signature. He also scanned the sign-in sheet for a few seconds.

"Does Barry have any close friends?" Bishop asked.

"Yes. He has several I'd call his friends, but he hangs around most of the time with Reese Warner. Both are married and more or less, I guess you'd say, working their way, with their wives' help, through school."

Bishop looked at the attendance notebook again. That time, he took a little longer.

"Is Barry a good student?" Bishop asked.

"He is. Maybe not the brightest I've ever had, but smart enough to make a decent engineer. Makes Bs and Cs in most of his math classes."

Bishop nodded. "I've heard tell … in fact, I know that now and then, one friend signs the attendance book for another friend. I couldn't help but notice that the signatures of Barry and Reese on the day you've turned to, the day I'm asking about, look like both were done by the same man. Take a look and tell me what you see."

Bishop shoved the notebook back to Hatch who touched the sheet with his index finger, held it for a second before moving it."

"I see what you're getting at. They do look the same, nearly the same anyway."

"I don't guess you remember if Barry was in class that evening," Bishop said.

Hatch half laughed. "No. I go on the honor system. That's why I use a sign-in sheet so I won't have to waste time calling roll. If somebody wants to cheat, it's their loss. I don't recall calling on Barry in that class and getting no response."

"Can you show me the sign-in sheet for the next class?" Bishop asked.

Hatch flipped a page and pushed the book back at Bishop.

Bishop scanned the sheet, stopping twice. "Look at this," he said and turned the notebook around so Hatch could see. "The signatures don't look the same on this sheet."

The professor looked at the two signatures, twisted his head, frowned and said. "I'd say you're right. Reese signed in for Barry the night you're asking about. Against the rules. I'll have to report it. Is that important?"

"Could be. I want you to type a note to that effect, sign it and give it to me. It's important to an investigation going on in San Diego, a murder investigation. I'll also want copies of both sign-in sheets. Also, give me Reese Warner's address and phone number. I may need it."

Hatch seemed reluctant but left to do as Bishop had asked.

Probably doesn't want to take the time, Bishop thought.

He waited a few minutes until Hatch returned with the note and the copies Bishop had requested. He'd also included Warner's phone number and address.

The note Hatch gave him was typed on the school's letter head. "I hope this isn't something that'll get me into trouble."

"I don't see how it could. Law enforcement these days have become gun shy. They want every t crossed and every i dotted. Lawyers are always looking over our shoulders."

He instructed Hatch not to mention his visit or anything he'd discussed or asked about to anybody, especially not to Barry Talbert or Reese Warner. Not even the Principal. If he wants to know anything, have him call me. "If you do tell anybody, trouble will hit you in the head, big time."

Hatch's face went white. "I won't say a word. If you hear anything, it didn't come from me. It's not really my problem. If one of the boys wants to skip a class, they miss my lecture and have to do self-study to catch up. As I said, it's their loss but I do have to ... well, I'm supposed to report it. I don't think it's essential that I do."

"I'll tell you when you can, if you elect to report it." Bishop said, looked at him and asked, "I assume the students have lockers."

They did.

Bishop asked for Barry's locker number. Hatch called somebody on his phone, asked for the number and gave it to Bishop who thanked him.

*****

During the drive back to San Diego, he turned on his phone and had a message from Raoul, a somewhat cryptic message. It said, "Mr. Bone, this is Raoul. I'm on my way to Quartzsite. I thought you'd want me to, based on what I found out in Weldon. I'll give you a call tonight with a full report."

What the hell? Bishop thought when he heard the message which he played twice to make sure he hadn't missed anything. "Based on what he found in Weldon. I wish to hell he'd have said what that was," Bishop said. He wanted to call the young man but didn't want to catch him in the middle of an interview so he elected to wait until the evening when Raoul said he'd call.

Chapter 24

When he was back at the apartment, Bishop typed a report on his Orange County trip and emailed it to Ellen. He recommended that she get a search warrant for him. He included copies of everything he'd been given by Hatch.

She called him a couple of hours later.

"You're making progress, Bishop," she said somewhat more cheerfully than she had been the last few times they'd talked.

Damn, he thought when he heard the word "progress." That meant he wasn't where he needed to be as far as she was concerned. But he could tell she was encouraged.

She continued. "The City Attorney just wants a little more. He wants you to nail down that the boy wasn't in class. He says sometimes one classmate will sign the sheet, as a favor, for another even though both are in class. Can you check that out? I don't see that as a problem, do you?"

"No. Just another trip to Orange County."

"But, you're almost there. Do it and let's get the show on the road. You may be onto something!"

"I hope so," Bishop said.

He drove back to Orange County and caught Reese Warner at his home. Following an introduction, he took him to a local police station to intimidate him, swore him in and asked questions about his sign-in for Barry."

Initially, Reese was belligerent and swore that Barry was in class. "I only signed him in because he was busy with something. He asked me to sign the sheet for him and I did. No big deal. We all do it. He didn't miss class."

Bishop, using his lawyer's skills, ran a little fabrication trick on Reese, telling him that Barry's seat mates had already testified that Barry wasn't there that night. Not only that, Reese was risking being expelled from school for lying about it.

Faced with that, Reese changed his story. "Okay, Barry's kids had a thing at their school that evening. He wanted to see them. So, I covered for him. He's my best friend. He covers for me when I need him to. Okay! Big fucking deal! You act like it's a Federal case or something."

"Well, I guess I got it wrong. Excuse me for a minute." Bishop faked punching in a number on his cell phone. After a couple of seconds, he said, "Yeah. What'd you find out? ... Is that right? You sure? Okay. Thanks. See you at headquarters."

He looked at Reese with a frown. "What would you say if I told you Barry's neighbors saw Barry's kids playing in the yard that evening? But Barry was nowhere in sight." Bishop stood and picked up the papers he'd put on the table.

"Looks like you're going to be looking for a new school, old buddy. Expelled for making false statements. Signing in another student and lying about it. Sorry. The DA might want to charge you with perjury. They'll call you ... maybe send somebody to arrest you." He turned to leave.

Reese said, "Wait! Listen, I'll tell you the truth. You must have been asked by a friend to bend the rules now and then."

Bishop just stared at him. "What are you saying?"

"He told me he had something to do for his dad. They work at an eatery. I think he had to work a shift for his dad or something. I told him I'd cover for him. Can you overlook what I said ... before. I'm sorry. It was for a friend. No harm done. I gave him my notes so he wouldn't miss anything."

Bishop sat down and wrote something on a sheet of paper. "Here," he said and shoved it toward Reese. "Sign that and we're even."

Reese looked at it. It was a statement of what he'd just told Bishop. "And, you won't report me?"

Bishop shook his head no.

Reese signed it and Bishop left.

Knowing Barry was working, he went to the grocery store where the wife worked as a clerk to talk to her. He asked her if Barry had recently driven to San Diego?

She didn't look him in the eyes and said, hesitantly, "No, not that I know of. Why?"

"You can go to jail for perjury," he told her. "This is a serious matter. We are investigating a murder. Barry may be involved in it with his dad."

"Oh, damn. I told him not to do it. Damn, damn, damn! I think he might have driven to San Diego a while back. I'm not sure but I heard him talking to his dad about doing something for him in San Diego. You're saying somebody was killed?"

"Yes. We're investigating. Somebody his dad had dealings with … Snapper Cornwall."

"Oh, God. That man his mother married. Damn. That's all he ever talks about with Barry … how the man stole from his mother and from them, the children. Damn. He was obsessed with it!"

"I'm sorry. You'll likely be asked to testify if it goes that far. As I said, we're still investigating."

He didn't ask her to sign anything but would include what she'd said in his affidavit for the City Attorney. However, he'd recorded their conversation on his cell phone which he'd get transcribed.

*****

When he was back in San Diego, Bishop sent Ellen another report and asked her once again to get authority, a search warrant, for him to search George's locker where he worked, Big Plates, Small Prices, and their homes, his and Barry's. It was his hunch that George kept the gun in one of those places, probably the restaurant, and gave it to Barry to shoot Snapper.

Damn, finally, I've found something out. I think I've cracked the case. Took too damn long. Son of a bitch! I'm getting slow in my old age.

Ellen called back right away. "Okay, you've done it, Bishop! You've got what I need to help you out. Help *us* out, really. Finally! I'll get you a warrant to search everything the Talberts have. I believe you've cracked it. Looks like it. Congratulations! I also told the Mayor.

He sends his congratulations as well. He can't wait to make an announcement."

"I agree, it looks good. First sunlight I've seen since I started, but I don't smile until I see somebody behind bars, Ellen. And, we still have a way to go before we can do that. I think it looks good though. I'd sure like to find the gun. With the gun, I'll feel like we've found the killer." *At least Snapper's killer. I don't see a connection for Vince's yet. I'll look at his computer again. Maybe I missed something.*

He had missed something, but it wasn't what he was thinking he'd missed. Raoul called him early that evening with a full report. He couldn't believe what he was hearing.

*****

"Mr. Bone," Raoul said, "I'm in Quartzsite. I think I'll spend the night here if it's okay with you."

"What the hell are you doing there? I thought you were in Weldon," Bishop said. "I've been waiting for a report."

Have I lost it? Too much frustration must have pickled my brain. I know I talked about Quartzsite but I don't remember telling him to go there. I need to go home. Damn.

Before Bishop could say anything else, Raoul said, "When I went to the City Hall in Weldon, the woman there had no record of any permits issued for a Taco Wagons business and had no knowledge of any such business being in town. To her knowledge, nobody was selling tacos out of a street wagon anywhere in Weldon."

"What? No taco wagon?"

"That's what she said. I accepted that but went out driving around looking for one just to make sure. I figured they might have decided to go without a permit. I drove all the commercial streets in Weldon. There weren't that many. I didn't see a taco wagon. I also looked for any business selling tacos. You'd said sometimes they sold out of store fronts."

"And, you found nothing?"

"Not a thing. So, when I couldn't reach you, I decided to drive to Quartzsite and check it out. I figured that's what you'd tell me to do. It wasn't that far, under a hundred miles."

Bishop, somewhat stunned and still absorbing what Raoul had found, agreed. "Yes. I would have told you to drive up there. You did the right thing. What did you find there?"

No Taco Wagons in Weldon. What the hell does that mean? Was McNally lying or … mistaken? What's going on? At least I haven't lost my mind.

"Well, when I got here, all the city offices were closed. So, I drove around looking for a taco wagon like the one in the brochure you gave me. I couldn't find anything but I saw a patrol car driving around and followed it until it stopped. I told the patrolman who I was … you know on special assignment and why I was there … looking for a taco wagon. He looked at me like I was crazy. 'What?' he asked. 'A taco wagon?'

"I showed him the brochure and explained what I could about how they operated. He shook his head and said he was damn sure there were no Taco Wagons in Quartzsite. His job was to patrol the city streets at night and he hadn't seen anything like the wagon shown in the brochure. Not only that, he said the only business selling tacos had been there forever."

"So, no Taco Wagons in Weldon or Quartzsite," Bishop said.

"No."

"Be damned. Good job, Raoul. Damned good job."

"Thank you sir."

"I'll make sure the Chief knows about it. Good initiative to drive to Quartzsite. You'll be starting work here with a big plus beside your name."

Raoul thanked him again.

"Come on back," Bishop said. "I want you to make a full report to Chief Wasserman when you get back. I assume that'll be tomorrow unless you have another flat tire."

He laughed.

After he hung up, Bishop let his thoughts wander. *No Taco Wagons in either town. McNally might say he made a mistake about one town, but how could he make a mistake about two. I'll call Beaver in the morning and ask if there are any Taco Wagons in that town. Then, I'll send Ellen a report. That ought to make her day.*

But, what am I going to do next? I have to think about that carefully. Something is going on with the Taco Wagons Investments. Maybe some kind of scam. Maybe. But, what kind? They're selling bonds and paying dividends. I'd like to know how many they've sold. Boxman said the last time he looked, they'd sold around fourteen million dollars worth. Where are the dividends they're paying coming from if they don't have income from the Taco Wagons? McNally told Snapper, Boxman said, that they were netting a hundred thousand a week from the Wagons. No Wagons, no money and yet, they're paying dividends. That must mean they're using bond money to pay dividends. Or, I'm missing something. If McNally's eating into the bond money, he must have an exit plan brewing.

Bishop did a quick calculation to determine what the company had to pay out monthly using an eight percent dividend.

"They'd have to pay out almost a hundred thousand dollars a month unless I screwed up my calculations. Boxman said when McNally and Snapper were talking in his office, McNally said they were netting more than enough to pay that. It doesn't make sense. They must have Taco Wagons someplace. Question is, where? And, if not, how in the hell are they doing what they're doing? Unless McNally's getting ready to split. Those are the questions I need answered."

I'm probably missing something. I need to know more about the business. I hope I'll find out more when I call Beaver in the morning.

But, taking it on face value, He asked himself, *what does McNally plan to do with the bond money if he doesn't have Wagons selling tacos? There may not be a business at all. Is that the scam? He takes the money and runs. And, where did Snapper fit into any of this mess? Did he find out and was threatening McNally? Was that why he was killed?*

Damn, lots of questions. Not many answers. Well, I'll call Beaver, Utah, in the morning and see what I find out. Are there any Taco Wagons there?

Now I'm worried about the Talberts. Am I wrong about them? Maybe they didn't kill Snapper. Hell, they had to, the boy anyway. He fits the description of the witness and he drove to San Diego. The old man would be an accessory. They had motive, George anyway, and the boy's wife practically said he'd done it.

Well, one step at a time, Bishop. One step at a time. First we get a search warrant. Then, we see if we can find a gun that matches the one that killed Snapper. And, while that's going on, I'll be on the lookout for some Taco Wagons someplace or something that tells me what's going on.

Bishop didn't sleep much that night. His brain kept searching for answers to his questions. What the hell was going on?

The next morning, before he had breakfast, he called the Beaver City Hall. After he'd identified himself, he asked if the City had issued permits for Taco Wagons. He described a wagon and explained how they worked and the need for wide sidewalks.

The lady who'd answered put him on hold to check out his request. After almost a minute, she came back on line and said, "Sorry I took so long Mr. Bone, but I had to do some searching. I couldn't recall such a business off the top of my head. As it turns out, I couldn't find any record of a permit to operate such a business anywhere in town.

"I checked around to see if anybody in the office had heard of Taco Wagons operating in town. Nobody had, Sir. I drew a complete blank. I'm sorry."

"That's okay," Bishop said. "I'm not surprised. My source of information was not reliable anyway. That's why I called you. Looks like I was given a bum steer."

"If I see one, do you want me to call you?" she asked.

"Please do, but I don't think you will. I think somebody got the wrong information," Bishop said and hung up.

"Struck out. All three towns. No damn Taco Wagons. Well, it's coffee time," he told himself.

So, he went out for breakfast to think about what he was going to tell Ellen in his report. No Taco Wagons anyplace! Three towns anyway.

Damn, that was a big discovery. Was he going to speculate about it in the report or just tell her what they'd found out, he and Raoul? He decided he'd just report the facts with slight implications and let her ask questions. The facts raised a lot of questions in his mind. He imagined they'd raise a lot in hers. One in particular was the impact the lack of Taco Wagons would have on the two murders they were investigating.

"That ought to make her day once she comes off the ceiling," he said, half under his breath.

What kind of scam was McNally running? Had to be a scam of some kind. Now, Ellen had that question to add to their investigations. People had invested millions in a company that, as far as he had been able to discover, wasn't doing business!

"Be damned!" The waitress looked at him, wondering what he was talking about. He had coffee.

He switched to thinking about it.

I'll assume for now that McNally's invading the bond proceeds for money to pay the monthly dividends. If that's the case, why? And, how does that play into Snapper's murder ... and possibly Vince's?

Has McNally been planning a quick exit? He has a house on the beach he would want to sell first. Why would he want to leave a property worth in the millions? I wouldn't. I'd better check to see if he has a pocket listing with a broker. Lots of damn questions and no damn answers.

When he returned from breakfast, he sat down and wrote Ellen a report that contained most of what he'd thought about over breakfast without the expletives. When he was almost finished, Raoul called to say he got an early start out of Quartzsite and was back home.

Bishop told him what he'd found out from his call to the Beaver City Hall.

"Okay, for now," Bishop told him, "you can report for work. Keep what you found out under your hat. I'm making a report to the Chief. She'll most likely want one from you but let's wait till she decides what she wants. We've opened a can of worms, I suspect."

He finished his report and sent it to Ellen. Then, he was going to sit back and wait, but decided to drive to her office. He wanted to see her face as she'd read the report.

Chapter 25

He passed the conference room and saw Raoul with other new policemen receiving their final orientation talk. From the sound of it, Bishop concluded it was a talk about political correctness on the job. He smiled. Such a talk wasn't in the orientation process of police officers in earlier times, Bishop recalled.

An evolution in thinking, Bishop thought.

As Bishop walked into the office area, he saw Ellen in her private office at a computer but she was on her phone. Her door was open. She finished her call and pushed a button on her keyboard. The screen flashed on.

Ah, she's going to check her mail, Bishop thought with a smile and hurried to get closer. She was so engrossed, that she didn't notice his presence behind her.

Although she had a number of email messages, she opened Bishop's email first and began reading it. As she did, her eyes widened; she frowned and leaned forward as if that would get her more of the report.

After reading it once, she pushed back in her chair, stared at the screen pensively and bent forward to read it again, just as studiously as before. When finished that time, she directed the computer to print out a copy. While it was printing, she reached for her cell phone and began punching in numbers.

Bishop said, softly, "No need, I'm right behind you."

She turned as if shocked to hear his voice. "Bishop! I didn't hear you come in!"

"I wanted to see your face as you read my report," he said.

"Well, I guess you did. I would have read it sooner, but I had to read my morning drug report. More killings last night. Drug dealers shooting it out."

"I'd hate to be wearing your hat," he said.

"Yeah. Me too sometimes. About your report, I was shocked. Surprised and shocked. Can you believe it? I'm not sure I do after reading it twice. Three towns where McNally said they had Taco Wagons. And none exist. Not one! What do you make of it? By the way, let me apologize for ever doubting your gut instincts. The results might not have been what you were expecting, but there was something smelly about the company's operations and you found it."

She walked over, pulled the printed report from the printer tray and walked back. She sat down in her desk chair.

"I never thought you'd find anything, frankly. I'm damn glad you did. As you say, what impact do the findings have on the Talbert situation?"

"Thanks to your support and Raoul's help. He did a great job. I'll get to Talbert."

"You said ... about Raoul," she said, tapping the printed copy of his report. "Hold on a second." She picked up her phone. "Get the door. Okay?"

While Bishop closed the door, Ellen told somebody to hold her calls. She was going to be in conference with Bishop for a while.

When she hung up, she looked at Bishop and asked, "Where do you suggest we go from here? I know you have some thoughts and some ideas. Let's have 'em."

Bishop pushed a chair closer to her desk, sat down and said, "I do. First of all, I want to know where McNally is getting the money to pay the monthly dividends to the bond holders. Is he taking it from the bond proceeds or does he have another source. I've had a couple of thoughts about other sources but I don't want to go off half-cocked until I do some checking."

He had the glimpse of another thought but it was so bizarre, he wondered if he might not be losing a step ... or two.

Might be time for me to wrap it up and get back to something I understand, bad loans.

"How do you propose to check? Ask the attorney?" Ellen asked.

Bishop shook his head. "No. If I ask him anything, he'll call McNally. In effect, he's McNally's attorney and has a duty to tell him anything suspicious that he hears. If I ask McNally why there are no

Taco Wagons where he said there would be, he'll give me some bullshit. Say he made a mistake or they closed up. If I ask for locations where he can guarantee that Wagons are selling tacos, he'll know we're onto him. I'd guess he'd begin a stall to have time to get out of town with what he has in the bank."

"I guess he'd say the franchisees don't want anybody bothering them. Wouldn't you?" she asked.

"You're most likely right. He's kind of said that already. He could also say … well, he could say the franchisees have an association or something and have decided not to give out interviews until they've been in business for … say a year or something like that."

"That would shut us down if he did that. Unless we get a court order and I don't see that we have enough rationale to present to a judge to convince him to give us one," she said.

"That's how I see it too. That's why I want to find out what I can without telling or asking him anything until I already know the answers. And, by then, you'll be ready to make an arrest," he said.

"We'll do it your way, Bishop. Have to. So, what are you going to do?"

"I'll be calling the two guys I had breakfast with to ask them for the name of the bank that's been issuing their monthly checks. Once we get that, I think the Chief of Police and I should show up at the bank and put the pressure on the bank manager to let us see their records or at least answer our questions. If necessary bring the City Attorney."

"Sounds like a plan," Ellen said, quoting a line from a movie or a television show she'd seen. "I think I can put the fear of God into the manager to tell us what we want to know."

"Good. After that, we'll have another talk to decide what to do next. I also want to know if McNally has a private listing on his house on the beach. I'll call Amy and ask her to check around about that. There might be a way she can find that out."

"You're thinking he might be getting ready to bail out?"

"A distinct possibility if he's been invading bond proceeds to pay dividends. If not, we have to consider other possibilities."

"I guess you have some," Ellen said.

"Well, one thing popped into my head a few minutes ago but it seems too damn farfetched, I don't want to get into it unless my first thought … about using bond money to pay dividends … doesn't make it."

"Okay. We'll play it your way. So, you're going out of here to find out the bank Taco Wagons is using and whether McNally is trying to sell his beach house and leave town with millions in bond money."

He agreed.

"Let me know what you discover," she said.

He would. "First though, before I do anything else on Taco Wagons, I want to finish what we have in the mill on Talbert. I want the search warrant you are supposed to be getting after my two boring drives to Orange County and I'll want some men to search every crevice and hiding place Talbert and his son have in Orange County. If we find the gun, we'll charge both men for the murder of Snapper. Then, we'll see what McNally is doing with his damned Taco Wagons. Where in the hell are they?"

She picked up her phone and made a call. She told whoever answered who she was and asked whether they had the search warrant she'd requested.

"Good. It is. Good. I'll be expecting it." She hung up and told Bishop the judge had issued it and a courier was bringing it over now.

She made another call and told somebody to have two crews ready to drive to Orange Country within the hour to search residences and a restaurant. "Bishop Bone will lead the search," she said as she hung up.

"It's all yours, Bishop. You can leave within the hour. I assume you'll send one crew to the residences of Talbert and his son and take the other crew to the restaurant and search that."

That's how he'd planned to proceed, he told her. While they waited for the search warrant and her crews to show up, he said, "If we didn't have the Talberts in our sights for the Snapper killing, I'd think McNally was behind it. As it is, if we find the gun, I think we can file charges and put that murder to bed, Snapper's. Still got Vince's hanging out there."

She agreed. "Solving one, Snapper's will make the Mayor piss in his expensive pants. He'll be thinking how that conviction will look to the public the next time he has to run for re-election. Shut the councilmen up too."

"I'm glad it's not me. I couldn't stand being that much of a phony. I wonder if a politician ever thinks about doing what he said he'd do if elected."

She didn't know and, she said, "I don't really give a damn! My only interest is in running this office and catching criminals." *And hanging onto my job,* she thought.

"Good way to look at it. Has to keep you from getting an ulcer," Bishop said.

*****

While they waited for the search warrant, Bishop called Amy. She was at her office, looking at new listings to see if any matched up with the needs of people she'd been talking to about buying a house.

"Bishop," she said after he'd said 'good morning.'

"What can I do for you? You want to buy a house? Gots some new listings on my desk. Prices are down a little. Good time to buy."

"Save it, Amy. I'm calling for a favor."

She asked what it was. He told her about McNally beach house. "I doubt there's a sign out front, but he could have given a broker a pocket listing. House like that should sell without much publicity or advertisement. I'm asking if you'll ask your broker to check around to see if anybody has, what I call a pocket or private listing on his house, one he keeps in his pocket?" He gave her the address but she knew it already. She and Cindy had been to parties there before.

She told him she'd get on it as soon as her broker showed up. He was showing a house that morning but she expected him within the hour. She'd call as soon as she found out anything.

He thanked her.

After he'd hung up, he called Fred Hillman, one of the men he'd had breakfast with to talk about their bond investments in The Taco Wagons Company.

"Fred here," he said into the phone.

Bishop told him who he was and said he had a question for him.

"Sure, Bishop Bone. I remember. You bought our breakfasts a while back. Fire away. I'll give you an answer if I have one," he said cheerfully.

"What I'm going to ask is part of an on-going police investigation of Snapper Cornwall murder. Everything I say is highly confidential and I'm asking … well I'm directing you, under police sanctions, not to mention anything I say to anybody."

"In other words, keep my mouth shut," he said with a laugh.

"Couldn't have said it better myself," Bishop said, also with a laugh.

"Well," Fred said. "I can keep a secret especially if telling somebody would land me in the pokey." He laughed again.

"Good. Here's the question. What bank issues your bond dividend checks? I need the name for a report to the Chief of Police."

"Hell, that's easy. I thought you were going to ask something that'd make me sweat like they do in the movies."

Bishop forced a laugh.

Fred gave him the name of the bank. It was a small bank, in Escondido. Bishop figured it hadn't been chartered long and would do favors to get deposits.

"I thank you Fred. That will finish my report."

"I won't say a word," Fred added. "My wife won't even know." His third laugh.

"I knew I could depend on you," Bishop said as he was hanging up.

"I am dependable," he said as he hung up.

Bishop thought the man sounded unusually cheerful. "In my Army days, he'd have asked if he'd just got laid."

Bishop put the thought aside and made a note of the bank. He and Ellen would drive to Escondido after they'd finished the investigation of the Talberts.

Chapter 26

The two police crews arrived about the same time as the search warrant. Bishop had made copies of Ellen's Talbert file for the leaders of the two crews. During the briefing he told them that they'd be searching for the thirty-eight caliber hand gun that killed Snapper Cornwall to see if bullets fired from it matched the bullet they dug from Snapper's head.

"It could be an automatic or revolver. It doesn't matter. Confiscate any hand gun you find. Also, look out for maps of La Jolla." He gave them copies of the file that showed Snapper's address.

"And, if you find any old clothes that look a homeless person might have worn, take them as well. The killer may have been dressed as a homeless person.

"I'll lead the crew that searches the restaurant, Big Plates, Small Prices. I think I can take you guys in my car," he said, looking at the second crew.

"The other crew will divide into two parts. One half will search George Talbert's home. The rest of you will search Barry Talbert's place." He gave the teams the addresses of both men.

"Okay. Let's go. It'll take us about two hours to get there. Probably no more than two hours or less to make our searches. And … make our arrests if we find the gun. I expect us to be back here before five tonight."

He looked at Ellen as they began to file out of the small conference room attached to her office. "I'll call you if we find anything."

"Call me if you don't find anything," she said. "Any news is worthwhile."

He would.

They loaded up and were on their way. The time was a few minutes before ten.

Bishop had called when he knew the search warrant had been issued and was told that both the son and father would be working at the restaurant that morning. So, Bishop's search crew would be at the restaurant while both Talberts were working.

Could work out to be convenient, he thought.

*****

He received a call from Amy when they were about fifteen minutes from the restaurant. He was driving but took it anyway. *Hell, I'm a policeman today. I can break the law if I'm trying to solve a crime.* He doubted that authorization existed but took the call anyway.

"Bishop," she said. "My broker called every broker in town. In particular the brokers who get the beach house listings. Nobody has heard anything about McNally listing his house."

"Not a thing?"

"Nada. If it's on the market, McNally's either selling it himself or somebody out of town is handling it. My broker said that could be the case. Now and then, some high roller lists with an out of town broker, say somebody from Beverly Hills who sells down here. He says he knows a couple of brokers. Do you want him to call around?"

"Not just yet. Let me finish a job I'm on and I'll call you."

He thanked her and told her to thank her broker.

She said the broker remembered him from the Flint case. "He says the Apogee development is doing very well. He gets a listing out there now and then."

"Thank him again then. I wish him well. I'll call you later."

He'd be told later that the broker had also called brokers in Beverly Hills and wouldn't find anything about McNally listing with anybody. So, Bishop could conclude that McNally didn't appear to be selling just then.

So, he's not getting ready to run. That's how I read that. Interesting but what does it mean?

*****

Bishop and two other officers came in through the back door of the restaurant a few minutes before twelve. They showed the owner the search warrant. He seemed shocked but told them to go ahead with their search, "but please don't disturb the guests."

Bishop didn't think they'd have to. The first places they wanted to look at were the employee lockers where George and Barry Talbert kept their belongings. Barry's locker was practically bare. It held some school books and school clothes he'd change into after his shift.

George's locker however held what they were looking for, a thirty-eight automatic hand gun. The smell told Bishop it had been fired recently.

Son of a bitch! Bishop cursed to himself. While he anticipated finding a gun, it was none the less exciting to have found it. Also in the locker was a map of La Jolla with Snapper's street address marked.

His team bagged both items wearing gloves. While they did, Bishop called the other teams and let them know what they'd found. They wanted to know if they should proceed.

Bishop hesitated but told them to go ahead. Who could tell what they might find. The gun they'd just bagged might not be the right one.

But, it was. And, the lab would find the fingerprints of both George and Barry on it.

The other teams would find old clothes and an old blanket in a clothes bag in a closet that Barry used for his clothes. They didn't find anything else of value, no other guns and no map.

Bishop and his team arrested both George and Barry although at the owner's request, they stayed out of sight and waited to make the arrest until the noon lunch was over at two.

George Talbert objected and cursed at them when they read him his rights but he didn't put up a fight.

Barry didn't say anything. However, his shoulders did slump when Bishop told him he was being arrested and would likely be charged for the murder of Charles Cornwall, aka, Snapper Cornwall, if the gun they'd found was the one used to kill the man.

Neither man talked on the way back to San Diego where they'd be arraigned. They were transported in the car of one of the other crews.

Bishop called Ellen with a report. She was beside herself.

"Have somebody ready to check the gun when we get back to make sure it's the one that killed Snapper. I'm pretty sure it is, but I want to be certain, before I make a fool out of myself," he said.

She would, and it would turn out that he was right. The gun found in George Talbert's locker at the restaurant was the one that had shot and killed Snapper. That had brought a smile to her face.

When both Talberts were arraigned the next day, attorneys were appointed to represent them. They claimed they didn't have the money to hire one. They also pleaded not guilty, the usual plea to see if there's a deal they can negotiate.

*****

The Mayor held a news conference with Ellen to announce the arrests. Bishop was also in attendance and was given credit by Ellen for his role in finding the men charged.

After consulting with their appointed attorneys, George confessed to killing Snapper Cornwall. In his statement, he said his son, Barry, had nothing to do with it.

Bishop didn't believe it for a minute.

Ellen had two line-ups for the witness who'd seen somebody he thought was young and in good physical shape.

He couldn't pick either man out of the line-ups.

"Hell, it's obvious that the boy, Barry, shot Snapper at his father's request," Bishop said. He went on to explain that George was obsessed with the way Snapper took money from his mother. That was the money, Bishop told her, George was obsessed about.

"That money, George felt, belonged to him and his two sisters, even though they had come out of it okay," Bishop said. "It was all he talked about from what I've heard. I think the day Snapper laughed at him when he asked for money, sealed the deal. That was most likely the day he decided Snapper had to die. I'm sure he drove his son to do it, his confession notwithstanding."

Ellen agreed. "But, with the old man's confession, and without a witness to point at the boy as the shooter, I think we have to go with the confession. There won't be a trial. Talbert will enter a plea with a statement and the judge will decide what sentence to pass."

Bishop didn't argue about it. He suggested that even with the confession there was enough evidence to charge George and his son with conspiracy to commit murder but it seemed more equitable to handle it the way Ellen had said.

The proof pointed toward Barry as the killer. He fit the description plus his wife had said he'd gone to San Diego that night. And, he had a map that showed where Snapper lived. Not only that, they had the weapon that killed Snapper and it had George's fingerprints on it as well as Barry's. George said he'd let his son hold the gun. George's confession was the only thing that disputed any of that.

After listening to Bishop's suggestion about "conspiracy" she said. "I agree we could do that and frankly, I have no doubt that the boy actually shot Snapper, but whether you believe it or not, I'm human and I think justice will be done with the old man's conviction. Don't you?"

Bishop agreed. "I guess so. I just thought I'd mention it because it crossed my mind. You could get both of them that way."

"The DA had also brought it up," she said. "We both figured having George plead would be justice enough. The boy was just doing what his dad told him to do."

"Suits me," Bishop said. "I'm just a hired hand."

But Ellen wasn't quite done with George Talbert and asked Bishop to join her for lunch to talk about it. She wanted him to search for a connection between the Talberts and Vincent Valley.

If Bishop could connect the Talberts to the Valley murder, it would make a difference in her decision, and the DA's, to let the son off the hook.

Ellen asked. "If you could connect them, I would ask the DA to change his mind about letting the son off. We'd have no trouble charging both if they were involved in two murders."

Bishop answered, "I understand, Ellen, but I'm not sure there's a connection between the murders. I interviewed Barry's wife to see if

Vince's name had ever come up in any of their conversations. It had not, she told me. They'd only talked about the Snapper guy she said.

"I did the same with George's wife. Same answer. Snapper was the only name she remembered them talking about and that name came up all the time.

"I asked if they'd talked to their husband's attorneys about Snapper's murder or Vince's. Both said they'd had had some conversations with the lawyers and were told not to discuss the case with anybody, especially anybody from the police department. But, since George was pleading guilty and Barry was going to be let go, they didn't see why they couldn't talk to me.

"I figured they didn't see any reason not to since what they were saying was in Barry's and George's best interest. I knew their lawyers were worried that they may say something that could open up a can of worms for their clients but that was yesterday's news after George had agreed to a plea deal."

"So, apparently there's no connection between the Talberts and Vince," Ellen said. "The Talberts didn't kill Vince as of this reading of the tea leaves. I'm concluding that's what you're saying."

"Right on. I don't see any of the Talberts as being so sophisticated that they could lie that convincingly. I also talked with both George and Barry. Both swore they didn't know Vince. Had never heard of him. And, they hadn't talked about Vince with their attorneys. I believed them as well. Vince's death didn't make the Orange Country papers or television reports."

Ellen said, "In short, then, we're no closer to finding Vince's killer than we were when we arrested the Talberts."

"'Fraid that's the case. However, maybe there's something on Vince's computer pointing at the Talberts. I didn't see any before, but I was focusing on Cornwall then. If I find anything that ties the Talberts to Vince, you can have another go at them."

"I'd sure as hell like to kill two birds with one stone," Ellen replied.

"Wouldn't we all. But," Bishop reminded her, "you hired me to find who killed Snapper. I think I've done that. Time for me to turn in my badge, don't you think?"

"I was wondering when you'd bring that up," Ellen answered with a grin.

"Yeah. Well, I'm ready to go home. Your new guy can solve the other murder, Vince's, and the Taco Wagons scam, whatever that is."

He hadn't shared with her his odd ball thoughts about how the scam might be working, but that was something he figured he'd put in a report.

To hell with the Taco Wagons scam. I'll email my thoughts to her from Mississippi about I've boiled them down some. I might be full of it anyway. I'd rather be in Mississippi when she reads what reared its ugly head in my thoughts.

She told him that her Orange County hire would start the following Monday and would need a few days to get his feet on the ground before he'd be ready to take cases.

"See what you can find, will you?" Ellen said.

"Okay," he told her. "But unless I find some connection in Vince's computer that links the Talberts to his murder, I think I'm done as a policeman. I did what you … I guess, and the Mayor hired me to do. Even gave you a new case, two cases in fact, Vince's murder and the Taco Wagons scam. Solving those will give the Mayor two more opportunities for press conferences."

Her face showed a grimace at what he'd said. "Yeah, I hear you, but, I know this loose end will bug you till it's solved anyway. So, what is your gut saying about the Taco Wagons … I'll call it an apparent scam, and Vince's murder? Just tell me your thoughts," she asked. "You're still on the payroll."

"Yeah. I guess you're right. My gut is telling me there's probably no connection between the Taco Wagons Company, what we found out about the franchisees, the missing Taco Wagons and Vince's murder. And there's likely no connection between Snapper's murder and Vince's. Different murder weapons for one. And, from the witnesses' vague description when Vince was murdered, the man seen on the street after Vince's murder was heavier than Barry."

"Could be that George killed Vince after his son killed Snapper," Ellen supposed.

"Could be, but why didn't he use the thirty eight?"

She had no answer to that question but suggested, "A hammer wouldn't make any noise."

"So, all of a sudden George got some sense, eh? Didn't mind a little noise in front of Snapper's place but got shy in front of Vince's camper."

She shook her head. "Hell, I don't know. Maybe something from the first murder scared some sense into him."

"I agree that's a possibility. Oh, I meant to ask. You said you were sending out people to canvas the neighborhood for heavy set men with cars. How did that work out? I'm thinking about McNally."

"Glad you asked. I was going to tell you. We found the heavy set man and his car. Lives in an apartment by the campground. He was going out for a six pack that night. Has no connection with the campground or anybody in it. So, that takes McNally out of the equation. Don't you think?"

Bishop shook his head. "Yeah. I guess it does. McNally didn't look good for it anyway. I only saw him as a slight possibility in any case because I didn't have enough evidence other that what the witness had said, to link him to Vince's murder."

Don't jump that far ahead, stupid. Bishop thought. *All you know is that the heavyset man the witness saw didn't do it. You still don't know that another heavy set man, McNally, didn't do it.*

He didn't want to share that with Ellen yet however. He only shared his thoughts when he had something that would give them some substance.

"What else have you been thinking?" she asked.

"You said the new guy starts Monday. It's Wednesday now. I guess we could, you and I, call on the Escondido bank while I'm still on your payroll. Depending on what we find there, I'll tell you the rest of what I've been thinking."

She smiled. "Good idea. I was going to suggest that myself. By the way, the Mayor and I agree, Raoul's trip is on the city."

Bishop nodded his head, agreeing. "Thanks. It should be, but it was my agreement so I was going to let it go."

She'd pick him up at his apartment the next morning at eight for the trip to the Escondido bank.

Chapter 27

They parked in the bank's lot a few minutes to nine and went inside. Ellen had brought a file with all of Bishop's reports to look more official and for reference purposes. She'd worn her official uniform for effect. Bishop stayed with his dark suit which looked official enough, he figured.

They walked to the back of the bank where the offices, with their glass windows, were located. One office bore the name "President" so that's where they stopped. A man in a dark suit, like Bishop's but more expensive, with a full set of dark hair and a face without emotion sat bent over a desk at the back of the office.

Probably looking at who he can foreclose on today, Bishop thought, tongue in cheek.

Ellen showed the secretary her police card as she identified herself and introduced Bishop.

"We'd like to see the President," she said.

"Is it something I can help you with?" the secretary asked using her serious look as she'd been told to do when people wanted to see her boss. "Get rid of them if possible," had been her charge.

Ellen restrained a smile and shook her head. "Official police business. I think only the President will do."

The look left the secretary's face. She stood and went into the office, closing the door behind her. She said something to the President which they couldn't hear. The man looked around her at Ellen and Bishop, still no emotion on his face. Then, as if it had just hit him, he smiled broadly at them, showing his perfect teeth. He stood and motioned for them to come in.

The secretary, looking embarrassed, passed them on their way into the office. She closed the door behind her.

Ellen reached over the desk, extending her hand, and introduced herself and gave her title as the Chief of Police in San Diego. The name place on the edge of the man's desk identified him as Abraham Culpepper.

He took her hand and gave his name, smiling broadly. Bishop followed Ellen. He extended his hand and introduced himself.

"Well, have a seat," he told them and sat down himself. "So, to what do I owe the pleasure of your visit?" He asked, still smiling.

Ellen said, "I'm sure you are aware of the murder of Snapper Cornwall. We're trying to wrap up the details of his murder. You may have read that we've arrested the man who killed him. I think it was reported on most television news reports that the man has confessed."

"I did see it. Congratulations! Good job. Mr. Cornwall and Mr. McNally are good customers of the bank. Well, Mr. Cornwall was. Snapper, we called him. They … well, McNally now, uses our bank for the company that does the business, the Taco Wagons Investments."

"That's why we're here," Ellen said. "We want to nail down a few details about the company in case it comes up in connection with the sentencing hearing for Snapper's killer, George Talbert."

Bishop said, "The judge may ask questions about the company. So, we're trying to anticipate what he may ask. We need to ask you some questions about how Taco Wagons did business."

Culpepper said, "They sold franchisees to … well usually to retired people to sell tacos and other Mexican food dishes to street buyers in small towns in the west. At one time, I believe they had sold over a thousand franchisees. Mr. McNally, I think, told me they're in five states now and hope to expand in those states and into other states in the future." He looked at them and asked, "Does that help?"

Bishop said, "Yes. By the way, before we get too far into our questions, we need to caution you. All we say today and all of our questions and your answers have to remain confidential. Under our police mandate, we are required not to reveal anything anybody says unless we are asked in court by the judge. Will you be able to observe that mandate? You cannot tell anybody anything, including your depositor, Mr. McNally until after the court hearing for George Talbert. He's the man who killed Charlie Cornwall, Snapper."

The man said he knew that and "Yes, I understand what you're asking me and I most certainly will not repeat anything that is said here today. Do you have any other questions?"

Ellen nodded toward Bishop who said, "We've been told that the investment company sold bonds as well as franchisees."

"That's right. We didn't get involved in the franchises. We have only been concerned with the bonds. We were told that they've sold something over five million. We process the monthly checks to the bond holders."

Five? Boxman said fourteen! What the hell. Big assed discrepancy! Bishop decided not to bring that up. He'd go with the information Culpepper was using for the moment.

"That's our understanding as well. And, that's what our questions are about, the bonds," Bishop said. "They may have been behind the killing of Snapper. Can you tell us where the money to your bank comes from that's used by the company to pay the bond premiums?" He asked.

The man's face went blank. "Ah, well, you know, we … the bank doesn't … we don't disclose specific details of our depositors business without their permission or a court order directing us to disclose."

Ellen said, "Yes. We understand. The DA and the City Attorney stand ready to get a court order if we can't do it informally and friendly. We don't want to drag you into court with some of your staff just to get some answers to our questions. The nosy reporters might have a field day supposing why." She smiled at him.

"But, none of these questions will disclose anything that should be confidential about the banking activities or the Taco Wagons Investment company. I think you will agree. These questions are fairly mundane. Things the Judge likes to ask, folksy things. Why don't we ask the questions and see?"

She nodded at Bishop who again asked, "Where does the money the bank uses to pay dividends to the bond holders come from?"

"See," Ellen said, using her police smile. "No depositors names. No bond holder names. No bond amounts. Just an innocuous question in case the Judge asks us before he sentences the defendant."

Culpepper looked at Bishop with a frown for a few seconds. "I guess you're right. There shouldn't be a problem that we can't handle informally. Let me see what I can find. I don't know the answer myself but my computer will have it, I'm sure."

He turned to his computer, got the screen up and typed in a request for information about the Taco Wagons account.

Within seconds, information appeared on the screen. "Okay," he said, leaning forward to read. He read off the names and addresses of five banks in five states. "Those are the banks that make wire transfers to us on a monthly basis. Usually those transfers are in the thousands. That's where the money for the bond premiums comes from."

The President stared hard at the screen and said, "Looks like we're getting ... well, were getting, almost a million a week. Lately though, the transfers, according to what I'm looking at, have been down quite a bit but usually they're in the thousands from each bank."

Why in hell is that? Bishop wondered to himself. *No damn Taco Wagons selling tacos? Boxman said they had a thousand wagons selling tacos, netting the company a hundred thousand a week. Hell, on their best week, a wagon couldn't sell enough to generate that much in sales, a million every week, net to the company. And, now, not nearly that much. Why? There must be a reason the money has dropped? I bet I can guess what it is. Off the wall reasoning, Bone. Off the wall.*

Both Ellen and Bishop were writing as he rattled off the names and addresses.

"Would you like a print out of the names?' he asked, noticing what they were doing or trying to do.

They would.

He punched in more instructions and his printer printed out a sheet of paper with the five names and addresses on it. Also, a contact for each bank was listed.

"See," Ellen said, "Nothing confidential had to be disclosed. Those bank names are well known, I assume, in the states where they're located."

Culpepper nodded his head. His smile had faded but he appeared relieved.

"Any other questions?" he asked Bishop.

He did, but to put the man off, he said he didn't. Then, he acted like he'd had a thought and asked, "Oh, I did have another question, if you don't mind." Bishop said.

Culpepper extended his arms toward Bishop, telling to ask his question.

"I'm not asking names or bond amounts, but I would like the total bond amounts the Taco Wagons company has sold."

He looked at his computer again, punched in buttons and said, "Looks like they sold something over five million. Five million and one hundred thousand. As I told you, we process checks to the bond holders."

Not fourteen million? I guess I'll have a couple more questions.

"You pay out less than half a million to the bond holders. Your bank must have one hell of a deposit for the Taco Wagons Company. Or, do you show other payments?"

The President laughed. "We don't have much of a deposit actually. We process checks to their management company for supplies and maintenance ... and salaries. That's the Taco Wagons Management Company headquartered in Reno."

"That makes sense," Bishop said. *Hell, it doesn't make sense at all. But, it ties in to what I'm supposing.*

Culpepper gave them the name of the Reno bank.

"That'll do it for me," Bishop said. He stood.

Ellen said the same thing but added, "Remember, you are under a police mandate not to disclose anything we've discussed with anybody, especially anybody associated or even involved with the Taco Wagons Company. Do you agree?"

He nodded his head. "Yes. I won't say a word."

They thanked him and left.

*****

On the way back to San Diego, Bishop did most of the talking. He told her she needed to do two things. First she had to contact her counterparts in the five cities where the banks were located and have them question the bank managers about the details they had given for the Taco Wagons deposits. If there were none, then her counterpart would shift the questions to any details they can find about funds collected and used for wire transfers to the Escondido bank for the Taco Wagons account.

The second thing she needed to do, actually she should do it first, was to have the Mayor of San Diego contact the Mayors of the small towns and tell them the City of San Diego had an active criminal investigation underway and needed the cooperation of the named bank in his town.

"The Mayor will ask the Mayors of the small towns to ask the banks to cooperate with us in completing our investigation. If they don't want to talk to their local police, they can call you directly and you can ask where they get the money, maybe also, how they get the money, they use to make wire transfers to the Escondido bank."

Ellen asked, "If, as I suspect you're thinking, there are no Taco Wagons in the states to generate money, where do you think the money is coming from?"

"I can give you a theory or my suspicion, Ellen, but frankly I'd prefer to have the answers the banks give before I tell you. Otherwise, you might get distracted and wreck us, laughing so hard."

"Come on, Bishop. I've heard your off the wall suppositions before. Fire away. I can take it, as wild as I figure they're going to be. I promise not to laugh ... or throw anything. Okay?"

Bishop sighed and said, "Okay. Don't say I didn't warn you. This is what I believe. I don't know if this tells us anything about Vince's murder, but it might."

"This must really be off the wall. I'm waiting, Bishop."

"Here it is. The lack of taco wagons, I'm assuming in all the states, got me wondering where and how the company got the money to make the monthly bond premiums. From what Culpepper said they sold five million in bonds, not the fourteen million McNally and Snapper talked about in Boxman's office. I'm thinking that was a cover for what they're really doing.

"Of course, before today, I had thought McNally might be taking bond proceeds to pay bond dividends, figuring on bailing out when they had as much money as they were looking for. I thought that was McNally's scam from the beginning. Snapper was indeed just a figurehead.

But, knowing what we now know from Culpepper. The company is getting, well, were getting, a million a week, and don't have the Taco Wagons generating any of that, I backed into what I think is the likely scenario for what McNally's doing. Maybe Snapper was in on it as well. Too late to worry about that now. "

"What," Ellen asked. "Don't keep it a damn mystery!"

He smiled. "I'm getting to it. You said something a while back that made me think a bit. Drugs. You've been having an epidemic of new drug dealers in San Diego, drug wars, fighting for sidewalk spaces. So, how about this scenario?"

"You think McNally is in the drug business?" she interrupted to ask.

"I do. I think he's getting money from drug sales to pay the monthly bond dividends with a hell of a lot left over. The left over goes to the Reno bank, I assume to pay off drug buys and everybody who's part of the drug network. If McNally thinks we're onto him, he'll close his doors and leave town with the money. Maybe set up in another town someplace."

"I'll be a son of a bitch," she said. "You know, you may be right. In fact, I'm betting you are. How about that? For once I'm agreeing with you up front."

"Hell, now I'm worried."

"The drug wars have heated up. Nobody is selling a hell of a lot of drugs. They're too involved in killing each other. And Culpepper said the wire transfers have been down."

"And McNally has said about the same thing. He's not selling anymore franchisees because China isn't sending him anymore wagons. That's his excuse for not expanding. Remember what he said. He takes the money from the taco wagons to pay the bond holders. If there's no money or reduced money because of the drug wars, there isn't money to pay more bond holders. He probably doesn't want to invade bond deposits but I bet he's having to at least partially invade the deposits right now to make the monthly dividends."

She agreed. "We may find out more when we talk to the banks about the money they're supposedly getting from the Taco Wagons franchisees that don't exist."

"We will. In the meantime, also talk to your informants to see what they may know about the new drug players in town. Show them McNally's picture. Find out what you can. We'll need to somehow, eventually, tie the drug dealers in town to McNally if we're going to charge him for selling drugs."

She agreed. "Might be a hard hill to climb. Those top guys usually cover their tracks very well. They use go-betweens."

"I figure. Anyway, I'll be calling McNally after you get your answers from the banks sending money to Escondido."

"You going to tip him off?"

"I'm not that stupid, Ellen. I just want to put him under some pressure. I know about what he's going to say, just like I just about know what you'll find out from the five banks."

"What are we going to find out? Might help me to know."

After a second or two, Bishop said, "Yeah, I guess you're right. I think you'll find that the people bringing money to the banks, maybe just one guy, most likely showed up at the banks one day with a story about how they were opening a cash-only business and described the Taco Wagons business, even gave the bank manager one of those glossy brochures. And, they wanted the bank to handle their account for the state. That story would give the bank a legitimate reason for allowing cash deposits. Reporting of violations for drug dealings would not be required."

"Damn, you have been doing some thinking, Bishop."

"A little. Once the drug money is in the bank, it's clean and can be wire transferred to pay the bond dividends and the other stuff, for supplies, maintenance and salaries, McNally told the bank it went for.

The Taco Wagons Management Company, he also told the bank, handles that side of the business. All above board."

"And, you got all of that from something I said?"

"Partly. You said drug sales were down because dealers were spending more time killing each other than selling drugs. McNally said he couldn't sell anymore bonds or franchisees because the Chinese hadn't delivered wagons. Translated, that could mean he was worried he wouldn't get enough drug money to pay the dividends on the five million dollars' worth of bonds they actually sold. He didn't want to invade the bond fund. I put the two things together and got what I told you."

"I'm impressed, Bishop. That's worth what we're paying you. And, you were going to sneak off without telling me."

"I was going to send you a report, Ellen, from Mississippi until you reminded me I was still on your payroll."

"And, how does that tie into Vince Valley's murder?"

"I don't know yet. That's something my brain hasn't gotten to yet."

She sighed. "Damn. I don't know how you do it but you do."

"Is that some of the Wasserman bullshit, Ellen? Or do you mean it?"

"What! Of course I mean it. And, you know it."

"I'll tell you this. Lawyers are trained to solve people's problems. That's how we think. So, when we have to face a problem, even complex problems like yours, our training kicks in and we think. Vince did that too when he was thinking about his people lectures."

"I'm glad we brought you in," she said.

"I could have lived without it. More frustrations than I usually run into on a case. I was content to handle the relatively simple problems the banks in Mississippi run into when one of their loans go bad," he said.

"This case had more players than we usually run into. That's why we ran into so many dead ends."

"And, we're not done yet. Supposing is one thing. As you know, we still need proof," Bishop told her.

"At least we know who killed Snapper and we've cracked a drug ring, a major scam. That's more than we've had till now."

He agreed.

"One more thing," Bishop said. "Sooner or later you're going to have to bring in the FBI. We've got out of state banks. I don't know if you can handle it with the police in those states."

She agreed.

*****

Soon they were back in San Diego. They had stopped along the way at a Starbucks to relax with cappuccinos and croissants.

She made the calls she needed to make from her office. The first went to the Mayor. Bishop stayed for that one. It didn't sound like she was getting any static from him. In fact, it sounded like he was very pleased with what she was saying.

He'll be able to say, at his next press conference how he helped crack the case, Bishop joked to himself.

After that call, she had to chase down the names and phone numbers of the police chiefs of the five towns the banker had given them. That would take some time so Bishop left her to it.

He went to the apartment he was using and called Kathy to bring her up to date with all that was happening. After that, they talked about more important things, such as how much they wanted to see each other and the things they were going to do.

Then, he had to think about his next move in the cases he had. He would call McNally to spook him a bit but had to wait for Ellen to complete her investigation first. He didn't want to scare him into leaving town prematurely.

"Hell, for all I know Ellen'll find some Taco Wagons selling tacos when she calls the Police Chiefs and I'll feel like a fool when I get on the plane in disguise, headed back to Mississippi."

He had dinner at a Denny's that night, his usual, bacon and eggs. It was good, but mostly he thought about the case, cases really if it turned out that Vince's killing was related to the Taco Wagon scam. He had to shake his head at that thought. That was a puzzle he hadn't solved. So far, he hadn't found anything to connect Vince to the Taco Wagons scam in any material way. He was killed before he could find out anything.

I'm going to look through his computer files like I'm searching for gold. Hell, in a way, I am.

Chapter 28

The next morning, he arranged to pick up Vince's computer for another go at his files. Ellen said she'd have it in her office waiting for him. He had told her he wanted it during their drive back from Escondido.

If there was anything in it that pointed to Vince's killer, he intended finding it.

Somebody killed him and, I seriously doubt it was a random killing. But if I can't find anything, I'll broaden my thinking in the last few days I'm here. Hell bells, maybe I should hang in here a bit longer.

He thought about searching the computer in Ellen's office in case he had questions about anything but it was a melee of telephone calls and shouts across the room so he decided to take it back to the apartment where he'd have some privacy.

Before he left to do that, he went into Ellen's office – she was off the phone – and told her what he planned to do on the computer.

"Listen, Ellen, I did some thinking over the night. Your new guy, my replacement, starts Monday, the end of my pay period and I figure, the end of my contract with the City. Trying to be fair to you, I'll say that it's going to take a couple of weeks before he's going to know shit about your cases, namely the cases we are currently trying to get before a judge."

She looked at him. "Of course. I know that. What are you saying? You are willing to stay on a few more weeks?"

"I don't know how long, but long enough to see if I can find out what'd going on with the Taco Wagons scam. That's what I'm calling it. And, hopefully find out who killed Vince Valley."

"I knew you wouldn't leave me half way across the river, Bishop. Okay. I'll extend you indefinitely. When you reach an end or the new guy is bitching because he can't take over, you can go home to your … Kathy and your beavers."

"That's about it, Ellen. Right now, I'm going to take this computer and turn it inside out. I'll be looking for a connection between the Talberts and both murdered men. If it's there, I'll find it. Or, maybe I'll find something else that points to who did it. I'll also be looking to connect McNally legally, as in with proof, to the Taco Wagons scam. I know now why he was back peddling on Snapper as the figurehead. He was building himself a back door should he need one. Right now, I'd say I won't need more than a week or so to find out all I can find. Then, it's yours and your new guy's."

Ellen sighed. "Okay, We'll talk when you get to that point."

"I think we've talked, just now, don't you. This is not the Army. We don't have to wait for a commanding officer to make a decision. It's been made."

She laughed. "We'll talk, Army or not, when you come in with what you find, two days or two weeks."

Bishop picked up the computer without replying and left for his apartment. Someone in the City Attorney's office had printed out copies of all files on the computer. Bishop took those as well. He'd read those first.

*****

With hot coffee by his side, he scanned the print outs of the files. Of particular interest were the "Note" files, the files he used to save his thoughts about future "people" talks. Vince wanted to talk about the "welfare" system. He thought the welfare system should be revised to include some kind of work program including training so the welfare recipients weren't doomed to remain dependent the rest of their lives without the dignity that came with self-sufficiency.

There were other notes. From what Bishop knew, Vince had already talked about some of the thoughts he'd recorded in his notes. And, Bishop supposed, he may have talked about all of them before he got involved.

Vince also had references to frauds and scams that had been perpetrated on people over the years.

From the dates of the searches, he'd done that recently, before he was hit over the head with a hammer.

Damn, no mention of Taco Wagons. Was he thinking of that? Apparently he hadn't finished his research before he was killed. I bet he was searching for something that'd tie into the Taco Wagons' venture his client had asked about.

But, he was killed before he could ... before he could record anything if he had found anything. Damnit to hell.

Bishop spent that day and half the next with the computer and the printouts and found nothing that referenced McNally or either of the Talberts, George or Barry.

He did find a curious entry in the "Notes" file. It said, "Problem. Jennifer, good Sx. Relief. Del Mar ??? Beatrice, good person, good fd, good cmpany. More ??? MAKE A Decision."

The computer date for the last entry was a few days before he was killed.

Obviously Vince was wondering what to do about the two women. He liked both of them for different reasons but nothing indicates he had made a decision about what he was going to do about them. I can't remember for sure, but I think he said something about telling Beatrice he was moving or something. I wonder if he had gotten to it. From his computer note, I'd say not. More damned frustrations.

Ellen called mid-morning the next day. "You were right, as usual, Bishop. Here's what we found out from the five banks."

She told him that two men, one for three banks, the other man for the other two banks, showed up on Monday mornings with stacks of cash bundled according to denomination to be deposited into a Taco Wagons account. "They wore suits, by the way. Looked respectable," she said.

"No doubt," Bishop agreed.

She continued with her report. A minimum amount of five thousand dollars was kept in each account. The balance was wire shipped to the Escondido bank.

When the men set up the accounts in the banks, she told him, they first talked to the Presidents of the bank and explained why they wanted to set up the accounts. The banks were relatively small, having just been chartered, and were looking for deposits. They talked about the Taco Wagons franchise operations, how franchisees would set up on wide sidewalks in small towns and sell Mexican food, namely tacos, for cash. They talked with a copy of their brochures on the desks in front of them and offered a copy of the grand opening of the Taco Wagons operations.

The men explained how, with a business like that, they didn't have the time to process credit card transactions so they only took cash. And, that was why they were talking to the bank before opening the accounts. When told by the President of the bank that they'd have no legal problems. They'd set up the accounts.

"We know the money didn't come from selling tacos, don't we?" Bishop said.

"We do. Unless they have the wagons hidden from us."

Bishop said, "I recommend that we put bugs on all of McNally phones. I'd assign somebody to follow him. I'd also put an electronic bug on his car so the tail can stay well out of sight."

"The DA said the same thing a few minutes ago when I talked to him. He'll be getting court orders to do just that. Also, next Monday when the two guys show up, bugs will be installed on their cars while they're in the last bank and somebody will follow them."

"Have you identified the men?" Bishop asked. "I assume the banks have security cameras."

"They do. The people I talked to will be sending us photos of both men. In fact, I suspect they're already here. I'll be running the photos through our database to see if we can find a match. I'll also be running the photos past my informants to see if they know them."

"Good. I believe we may be closing in on a drug ring that's run by McNally. Although, that's speculation until we can connect somebody involved in the drug sales to him. I think circumstantially we're there, but until somebody can say he's involved, I won't be sure."

"The DA and I agree with you there, Bishop."

"So, we're going to be in a surveillance posture for a while," Bishop said.

"Yep. I'll keep you posted. What are you going to do next?"

"I'm going to call McNally after you have all your bugs in place and ask for permission to visit a Taco Wagons' franchisee. I want to see what he says."

"I bet he will turn you down," Ellen said. "Like you said."

"I assume so, but my call might shake him up some. Make him think we suspect something. See what he does, if anything. I'll press him hard."

"Rattle his cage," Ellen added.

"Yep. I'm curious to see if he starts pointing at Snapper."

"You haven't been wrong yet. By the way, the Mayor sends his congratulations and thanks for a good job."

"I'll accept both when we have McNally behind bars and somebody, even if it isn't McNally, on the hook for Vince's murder."

"Well, keep looking. You'll find them."

"Don't I wish? Vince had a note in his computer about Jennifer, a woman he was sleeping with and about his next-door neighbor, Beatrice, a woman who wanted him to sleep with her. I had interviewed Jennifer after Vince was killed. He'd told me about her. I'm going to revisit the camp ground one more time. I had a thought I wanted to squeeze."

"Do it. When you start squeezing, things happen." She laughed.

Bishop replied with a laugh of his own.

*****

He'd take the computer back to her office in the afternoon. Then, he'd revisit the camp ground to follow up on what he'd found or at least thought he'd found. While he was delivering Vince's computer, he asked Ellen for a couple of policemen to come with him should they be needed. She assigned two men without argument or question.

I'll use them, he thought. *Something I should have done before now. Getting too soft, Bone,* he told himself. *Maybe. Damn, probably. I guess I'll find out.*

*****

He parked on the street beside the camp ground and walked inside. The two policemen he'd brought with him waited in the car with their cell phones.

"I'll call you when I need you," he told them. *If I need you.*

He didn't want anybody in the camp ground to see him officially until he saw them. He wore, what he called in Mississippi, his working clothes, khakis and tennis shoes.

Bishop glanced toward Beatrice's camper. She was nowhere in sight. Neither was Vince's dog, Rascal. He was glad about that. He wanted to see Jennifer before he saw her.

He stopped at Jennifer's camper and knocked on the door. Hers was about the same size as Beatrice's, probably more expensive, Bishop decided. He saw her inside at the sink, rinsing her hands, obviously in the process of preparing something. She turned.

"Oh, Bishop Bone. You want to talk to me?"

"For a minute or two. I need to ask a couple of questions."

"Come in then. You want coffee. I'm perking a fresh pot. My friend from Del Mar called to say he was coming over. He said he has something important to ask me. I hope it's what I've been waiting for. So, I'm fixing bread pudding with whipped cream topping and coffee."

"I hope you're right," Bishop said. "I love bread pudding myself. A southern favorite!"

"Come back later. If there's any left, you can have a slice. My husband never liked it."

He promised he would and said, "Your husband must have had an arrested sense of taste."

She laughed lightly and turned as if to ask why he came.

"I realized that most people keep tools in a kitchen drawer for odd jobs, like hanging pictures or tightening screws, things like that. When I was here before, I forgot to ask if you did."

Her face took on a puzzled look. "Yes, I do. Drawer's over there." She pointed at a drawer under her coffee pot. Steam was drifting up from the fresh coffee dripping into it.

"Be my guest," she said with a nod at the drawer.

He pulled it out and looked inside. There was a small hammer and two screw drivers one for both types of screw heads.

"I should have asked. You forgot to tell me about this hammer." He didn't think it was big enough to have caused the indentation in Vince's head, but knew it was a mistake not to have taken the hammer for tests.

"Can I take it?" he asked.

"Take it," she said. "Bring it back when you're through with it."

"You got the one I took before?"

She had.

He put both hammers in the bag he'd brought and told her good bye. As he headed out the door, a thin man with graying hair, about as tall as Bishop, came up the walkway to her camper. He was casually dressed. In his hand was a bouquet of flowers.

Jennifer's Del Mar suitor, Bishop thought.

He hesitated when he saw Bishop, looked puzzled.

Bishop knew he'd be suspicious, seeing a strange man coming from the camper of a woman he'd been seeing.

He reached into his pocket and pulled out his police identification card. "Bishop Bone," he said. "I needed to ask Jennifer a couple of questions regarding a police matter I'm investigating." He figured Jennifer could tell him what she wanted him to know about Vince's murder.

The man uttered something Bishop didn't catch as he brushed past. Bishop nodded and walked on.

Behind him, he heard Jennifer greet him like he was her "very closest dear" and gushed over the flowers. Her camper door closed.

He'd call later and find out that the man had proposed and that she'd accepted. And, he loved the bread pudding. She apologized when she told Bishop there was none left.

He called the two policemen who were waiting in his car and told them where to meet him, in front of Beatrice's camper. He left the bag with Jennifer's hammers on the little table under the tree that Vince sat under to have his afternoon beer and think about his late wife, Carolyn.

Chapter 29

Even before Bishop reached Beatrice's door, Rascal had begun barking. *He's adopted Beatrice now. Protecting her from intruders. Vince who? Bishop thought with some irony.*

He knocked but Beatrice, having heard Rascal barking was already there, smiling. "Mr. Bone," she said. "What brings you back?"

He explained that when he submitted his final report of Vince's death, his boss got all over him.

"Police procedure required me to check everyone's hammers," he said. "I knew you had nothing to do with his death so I didn't check yours. But, I need to do that now to get my report approved. Do you mind if I let these two policemen get your hammer and search your camper. Only take a couple of minutes."

He told her he had a search warrant if she wanted to see it. She said she was more than happy to let them search all they wanted but she frowned as she did, like it was an intrusion.

"No," she said adding a cheerful tone to it, like she was happy for their company. "I'll show them my tool chest."

"Good. By the way, I'd like to look at Vince's camper one more time as well. Can I borrow your key?" He asked with his best disarming smile. She handed it to him and motioned for the policemen to come in. She told them where her tool chest was in case they wanted to look there. They thanked her and began their search.

Bishop went next door. He primarily wanted to search Vince's tool chest. It occurred to him that whoever hit him over the head might have been somebody who knew him and could get by Rascal to get his hammer. He didn't try to work out the details of that thought but decided he should look at Vince's tool chest for his hammer, just in case something like that happened. He had another idea but that one had to wait until he'd finished the search.

A quick look around Vince's small camper gave him what he needed. Under the bed was a storage area and Vince's tool chest. In it was a hammer. As he had with Jennifer's hammer, he picked it up with his clean handkerchief and put it in another bag he'd brought.

He checked around to make sure the man didn't have another hammer, like Jennifer had. He couldn't find one. The two policemen were waiting for him out front when he locked up Vince's camper. They had taken Beatrice's hammer. It looked new they told him.

He thanked Beatrice and gave her back the key. She wanted to know if he'd found anything.

"Nothing to write home about," he told her. He knew that might not be true and most likely wasn't true, but would only know what they'd found for certain after the forensic lab had checked out the hammers they'd picked up for traces of blood. None was visible on the one he'd taken from Vince's tool chest or from Jennifer's drawer. The policemen told him the same thing about the one from Beatrice's tool chest.

They took the hammers to the lab for examination. They'd have something for them by the next morning, maybe sooner.

Bishop dropped by Ellen's office to see if she'd made any further progress at her end.

"It's almost noon," she said. "Why don't we discuss it over lunch. How about the Bread and Cie."

He agreed. "Never had a bad meal there. The people there all act like I'm family when I eat there."

"Me too. I can totally relax."

She drove and he told her what he'd done that morning.

"The lab will finish their examination of the hammers by morning. I'm hopeful they'll find something. If not ..." He shrugged. "Back to zero on Vince's murder."

"So, you're thinking it could be one of the women, Jennifer or Beatrice? Why?"

He told her a little more about the cryptic computer note he'd found on Vince's computer. "I guess it didn't really say all that much, but I let my cynical side think about it. That's why I wanted another search of the two campers. Both women might have had a reason to kill Vince. He was using Jennifer to get rid of his uh ... tensions. She might have gotten tired of it, being used. Not much motivation to kill somebody, but it was a possibility."

"I'd say," Ellen replied and asked. "How'd you work the other woman into your equation?"

Bishop laughed. "It bothered Vince that Beatrice wanted more out of him that he was willing to give ... namely marriage. I think he told me he was going to tell her but he had to work up to it. He hated to hurt her feelings."

"So, you're thinking he told her and she got upset and hit him over the head with her hammer."

He nodded. "If not hers, his. She's not a dumb woman. She might have figured we'd come around looking at hammers."

"No! You think she switched her hammer for Valley's? You gotta be kidding me?"

"That's the possibility I wanted to eliminate. I know it's far fetched but who knows what a woman spurned in love might do?"

Ellen shook her head. "I'd think you've been at it too long but for the track record of your hunches."

"Well, don't get too excited yet. I've struck out a lot on these cases."

"Haven't we all?" she said. "But, regardless of whether your hammer theory turns up, it sure as hell looks like separate killers for both men. Cold blooded as far as Valley is concerned ... using a hammer. But, it could be the killer didn't want to raise the dead in the camp ground using a gun to kill him."

Bishop agreed. "In which case, I have to start my investigation all over. Well, you and the new guy will. I'll be looking at McNally again if I don't find something on the hammers we picked up this morning."

"I've been thinking McNally did it," she said. "He had the most to lose. And Vince was looking into The Taco Wagons Company for his client."

"That's true. And, McNally killed him to stop him for discovering what we found when we did our secret investigation. There are no Taco Wagons," Bishop said.

"Hell, Bishop, Vince's killer could have been anybody. Not necessarily connected to the Taco Wagons. We don't know who he pissed off while he was in practice or during one of his people talks. If Charlie Cornwall, ole Snapper, was still alive, I'd think he'd be a suspect ... the tennis fight and the Taco Wagons. I'm sure Vince was skeptical about anything that sounded as good as that venture."

"Yeah, but Snapper was already dead, so we can rule him out," Bishop said.

They arrived at the Bread and Cie bakery and cafe and ordered what they usually ordered.

Over coffee, she told him, "The Mayor called me this morning. He's very happy with what we've done. He asked me this morning how you're coming along with Vince's murder. I told him you were hot on the trail. He said he was very impressed with the results you get."

Bishop laughed. It was a hollow one. "He's more optimistic than I am. Hell, there may be nothing on the hammers. I wonder what he'll think then."

"I know you Bishop. You wouldn't have gone back out there if she didn't suspect one or the other of those women. And, usually I can take your suspicions to the bank. So, don't bullshit me, ole buddy."

Bishop laughed again. She was right.

The waitress brought their orders.

Both looked at their plates. Both had steam rising up.

"Looks good," Ellen said.

Bishop was already biting into his sandwich. "Damn good."

"I told the Mayor you would stay on until you had Vince's killer behind bars and we have arrested McNally for a drug scam."

"I didn't tell you that, did I? I thought I'd stay ... what a week or so, to finish up what I had on my plate."

"In my mind and the Mayor's, you agreed to stay on for the budgeted term and then some if you were hot on somebody's trail." She looked at him. "Well you are hot on a trail and I've always known you to be a man whose word was his bond."

"You're assuming more than I said but I'm not going to quibble just now. Maybe in the morning after the lab calls me. If it's bad news, I'll offer my badge."

"Call me when they do," she said. "I have some news to tell you."

"What? Hell, I'm been rattling on about worthless crap. What news? Tell me."

"Sounded good to me. It's got my attention. Anyway, my informant called me this morning."

"Must have been good news," Bishop said.

"It might be," she said and gave him the gist of it. "I like it. First of all, I talked to the FBI and told them I may have something cooking that'll involve them. A multi-state drug operation."

"The guy I was talking to was interested. Very, in fact. He said when we get ready to let him know. It'd take some organizing to put a plan together. He did tell me this when I told him about our drug war. He said it was happening in several large cities.

"He said they had been tracking drugs coming from Mexico City but recently a new supplier was bringing in drugs through Puerto Vallarta. They are trying to get a handle on it but he supposed they could be our new dealer in San Diego. An informant told him that the two suppliers are going to have a meeting to see if they can divide up territories and they can both sell drugs without killing each other. It could be, after their meeting, that the drug war will end."

"That'd mean money would start coming in again from McNally's Taco Wagons," Bishop quipped. "And China would deliver more wagons."

She laughed.

"We took the photos of the men depositing the drug money. The banks gave them to the local police and they sent them to us. We ran them through our ID data bases and got names. I'd give them to you, but they'd do you no good. I'll give them to you anyway. Riley Dunn and

Paul James. Both have connections to drug dealings in the past but have never been charged with anything."

"So, legally they're clean but you're watching them."

"We'd like to connect them to McNally."

"I'll second that," Bishop said. "Let me know if you do."

She would.

"As of now though, you haven't tied McNally to anything?" Bishop asked.

"Not a thing. He hasn't called either man or any other man we can connect with drugs. He hasn't had meetings with anybody suspicious. The two men have met with some local people, known to have drug dealings, but we haven't been close enough to see anything that could give us reason to arrest them. But, that may come."

"I may ..." He interrupted himself and said, "Actually, I will call McNally and see if I can spook him."

"Don't give us away," Ellen said with some alarm.

"Don't worry. I've been doing stuff like this a long time. It'll be morning before I do. I'd like to get a report from the forensics' lab first."

"Maybe they have something for you, now."

"They said tomorrow but they could have been giving themselves time for an emergency. I'll call them when we get back."

*****

Bishop called the lab late in the day.

The director said, "We've finished our examination of the hammers. The small hammer was clean. The fingerprints on it and the big hammer you brought with it matched the ones you had previously brought in. Jennifer's fingerprints."

So, Jennifer's clean, Bishop thought. *No surprise. I'm glad. The hammer was too small anyway.*

"How about the other big hammers?" he asked. "I designated one big hammer as 'one' and the second big hammer as number 'two.'"

The number 'one' hammer came from Vince's camper. The other one, number two, came from Beatrice's camper.

"Well, we found blood and a hair on hammer 'one.' Both belonged to Vince Valley. We did the autopsy on him."

"Damn. That's the first decent news I've had during this investigation."

"And," the director continued, "there was a smudged fingerprint on that hammer that matched the fingerprints on hammer 'two.'"

Hammer number two also had prints that matched Vince Valley's prints.

Bishop hadn't supplied Beatrice's prints. He decided not to ask her because he figured if there were prints other than Vince's on the hammer, they'd likely be hers.

"I'll get you prints to compare with it. I know whose print it likely is, the killers. Her name is Beatrice. I dread confronting her. She was in love with Vince."

"I don't envy you, Bishop."

He still had time left in the day so he got into his car and drove to the park. That time, he parked in front of Beatrice's camper.

He took a deep breath and slid out of his car. Rascal began barking right away. Before he got to the door, Beatrice was already there, looking out. Her face had a sad look to it.

She must suspect why I'm here.

"Shall I come out there?" she asked.

She knows.

"Yes. Let's sit in Vince's chairs, under his tree."

"Is this about … Vince?"

"It is. I assume you know what I'm going to say."

She nodded her head slowly. Tears ran down her face. "I know. I'm sorry. I'm so sorry." She looked up and added, "Please Lord, forgive me."

Then, she burst out crying, her head bowed.

"I think I understand," Bishop said after allowing her time to get it out of her system.

"Do you?" She asked. "He told me there would never be anything between us. He regretted having to tell me, but he was going to move his camper to another camp ground. He said he couldn't stand seeing me try so hard, knowing that he would never be able to respond like I wanted."

"He told me it bothered him, the way you tried to take his wife's place. He just wasn't ready," Bishop told her.

"But, he was ready for that bitch, Jennifer. He admitted that they'd been ... they'd had sex. That was too much for me. He slept with her but wouldn't give me a kiss on the cheek. I went inside and cried. When I looked out the window, he was asleep in his chair. I took my hammer and hit him with it. Nobody was around."

"What'd you do? Switch it with his hammer?"

She nodded her head. "I wiped it clean, I thought, with one of his towels. I threw the towel in the trash and thought I'd gotten away with it. I've cried myself to sleep every night since I did it."

She looked at Bishop and added, "I reckon, people would say I should have thrown the hammer away too. Nobody would have noticed. I'm glad you figured it out. I couldn't live with myself, thinking about it every day. I killed the only man I really loved."

Bishop gave a half nod to that.

She burst out crying again. After a bit, she looked at him and said, "When you showed up with the policemen and I saw you come out of Vince's trailer with that bag, I knew you'd figured it out. I've been waiting for you."

"I have to take you in, Beatrice. I hate it, because I know how you feel, but you committed murder and you'll be charged."

"I know. Let me get my purse and put Rascal out some food and water. I need to visit the bathroom too."

She went inside. He heard her putting out food and water for the dog. Then after a moments silence, he heard a shot, then a second shot. He ran inside. There she was, holding Rascal under her left arm, laying across the bed. The gun was in her right hand, close to her head.

"Damn. I guess I should have followed her inside. Son of a bitch. I didn't think. I should have."

He called Ellen and told her what had happened. She said she'd send an ambulance to pick her up. He'd have to make a full report which he already knew.

In the kitchen on the table was a glass. He put it in a bag he'd brought for that purpose. The glass would have her prints on it. It'd give the lab something to compare to the smudged print they'd found on the hammer.

When he went outside, a number of people had gathered on the drive in front of the camper to see what had happened. They'd heard the shots.

Jennifer stepped forward and said, "We heard shots. What happened?"

He started to tell her Beatrice had accidentally shot herself but there had been two shots and he knew the story would be in the newspapers so he told her.

"She was upset about Vince's death. She was in love with him and he told her, in effect, that he didn't love her and probably never would. That broke her heart and she killed him."

He left out the part of the conversation that involved Jennifer. He didn't think that part was necessary to answer her question.

The lab did match one of Beatrice's prints to the smudged print on the hammer. Even though she'd confessed, he felt better to have some actual proof to back it up.

*****

He and Ellen shared a beer on the balcony of his apartment that evening.

"I felt sorry for her. She was in love and Vince knew it but he didn't think it was fair not to tell her. Damn, it broke her heart."

"She may be better off dead. It's hard to live with a broken heart," Ellen said.

He agreed. "Now, I have to face our other problem unless you want your new guy to take over."

She didn't. "He's not ready. Besides, you've brought it this far. I couldn't stand to let somebody else take the credit, even if he could, which I doubt. I think he'll be a good detective, but frankly, he'll never be in your league, Bishop."

He thanked her.

I'll call McNally in the morning and see what happens when I shake his tree.

He told Ellen as much, and about what he was going to say.

She told him, "I know you'll be careful. I'm embarrassed to even tell you, but I'm a creature of habit and I'd feel like I hadn't done my job if I didn't tell you."

He laughed. "I know you, Ellen. I'm not even surprised. Thanks."

*****

After she had gone, he called Kathy and told her what had happened. She also understood what Beatrice had gone through and understood that her life was over when Vince told her he didn't love her.

"She did the only thing left for her to do," Kathy said.

Bishop didn't disagree.

"I just have to see if I can finish up the Taco Wagons case. Might take a couple more days. Damn, Kathy, I miss you. I love you."

"I love you too, Bishop. Wrap it up. I can't wait to enjoy a beer with you on the back porch, watching our beavers."

*****

Bishop slept nervously that night. Initially his thoughts were on Beatrice. How she'd suffered a love that didn't come. Finally, he was able to put her plight behind him and turn his attention to the Taco Wagons case, namely McNally. How could he bring him in?

Ellen hadn't been able to connect him with the two "bagmen" Riley Dunn and Paul James. They were likely using phones that weren't registered. *People like McNally know they are always at risk so they're extra careful. And, with millions on the table, he had a lot to lose if he screwed up.*

By the time the first of the morning coffee was pouring into his cup, he still didn't have a plan.

He decided to call McNally around nine and see if he would make a mistake. He'd keep his call simple, like he was spinning his wheels. No threat. He wouldn't know about Beatrice so he could keep Vince's murder on the table.

Chapter 30

McNally picked up on the first ring. "McNally," he said.

Bishop told him who he was but before he could say why he'd called, McNally congratulated him and the police department for finding out who'd killed Snapper.

"Great job!"

Bishop thanked him and proceeded to tell him that he was wrapping up his San Diego assignment.

"My contact with the City is about to run out," he said. He explained his arrangement with the City, the short-term contract. "They finally hired a guy who'll take my place. He started last week and has completed his orientation. I'll turn over my cases to him before I leave. I do have a couple of questions for you before I make my final report."

McNally told him to ask away. "I'll answer them if I can."

Bishop said he wanted to know if Vince had asked to contact one of his franchisees on behalf of his client.

"I'm technically still on the case until the new man takes over. I looked at Vince's computer notes and it appeared that his client asked him to personally interview a Taco Wagon operator to get a first-hand opinion about the company."

"Maybe his client wanted him to do that, but the man didn't call me again."

He told McNally he was a licensed attorney who helped Chief Wasserman now and then when she needed it as she did just then.

"As an attorney, I would have agreed that contacting one of your franchisees would have been the prudent thing to do if a client was asking for information."

McNally went silent for a moment or two. "I didn't know that. You didn't tell me you were an attorney when we first met."

"You think my status as an attorney is relevant?"

"I think you should have told me. It's misleading."

"Well, I disagree. Talking about Vince, I'll tell you his computer file was clear on the matter. He wrote that he was going to talk to one or more of your Taco Wagon people," Bishop replied.

"He must have been killed before he could. I don't mind telling you, if you want to know, that all our Taco Wagons' franchisees are doing well and are very happy. I have a stack of testimonials on my desk. The money keeps rolling in. I've been told that I'll soon have a new shipment of wagons from China. Once they're unloaded, I'll be able to sell more franchises and more investments," McNally said with some enthusiasm.

Yeah. China will send more wagons as soon as the rival drug gangs have worked out a deal in Reno to divide up territories. That's what he thought. What he said was, "Somebody told me the other day, that when something takes off like your Taco Wagons, it's only a matter of time until a competitor moves in. Have you heard of any competitors?"

He laughed. "Anybody thinking of competing with us would know they'd never stand a chance. We're too well organized. Our Taco Wagons offer it all, fresh and tasty food. Nobody can do it better."

"Sounds good. I'd sure like to see one. Think you could set up a visit for me."

McNally went quiet for a few seconds before replying, "I wish I could. You'd be impressed but, I got an email a couple of days ago from the President of the Taco Wagons' Association. He says they're tired of visits that interrupt their businesses. Apparently newspapers have been bothering them."

Bishop interrupted. "An association! You didn't say anything about an association the first time we talked. Hell, anytime. I'd call that misleading."

"I couldn't tell you because I didn't know. I only found out about it when I got that email from the President. It surprised me. No law against it, but it … well, frankly it shocked me. I had no idea."

"Is that right? So, what did the President say? Does he want to charge a fee for anybody to come see a Taco Wagon in operation?" Bishop said, throwing in a jab.

"No. His email just said they had voted not to permit any interviews until they've been in business awhile. He didn't say when that would be."

"Hell, McNally, I might just drive to Arizona and buy myself a taco. While I'm doing that, I'll ask how he likes selling tacos from a street wagon. I believe you said there was one in Weldon."

"Why would you want to? The Valley guy, Vince, never asked to see one when he was nosing around for his client. He might have been interested, but he didn't get around to asking. So, why in hell do you want to bother one of our franchisees? You've solved Snapper's murder and Vince's only contact with the company was his talk with me."

"Since the last thing Vince was doing before he was killed was investigating the Taco Wagons, my boss wants me to talk to a franchisee to see if there's any connection between your company and his murder," Bishop said.

"What the hell! I don't believe this. Good God! I'm going to call the Mayor about this act of stupidity by the Police Department. You can't solve your case so you're blaming us. You're making us your whipping dog."

Bishop laughed. "Good point, Walter. But, it was the Mayor and the Chief of Police who told me to talk to one of your franchisees before I left town. I told them it was a stupid waste of time but they insisted."

"I could understand if you wanted to talk to one of our bond holders. If there was anything wrong, that's where it would be … ah hell, I just remembered you've already interviewed two of our bond holders. Fred Hillman and Larry Friedman. I was just talking to Friedman about investing more money. He told me you had breakfast with the two of them. I think they both told you they'd heard nothing bad about the company."

Bishop agreed and told him that both men were very satisfied with their investment. "They love those monthly checks they're getting. Great return on the bonds."

"Well, there. Did you tell the Mayor and … what'd you say … yes, the Chief of Police about that?"

"I did. I gave them both a report about my breakfast and everything the two men said. My report said as far as they were concerned, they'd heard nothing but good things about your company."

"There you have it. What the hell will harassing one of our franchisees add to that?"

"I don't know. And, that's also what I told the Mayor and the Chief. They said they want to close the case but in case somebody starts asking questions, they want to be able to show that we crossed all the t's and dotted all the I's."

McNally signed loudly. "No wonder people think the police are stupid. If anybody asks me, I'd have to agree."

"Listen Walter. I'll just look at the wagon while I'm eating my taco and ask how everything's going. If they sell coffee, I'll buy a cup of that as well. While I'm doing all that, I'll casually ask about the company. Maybe tell 'em I'm thinking about buying a franchise myself. Probably take no more than fifteen minutes. What is harassing about that?"

McNally said nothing for a few seconds. Then, he said, "Okay. I understand. I'll contact our franchisees around Tucson, that's an easy drive from here, and see if one of them will agree to be interviewed by the San Diego Police Department about the death of a man not one of them has ever heard of. I assume one will be enough. You understand, it's not up to me. The franchisees are independent and they've said, through their President, they don't want anybody bothering them."

"I doubt they'll mind, frankly, Walter. And, if you can get permission for me to talk to two, that'd be even better. Then, I'm outta here. My contract will be over."

"You're a stooge for the Mayor who's covering his ass on a murder you guys can't solve. How many times did it take for you to pass the bar exam? I can't believe the stupidity I'm having to deal with. Asking me to inconvenience my Wagoneers so the Mayor can claim he has an IQ above the imbecilic level. I don't like it."

Bishop ignored the man's bitching and said, "I assume you can find out with a phone call if somebody will talk to me. So, let me know something today. Who can I see?" He gave McNally his phone number. "I'll call the name or names you give me and arrange a time they can live with. I'll ask my dumb shit questions and write a report to the stupid Mayor and lazy assed Chief of Police so they can close the file on Vincent Valley's murder. Another unsolved murder. Okay?" Bishop said the last, tongue in cheek.

"I hear your sarcasm, Bone," McNally said. "I'll call you if I get anything." He hung up.

*****

An hour later, Bishop got a call from McNally. "Okay, you bullying bastard, I found a Wagoneer who's willing to talk to you. Paul Cranston. He has a wagon in a commercial development this side of Flagstaff. Not even a town. The developer put in a special sidewalk to get us in. Cranston took the space and says he hasn't been sorry. Been doing great. Says he has no problem talking to you. Says you're wasting your time but come on. I couldn't find anybody closer willing to waste their time with you. Looks to me, considering your time, it's too far to drive, but you can spend the City's money and fly in."

"That's okay," Bishop said. "I'd like more information about the location. That sort of thing."

Son of a bitch. What the hell. I was certain there were no Taco Wagons. Now, he has one, Paul Cranston. I'll tell Ellen. I have to go. We thought we had the bastard in our sights. Damn.

"As it happens, I have a video of Paul setting up and selling tacos. His wife is helping. If you can come out here after eight. I'm finished dinner by then. I'll show you how to get there, show you some photos and the video. You may decide, after you see what I have, to forget the trip."

"Could be," Bishop said. "I'll be there at eight."

I'll wait until morning to give Ellen a report. Damn. I can't believe it. Well, look at it before you throw in your towel.

"He's buying one for his son," McNally continued. "His daughter has a Chic-Fil-A. Doing gangbusters, he said. His son is an underachiever, he says. He thinks the wagon will bring him out of it. The boy is on the video. He's buying a taco."

"Commendable. Cranston must have some bucks to throw around. Franchises for the whole family and a wife pitching in to help. I'm impressed."

"All our Wagoneers are top notch. That's what I've been trying to tell you. You're too st... well too stubborn to listen."

"Just doing my job, McNally. You do yours. I'll do mine. Let's keep the insults at a minimum, shall we? Sooner or later, probably sooner, I'll take exception and reply with some of my own ... not necessarily the wordy kind. Get me?"

"Yeah, I get you. It's just I hate for people to waste my time."

"Like I hate for people to waste mine, jerking me around," Bishop said.

Bishop said he'd be there at eight. He took the time to get a bite of dinner at Denny's. While he enjoyed dinner, he did some thinking.

I'd have bet the farm there were no Taco Wagons. Now this asshole says they have one. No way in hell would they have just the one. Has to be others unless he's running a game on me. What the hell could that be?

I could be wasting my time. Could be hell! I am ... unless ... What kind of game could be he playing? I guess I'd better think about that a little more.

If it's not a game, I have to go over there and look. I'll run it past Ellen, but I'll cover it myself. If it turns out to be some kind of trick, I'll know soon enough.

You do some stupid things, Bone. McNally might have been right when he started to say I was stupid. Coffee's good, even decaf.

I'd better think about McNally. He's a crooked bastard. I know that. I also know he lied about Wagons in Weldon, Quartzsite and Beaver. So, how, all of a sudden does a wagon pop up outside of Flagstaff.

I bet he's gambling that I'll look at the video and not go. That has to be it. He's taking a big risk though. What if I do go? What the hell will he do?

And, what the hell will I do? I'll be watching my back every second, that's what I'll do. He cursed to himself and resumed with the thought. *One of these days, I'll get a simple case with Ellen.*

"I hate to think what her new guy would do with the case at this point. First, he'd think I was a sloppy investigator, making decisions without all the facts. Ellen would agree and I wouldn't be asked to give anymore speeches for her. There's good in everything, I suppose." He smiled.

The waitress heard him mumbling and asked if he wanted more coffee. He did.

By the time he'd finished his last cup of coffee, he figured he was ready for anything McNally was getting ready to throw at him.

"We may end up having a come to Jesus meeting after all. Fists and all the rest." He laughed at the thought that followed. *I don't have a flak jacket if he answers my fists with bullets.*

Chapter 31

Bishop rang the doorbell and was let in in with a quick handshake. McNally looked out to see if he'd brought anybody with him.

"Come in," he said during the entry.

Bishop walked in without replying. He didn't figure the meeting was going to be friendly or cordial and was mentally prepared for it.

He followed McNally into the living room with its broad expanse of windows looking out at the waves sweeping over the sand bordering the back yard. Music came from someplace, classical music. It was pleasing. He'd heard none when he was there before.

To his surprise Fred Hillman was sitting in one of McNally's plush chairs smiling.

Son of a bitch. No wonder the bastard was so cheerful last time we talked. I was telling the enemy what I was doing. No doubt he hurried up and called McNally as soon as I'd hung up. So, McNally's been playing a game with me. I'd better watch my ass. I wonder what the hell they have in store for me.

A glass of red sat on the table beside Fred's chair. He stood and shoved out his hand which Bishop took with a nod.

"Fred," he said, giving his name. He acted like Bishop was a big surprise. "What brings you here?"

I guess he's part of it. Probably hasn't bought a single bond. I wouldn't have thought that. He and Larry seemed legitimate to me. I have to watch what's going on. I doubt anybody thinks I'll be leaving here with my eyes open. Fred would be a witness no one can argue with. He could say he saw me leave.

I wonder if the bond sales have all been as phony as the Taco Wagons' franchisee program has been. That's a scam to end all scams ... maybe they figure on an ending of me as well.

"Walter thought you might have questions about the company's bond program. I'm here to answer any you have," he said.

Behind him, McNally asked, "Red or white, Bone?"

Bishop turned and said, "Beer, if you have it. Us low brows like our beer." He smiled.

McNally didn't respond to the dig but did say, "I assume a glass."

Bishop said, "Sure, a glass when I can get one." Beer in a cold glass tasted better somehow, he told McNally.

McNally returned and handed him a glass of amber liquid. "More where that came from."

Bishop nodded and raised his glass. "Cheers,"

The two other men followed suit.

About that time, another man walked into the room. McNally turned and said with a wave in the man's direction, "Riley Dunn. He knows more about Cranston than I do if you have questions after seeing the video."

Well, be damned. I think McNally brought in a full house to deal with me.

Dunn switched his wine glass to his left hand shoved out his right. "Mr. Bone. Glad to meet you. Walter's been telling me about you ... and your pursuit of killers." He grinned. "I don't think you'll find any in Flagstaff. Paul Cranston's not one, but I'll answer any questions you can come up with. Paul's a great guy, good business man."

"No doubt, from what I've heard," Bishop said.

Dunn shoved his glass at Bishop's and said, "Good luck to you." After a click, he turned his glass up for a big swallow.

Bishop turned his up as well.

McNally announced that he was warming up some hors d'oeuvres in the kitchen. "The maid cooked 'em up before she left."

Fred looked at Bishop with a big smile and said, "Drink up, ole buddy. Might as well relax." He turned up his glass and finished it off.

Bishop followed suit. Fred went to the bar and refilled his glass.

Be damned. Everybody's friendly all of a sudden. Fred's a surprise. Just then, he remembered Dunn. He's a bag man for the so called Taco

Wagons collections. Ellen was looking to connect him to McNally. I guess I just have. Nobody in this room thinks I'll be around to tell anybody, I'm betting.

When Fred returned, Bishop handed him his glass. "I could use a refill. That one had a bitter taste. Try another brand. A Stella would be nice."

Fred called McNally with Bishop's request. McNally took his glass into the kitchen and returned with a fresh glass filled with beer. "I hope this one is more to your liking," McNally said, handing it to Bishop.

Riley came in with a tray of something tasty looking, cheese and avocado in the middle of crackers. Bishop took one when the tray was waved in front of him.

His hand wobbled a bit as he did. He shook his head. "Damn, feel kind of dizzy. Maybe I drank my beer too fast."

"Maybe you did," McNally said and sat down with his wine.

Bishop looked at them and shook his head again as if trying to rid it of cobwebs.

"I'm glad to see everybody," Bishop said. "Before we see ... excuse me, I'm still kind of dizzy."

No one said anything.

"Anyway, let me tell you what I know, Walter. I really came here tonight to make a deal. I want a cut of what you're taking in. My last day is day after tomorrow. I want to go home a rich man."

McNally laughed. "Bullshit, Bone. We all want to be rich."

He leaned back in his chair, sighed and began. "I guess I'd better tell you what I know. Only I know this, by the way. I'll make a report with it to Chief of Police before I leave unless we can make a deal."

"More bullshit. Tell us what you think you know, asshole," McNally said.

"I will. First of all, I'll tell you that the Taco Wagons Company is a complete sham. There are no taco wagons. I've checked on my own.

There are none in the towns you gave me, McNally. Not one and there never have been any."

No one batted an eye. Riley glanced at McNally who took a sip of his wine.

"Need more beer?" Fred asked with a gesture at Bishop's empty beer glass.

Bishop nodded weakly and said, "Your whole damn operation is a cover for drug money. A way to launder it. I know everything." He nodded at McNally. "You are the new guys in town. The first bunch has been objecting to you taking their street spaces and you have been killing each other. I understand … Excuse me, I might be going to pass out."

"If you feel faint, just sit back and take a break. We aren't going any place, Bone. And, I don't think you are either." McNally said. "If you can though, before you pass out, tell us more about what crooks we are."

Bishop nodded. "Riley and your other bag man, Paul James, take the drug proceeds for the week to five banks for deposit. Cash from taco sales, they told the banks. Pretty good scheme. Good reason for having cash. Your Taco Wagons franchises don't deal in credit cards or checks. Once the money's deposited, it becomes clean. Wire transferred to the Escondido bank and then to the bank in Reno for more cleaning. Used for drug payoffs." Bishop's eyes closed momentarily.

"You're not as dumb as I figured. Good job. We're making money and once you're out of the way, we will continue to make money. People love our drugs. And, we'll be dealing with the assholes who've been objecting to us."

"I … you put something in my beer," he told McNally. It was more a mumble than anything clear.

"I sure as hell did," McNally said. "I didn't intend for you to leave here tonight. From what you'd asked Fred and what you were throwing at me, I knew you had a pretty good idea about our operations. You had figured out more than I knew, however."

"You didn't kill Vince Valley. I'll tell you that. We have his killer behind bars."

"I told you I didn't, you shit!" McNally said.

"And, Snapper was only a figure head, wasn't he? Your dupe. Well paid, but a dupe."

McNally laughed. "Of course. The man was an arrogant fool. Never had a thought that got beyond his crotch. Except for money. He loved getting laid and getting paid."

Bishop gave a half laugh as his head drooped forward.

McNally said, "That shit works, Riley. The asshole is out. How do we do this? I don't want any blood on anything in the house. Cops are going to be all over it. I'll wash his glass and make damn sure we leave nothing for the cops to analyze."

Riley said, "Fred and I will drag his ass out to his car and drive it to a remote beach. I have a place picked out. No one goes there at night. People will speculate that he committed suicide. Maybe the case was too much for him.

"We'll leave his car there but put his body in the trunk of mine. I'll have somebody drive him to Arizona, a deserted place and bury him. Without a body, the cops can bitch all they want at you, but they won't be able to charge you with anything, Walter. And, Fred will swear that Bone left here at nine. He said he was happy with the meeting. Was going to recommend closing his case file."

McNally said, "Sounds good to me. What'll we do, choke him to death?"

Fred said, "That'll work. He won't ever wake up. Got a rope?"

McNally left to get a piece of rope from the garage. When the door to the garage closed behind him, Bishop stood and announced to the rest of Fred and Riley, "I guess I've had a miraculous recovery. I don't expect the rug under my chair will though. When I saw you, Fred, and this drug cretin, I knew I had to watch my ass and anything you gave me to drink. I guess I was right."

He pointed the automatic pistol at them and moved to one side so he'd be facing McNally when he returned which was a few seconds later. By then, Bishop had made an automatic call on his cell phone.

After he'd done his thinking at Denny's, he'd told Ellen what he was going to do and the concerns he had.

"I kind of expect McNally's plan for me is to leave in a prone position. I'll be careful however. Forewarned is forearmed," he had told her.

She asked if he wanted her to back him up.

"No, just stay by your phone. I'm taking a wire to record everything that's said and a gun if things get rough. I'll call you if it becomes necessary. I doubt it will, but who knows. McNally has been giving off noises like he's going to cooperate. I doubt that and that's why I'm going in prepared and on my toes."

But, Ellen knew Bishop and knew he was likely to end the evening with a life threatening fracas. So, she'd parked with a van of policemen a block away to wait for his call. She sent one guy down to the house to look through the windows to keep up with what was happening. When he saw Bishop pointing a gun, he let Ellen know.

"What the hell?" McNally said when he returned and saw Bishop standing in front of the two men, pointing his Glock automatic at them. He'd gotten it from the Police Department early on, just in case and just then was the "case" he'd been waiting for.

Bishop waved the gun at McNally and said, "Come closer, ass hole. I'd say your drug wagon has just lost its wheels. Tacos might have been better after all."

Ellen's team knocked open the front door and stormed in. "Thought you might need help so I decided to stay close. Looks like you were right. McNally figured on you leaving in the prone position."

"Things didn't go quite like I figured, but close enough, I guess."

He hadn't anticipated Fred Hillman being there but had figured McNally might have somebody lurking around, ready to kill him before the night was over.

Ellen wasn't totally convinced when Bishop had called, but given Bishop's record lately, decided the prudent thing to do was to stand by and wait for his call. She'd be closer than he figured.

*****

The Mayor had a big press conference the next day to announce the breaking of a big drug ring and the arrest of all principals. Ellen stood by his side. He gave her full credit for cracking it.

Ellen was asked questions about it. How she went about solving it, problems, that sort of thing. She pointed at Bishop and gave him credit for doing the hard work of going "hands on" with the main drug dealer.

"Bishop Bone figured it out," she said. "And, today's his last day with us."

She also introduced the new guy who got to say a few words.

Though not mentioned, the FBI made arrests at the meeting in Reno when the rival drug gangs met to resolve their differences. Unfortunately, for the FBI, the meeting was not a violation of law so no one was charged.

*****

By the afternoon of that day, Bishop was sitting on his porch back in Lawton drinking a beer with Kathy and watching the beavers work in their pond.

The End

Made in the USA
Las Vegas, NV
19 June 2021